CABOT STATION

WILLIAM S. SCHAILL

AVON BOOKS  NEW YORK

AVON BOOKS
A division of
The Hearst Corporation
1350 Avenue of the Americas
New York, New York 10019

First Avon Books Printing: April 1992

AVON TRADEMARK REG. U.S. PAT. OFF. AND IN OTHER COUNTRIES, MARCA REGISTRADA, HECHO EN U.S.A.

Printed in the U.S.A.

RA   10   9   8   7   6   5   4   3   2   1

ONE

CABOT STATION—
MARCH 5—DAY ONE

Lieutenant Commander Alfonso Madeira lay on his back and gazed at a deep blue sky filled with puffy, almost painfully white clouds. He breathed deeply, contentedly, inhaling the herb-like smell of the sun-bathed meadow—the grass, the wildflowers, the pines in the distance, the scent of the girl lying next to him on the blanket. He turned his head to look at her, but he couldn't see her face clearly. She looked so familiar, but he couldn't be sure exactly who she was . . .

The loud buzz of his travel alarm jerked him from his dream into the real world. Madeira rolled over in his bunk, slowly coming fully awake. Three hundred feet above him, the winter North Atlantic thrashed and foamed, a violent mass of towering gray water and wind-blown spume driven by powers greater even than itself.

Madeira opened his eyes and looked at the little wind-up clock sitting on the built-in night table next to the phone to Central Command. 0655, he read with the help of the small night light as he groped to turn off the alarm. He glanced at the dimly lit telephone. It hadn't buzzed once all night. He stretched, almost luxuriously, and tried to drift back to the meadow, to identify the girl on the blanket but reality had him by the neck.

[1]

There was no flower-filled meadow, just damp, repackaged air. He was still commander of Cabot Station's Gold Crew, one of two that rotated service aboard the United States Navy's most decrepit subsea station.

If the habitat were a submarine, its retirement would be long overdue. Since it was not, it was expected to last forever. So, apparently, was the station's crew.

Oh hell, Madeira thought. They warned me. Cabot was at the wrong end of a long, almost hostile supply pipeline. It was the runt at the bottom of the heap. It hadn't always been that way, but it was now.

Early in the Sixties, when Vietnam was just beginning to develop into the unexpectedly monumental struggle it finally became, the United States planted portions of SOSUS—SOnar SUrveilance System—an array of antisubmarine sensors on the bottom of the North Atlantic. Shortly thereafter, the Navy decided that SOSUS could be improved by using underwater maintenance stations equipped with specialized, deep-diving worksubs. Cabot had been built on Flemish Cap, an undersea plateau 400 miles east of Newfoundland, to service the Atlantic portion of the SOSUS net lying above forty degrees north latitude.

At the time of its construction, Cabot Station represented the most advanced undersea technology. It had been a secret, high priority project. Now, almost thirty years later, it had lost its glamour and become an insigificant, often overlooked support facility. There were many in authority who considered the SOSUS defense network obsolete. To them, SOSUS—and Cabot—were expensive anachronisms at a time when the world order appeared to be changing for the better. Budgets were tight, and the incredibly observant spy satellites seemed more than adequate.

Whether or not this assessment was correct didn't matter if you were a chunky, beetle-browed junior naval officer three hundred feet underwater, trying to get a repair part that nobody wanted to give you.

Oh the hell with it, Madeira thought. So what else is new?

There was a knock at his door.

"Enter."

Dumont, the tall, rail-thin messenger of the watch, walked

in, carrying a metal clipboard. "This message just came in over the landline, Captain."

Madeira sat up slowly, took the proffered message board and flipped it open. Holding it under the nightlight, he read:

```
FROM:  COMCONDEFSURVCOM
  TO:  CO CABSTA
INFO:  NORAD
       CINCLANT
       CINCLANTFLEET
       COMSUBLANT
       DIRECTOR CENTRAL INTELLIGENCE
       DIRECTOR DEFENSE INTELLIGENCE
```

AT ONE-ONE-ZERO-SEVEN HOURS ZULU SOSUS DETECTED SCREW AND MOTOR SOUNDS NORTHERN SECTOR AREA ZEBRA FOUR-ZERO-THREE/SCREW AND MOTOR SOUNDS ENDED ABRUPTLY ONE-ZERO-ONE-TWO HOURS/INTERMITTENT FAINT POPPING SOUNDS DETECTED FOLLOWING THREE-THREE MINUTES/ANALYSIS INDICATES SMALL NON-NUCLEAR SUBMARINE PRESENTLY RESTING SEA FLOOR VICINITY SENSORS ZEBRA FOUR-ZERO-THREE TACK NINE-NINE AND SEVEN-FIVE/NO DISTRESS SIGNAL RECEIVED THIS TIME/BE FURTHER ADVISED TWO SOVIET ATTACK BOATS APPROACHING ZEBRA FOUR-ZERO-THREE FROM EAST/BT

Holding the message board in one hand, Madeira grabbed the telephone with the other and pushed a button.

A voice on the other end responded, "Central Command, Mr. Merrill speaking."

"This is the Captain. What's *Molly's* status? Has she reported anything unusual?"

"No, sir. She's right on track about four hundred miles out."

"Are there any vessels near us?"

"None within a hundred miles, sir."

"Very well."

"Captain, do you want to forward that message that just arrived to *Molly*?"

"Yes. And tell them to be alert." Madeira hung up. He pulled a copy of the message for himself then initialed the original and returned the board to the messenger.

After Dumont left, Madeira remained seated. Shit! I thought they said they weren't going to do things like this anymore. What the hell is going on?

Zebra 403 was located at the mouth of the Davis Strait, a wide, icy alley that runs north from the Atlantic between Baffin Island and Greenland to Baffin Bay, and on into the high Arctic. Sensors nine-nine and seven-five were located somewhere in the northwest corner of Zebra 403. That meant the whatever-it-was was in, or very close to, Canadian—North American—waters!

Madeira looked at his copy of the message again. From the way it read, SOSUS hadn't been tracking it. It had just appeared!

Why hadn't they been tracking it? How had it gotten there undetected? Had it wormed its way through the Northwest Passage along Canada's roof? Had it made a sub-Polar passage?

But why bother? And, even if it had, it still should have been detected sooner.

Maybe they had been tracking it and just hadn't made that fact clear in the message. There were many things his superiors neglected to tell him.

The mystery sub could be practically anybody . . . but who really wasn't the question. The questions were how had it gotten there—and what was it doing?

An outright attack on SOSUS would be insane, Madeira told himself. But what about slowly and quietly pulling the net apart and then slipping a flotilla of missile subs through? In stormy weather like this, the satellites would never detect them. Nobody would, until it was too late.

The thought propelled Madeira back to before he was born, to Pearl Harbor. That had been a Sunday, too.

The tribal memory, common to U.S. Naval officers, chilled him. The Japanese fleet had disappeared into the Pacific. At least one mini-sub had been detected and the Japanese planes had even been spotted by radar. There was plenty of warning but nobody in authority had known what to make of it. Until it was too late.

Was he to be one of the unfortunates who saw the enemy coming but didn't understand what he was seeing? Fifty fathoms down, encased in an unarmed, rotting steel cylinder, Madeira suddenly felt very vulnerable.

He reached for the phone, intending to tell Merrill to put the station on Condition One readiness, then thought better of it. He didn't want to get caught with his pants down, but he didn't want to further exhaust his crew, either.

The problem, if it was one, was almost a thousand miles away and there was nothing he could do about it right now. *Mad Molly* couldn't be sent to investigate until she had returned and been reprovisioned. *Peppermint Patty*, his other worksub, was undergoing an overhaul along with her three remote controlled work vehicles. There was no way Madeira could speed up the overhauls.

Besides, it wasn't even his problem. Not yet, anyway.

TWO

CABOT STATION—DAY ONE

Susan Constantine looked down into Cabot Station's one-atmosphere porpoise pool and laughed when she caught sight of Old Sam, the boss porpoise. "Sam, you're a dirty old man."

As if able to understand her, Sam popped out of the water and did what looked like a hornpipe. As he danced, he clicked, whistled, and nodded his head. After falling back into the water, he swam over to the catwalk on which Susan was standing. Even before he rolled over on his side, Susan knew what he wanted. He shot a column of water vapor across the tank and chortled as she scratched his stomach.

Damn! she thought for the thousandth time, this water is cold!

Associate Professor Susan Constantine found the Porpoise Section utterly depressing. The dome was a dimly lit gray chamber dominated by the three porpoise tanks. The largest of these was an open, fifteen-foot deep pool spanned by catwalks. Next to it was the smaller, enclosed saturation tank, in reality a huge hyperbaric chamber half-filled with water. The third tank was a small, open pool used for treating seriously ill porpoises.

It all reminded her of a scene from an old-time black and white horror movie—a dark and evil workroom filled with giant vats and buried in the bowels of a moldy castle. Gray concrete and gray steel. The only colors present were the drab codes on the pipes and cables that ran everywhere, dripping condensation. With the exception of the porpoises' occasional puffy breathing, and a splash every now and then, it was quiet as a crypt.

Despite her heavily insulated, almost-waterproof clothing, the chill in the air struck deep into Susan. She retreated into the small control room not because it was really any warmer, but because its bright lights made things seem a little warmer. At least she wouldn't be splashed there. She plunked herself down in the seat behind the combination desk and console and checked the clock. 0705. Another forty minutes to go.

Susan scanned the grease pencil notations on the status board, although she knew the contents by heart: Two porpoises on saturation patrol around the station, looking for air leaks or other problems and ready to assist any human divers in trouble; two more in the saturation pot. She glanced at the TV monitor in the enclosed tank. All appeared well. Four more, including Sam, were in the one-atmosphere tank, resting from patrol and ready to assist any surface mariners in distress. Finally, four porpoises were on R and R, chasing ships and mackerels, or doing whatever they do on their own time.

Of course, she thought, I should know exactly what they are doing. I'm supposed to be an expert on porpoise behavior.

According to her original schedule, Susan had already left Cabot Station and gone on to Kamehameha Station, the last stop on her itinerary. Kam Station was in the warm Pacific. Cabot Station was in the icy North Atlantic. Kam was a research station, big and shining and almost new. Cabot was a utilitarian maintenance station, and a miserable old one at that.

Susan looked at the thick, looseleaf notebook on the desk. It contained all her data. Descriptions of non-natural behavior in every porpoise she had met at every station she had visited. Reports on the initial training of each porpoise. Interviews with every handler or diver who had spent a significant amount of time with each porpoise and psychological profiles of each of these handlers and divers.

She had all the data, yet she knew her project was going to be a failure. Visiting Kam Station would be futile. It would neither prove nor disprove any of her hypotheses. This was her first big project. This was the one that was supposed to make a name for her, but it was not to be. She was now convinced that the damn porpoises often acted out of whimsy and caprice. She even suspected that some, Sam and a few others, were playing with her, purposely confounding and confusing her.

Where, for example, did Sam learn that little dance of his that so resembled a sailor's hornpipe? Neither his species nor any other had ever been observed doing it in a wild state. According to his training records, nobody taught him to dance across the waves, especially not in that highly stylized manner in which he turns and bows to each spectator, and, up until six months ago, he had never been seen doing it. Did some trainer or handler teach it to him and neglect to note it in the records? Did Sam see sailors doing it in jest? Or, did he make it up himself?

Susan had no way of knowing. Even worse, she could think of no way to find out. She'd even tried asking him. His only response had been a smile. For all she knew, the crusty old bastard understood what she was trying to do and was toying with her. Was the hornpipe act really a hornswoggle? Who was crazy, Sam or Susan?

She should have moved on two weeks ago, but, instead of leaving on schedule, she had volunteered to stay and stand two watches a day so that the Navy porpoise handlers could lend a hand elsewhere. Now she was stuck until more personnel arrived. Well, she'd made her own bed. . . .

Susan watched the red light blink on and off on the console. Somebody, probably the Sound and Security Watch, the sailor responsible for wandering around looking for leaks, fires, and other potential disasters, had opened and closed the watertight door connecting the Porpoise Section with Central Station.

"Hi, Professor Constantine. It's me, Jamison."

"Hello, Jamie," replied Susan as the young sailor, one of several female crew members, walked into the control room. "How's the watch going?"

"Great. You know, my watch is much more interesting than yours. Sitting here, all by yourself, must be the real pits."

"You're right, Jamie. How's Cabot Station holding up?"

"Oh, drips and bulges in all the usual places. Nothing new."

The biologist watched as Jamison's blonde, tomboyish figure disappeared behind a book of pipes and valves. The gloom of the Porpoise Section didn't seem to bother her at all. Every so often she would stop and tap something or shine her flashlight under or behind this or that.

As Jamison crossed the catwalk over the one-atmosphere tank, Sam made a beeline for her and launched himself into his seduction routine.

"Is it still okay for me to scratch Sam's belly? He always acts like we're real close friends."

You and every other young female, of either species, thought Susan. "Go ahead, Jamie, but watch out. Sam's a dirty old man."

Jamison knelt down and scratched while Sam continued to pour on the charm.

Susan watched Jamison play with Sam. Wasn't she going to marry what's-his-name . . . yes, Dumont, the gawky kid?

"Jamie, I understand you're thinking about getting married."

"Ms. Constantine?"

"Sorry. I didn't mean to pry."

"That's okay. It's just that the XO'll kill me if he hears that I've been talking about it. You know, there's a lot of men here and not many women and we've all been here a long time."

"My lips are sealed then, but congratulations anyway."

Jamison smiled a thank-you and left.

Susan started to muse away the rest of the watch. Her eyes settled on a number of standing orders and directives posted on the bulkhead. All were signed by Madeira.

He's a strange bird, she thought. So aloof. So distant.

She pondered the possibility that he'd been sent to Cabot as punishment for some crime or impropriety, although that didn't seem very likely. In fact, he really was quite competent and had gone out of his way to arrange for his people to help her. She couldn't complain about that. He'd always been polite—but icy. There seemed to be a wall between them. And

[9]

maybe she'd contributed to that wall. She could, she realized, get a little distant herself when she was working.

Maybe it just went with their jobs.

Whatever he's really like inside, she thought with the flicker of a smile, he looks like a thug with that squat, almost simian build, dark hair crawling down his brow, and that huge, arched nose.

Who knows, though. Maybe he likes this place. It certainly matches his personality.

THREE

CABOT STATION—DAY ONE

The little wind-up clock now read 0705. Madeira glanced at the Navy issue digital chronometer mounted on the bulkhead. The travel alarm was accurate, as usual. The little clock always gave him a certain satisfaction. His grandfather, a Portuguese fisherman, had given it to his son who, in turn, had given it to Madeira. It was at least fifty years old, yet, with frequent cleaning and lubrication kept ticking away, rarely losing more than a minute or two now and then.

Madeira lay in his bunk, listening to the clock's soft ticking and to the equally gentle 'wsssh' of circulating air.

It was getting late, he realized with a start. He sprang out of his bunk and flicked on the overhead light, illuminating his small Spartan cabin. Even through the thin rug which covered the steel deck he could feel the faint vibration of machinery. So much like a ship, he thought. Always a hum, a vibration. Only here there's no real motion. We never go anywhere, and there's no wind or sun or rain.

He returned to his bunk and started his morning exercises. The leg lifts were first. Up. Apart. Together. Apart. Together. Apart. Together. Down. He hated each and every one for its utter tediousness.

He had considered, almost every morning, skipping the whole drill completely, "just this one day." The fear of what would happen to his naturally barrel-shaped body kept him honest.

[11]

The leg-lifts were followed by fifty pushups. Then he maneuvered his stocky frame into the only private shower in the station.

0720. He was running late. He removed his collar devices from yesterday's coveralls and pinned them on a clean set. The coveralls were dark blue and made of a thick, nonflammable synthetic material. They were supposed to keep him warm. Regulation blue sneakers and thick socks completed his uniform. By 0730 he was on his way to Central Command.

The walk was a short one. Although Central Section was the larger of the two cylinders which, along with the dome-shaped Porpoise Section, made up Cabot Station, it was not very large.

"Good morning, Captain," said the Petty Officer of the Watch as Madeira entered Central Command.

"Good morning, Falk," replied Madeira. "How're your joints today?"

"Creaking a little, Captain, but that's okay if you take my age into consideration," Madeira smiled. Falk was twenty-five going on ninety.

"Good morning, Captain," said the Officer of the Deck.

"Good morning, Mr. Merrill. Is your relief late?"

"She'll be along shortly, sir."

"How are things topside?"

"Sea state seven. Wind zero-seven-five, speed five-two knots. Air temperature minus twelve Celsius. Water temperature the usual for early March. All in all, the sort of day that honest sailors should be spending in front of a fire with a pretty girl and a hot rum toddy."

Madeira smiled politely. He wondered if Merrill had ever tasted a hot rum toddy.

"As for the important data, *Molly* is right on track. ETA is still zero five hundred tomorrow. Other than *Molly* there's very little traffic. According to ConDefSurvCom, those two surface ships, the two supertankers bound for Halifax, have passed out of 403." He paused. "Do you think there's any connection between them and that last message from ConDefSurvCom?"

"I don't know, Mr. Merrill. I wish I did."

"Oh, yes, and compressor number two is performing famously."

[12]

"Is that so very unusual?"

"No, sir. Didn't you know? It crapped out during the midwatch. When I relieved him, Mr. Sonneberg said that he and the XO had squared it away, though."

And why, Madeira wondered, didn't I feel it and wake up? "Why wasn't I called?"

"I don't know, sir. I'll have to ask Mr. Sonneberg or the XO."

"You're quite right, Mr. Merrill. *I'll* ask the XO."

God! he thought as he spoke, wouldn't it be wonderful to wake up some morning and find everything operating correctly, in order and under control!

Jamison walked into Central Command.

"Sound and Security reports all secure, sir," she said to Merrill," except for the damaged door between Central Section and the Submarine Section Tunnel."

"Very well," replied Merrill.

That damned warped door, thought Madeira. They'd received not one but two replacements, each more warped than the original. At least he had an idea that might solve that problem. All he had to do was get ashore for a day or two.

Madeira leafed through the Quartermasters' Notebook, the minute by minute record of the events occurring during each watch. It didn't take him long to find what he was looking for, the report of the compressor's failure.

Why the hell had Sonneberg called the Executive Officer and not him about a serious operational casualty! Number one main compressor was already down. The auxiliaries, together, had just barely enough capacity to carry the whole station and both could use an overhaul. If number one had failed, large portions of the station might have flooded. Hell! The whole station might have gone, thanks to that damned door.

Madeira knew the answer. Sonneberg had called the XO because the XO had told him to. The XO had decided that Madeira needed sleep and to hell with Madeira's night orders.

He looked around Central Command. Everybody present was dressed in blue coveralls like his. Two petty officers, talking quietly to each other, were sitting at large separate consoles, one for communications and the other for the station's engineering and life-support systems. The third console, which monitored the station's own net of external sensors, was unoccupied. The automatic alarm would alert them to any visitors.

One of the petty officers turned to Madeira. "Morning, Captain."

"Morning, Cunningham. I see your Bruins took another one."

"Yeh. They got the cup in the bag."

"Bullshit!" snorted the other petty officer. "Vancouver's going to skate all over them."

While the two continued to argue quietly over who would win the Stanley Cup, Madeira, considering what he might say to his XO, examined the large display of the North Atlantic. Cabot, perched on Flemish Cap, was marked by a star. About nine hundred miles north of the star, he made out the dotted lines marking Zebra 403.

Something was happening there. He wished he knew what. Whatever it was, he was sure he'd have to do something about it and hoped his crew would be up to it.

The watch at Central Command seemed alert enough, but what about the others in the Porpoise Section and in the machinery spaces below him? What about the people in the Submarine Section, working on *Peppermint Patty*? How many more eighteen-hour days could they take? What about the few who were still in their bunks?

He glanced at the engineering console, at an ammeter which indicated the current coming in over the underwater electrical supply cable from the mainland. Thank God he didn't have to worry about what would now be a thirty-year-old nuclear reactor at Cabot. The diplomatic and political situations at the time of the station's construction had prevented the installation of fixed reactors on the ocean floors.

"Mr. Merrill. What do we know about those two tankers?"

"One's French and the other's Greek, Captain. They're headed to Halifax I think, from the Arctic Oil Preserve."

"Has either behaved oddly?"

"No, sir, except that both hove-to for a few hours last night. It must have been the weather. It's just awful!"

One or both of the ships could be connected to the mystery sub—but as yet Madeira couldn't see the connection. He hoped there wasn't going to be one.

FOUR

COLORADO—DAY ONE

Rear Admiral Laneland Williams, Commander, Naval Section, Continental Defense Surveillance Command, was asleep when his secure phone rang.

"Good morning, Admiral. This is Commander Pendleton. We have just received a strange report from SOSUS Atlantic concerning Area Zebra 403."

"Yes?" The admiral spoke quietly, to avoid waking his wife of almost forty years.

Pendleton described the situation.

"We weren't tracking it?"

"No, sir. It just happened. There were two Soviet missile boats in the area a few hours ago but they've gone now. One's still southeast of Greenland. I don't think it's anything important. Based on my assessment of their current intentions, it would make no sense for them to start something now but, of course, we should look into it."

"Thank you for your analysis, Commander. Are there any units in the vicinity?"

"*Lion Fish* is about a hundred miles south, playing with a Soviet attack boat."

"Very well. Ask CincLantFleet to send *Lion Fish* to investigate.

"Pendleton!" The admiral's voice grew louder. "What about Cabot? Don't they have a worksub returning home from Zebra 403?"

"It must have already returned, Admiral. We don't show it on the display."

"That, as we both know, doesn't mean a damn thing. Did they report its return?"

"I don't know, Admiral. I'll check."

"This isn't the first time those worksubs have fallen between the cracks. One of your hotshots probably had an attack of neatness and dumped it from the display to reduce the clutter."

As he spoke, the admiral wondered why he was abusing Pendleton so. Cabot's worksubs *were* hard to keep track of. It was, he decided, Pendleton himself. The man was so damn blasé, almost indifferent. And he was too damn young to be a full commander!

But it wasn't Pendleton's fault, it was endemic. There'd been so many alarms over the years and never a major fire.

And now, much of the world seemed to be scrambling for Western-style freedom, or maybe it was just Western-style affluence they really wanted, and loudly forswearing aggression in the process.

Perhaps! But there were hundreds of nations in the world, each with its own self-interest and each with its own sharp elbows. Furthermore, today's democratic trappings were no guarantee against tyranny and warlust tomorrow.

Lacking an ever-present, gnawing fear, it was understandable that Pendleton might come to view his job as, at best, a complex intellectual game; that he might become preoccupied with the process and the dynamics.

"I'll check the communications file right now, Admiral," answered Pendleton, alarmed at the admiral's tone of voice.

"Before you start rooting around in the files, contact Cabot and ask them if this could be their sub and if it's in trouble." And, continued Williams to himself, prove you're the hotshot you think you are by getting those two Soviet attack boats to tell us what they're up to.

"Aye, aye, Admiral."

"God damn them!" mumbled Williams as he hung up.

"Is something wrong, Lane?"

Williams turned to his wife. "Nothing serious, dear. Just another screw-up. I hope."

The admiral lay in bed a few minutes, fuming. Despite his best efforts, nobody paid much attention to Cabot and its worksubs. If they didn't carry missiles or torpedoes, they weren't worth thinking about. Yet, without them, SOSUS would fall apart and without SOSUS he'd have even less idea where the Soviet missile boats were. . . .

He caught himself in mid-thought. The problem wasn't just that everybody else took Cabot for granted. It was also him. He was the one who kept cutting Cabot's budget. He did it because he'd found that only large sums of increasingly scarce dollars seemed capable of bringing about needed technological improvements in his strategic surveillance system. At the same time, he'd also found it was usually safe to gamble that most of Cabot's problems could be overcome by its crew's hard work and stout hearts.

He resented having to abuse Cabot but consoled himself that he did it for a good reason—not one that would get him into heaven but one that might keep him out of hell—while the others did it out of negligence or stupidity.

Feeling hungry, and no longer tired, he put on his bathrobe and went downstairs to the kitchen where he filled a bowl with the detestable bran cereal his wife made him eat. As he added low-fat milk, he switched off the kitchen light so he could look out the window while he ate.

To the east, as far as he could see, the High Plains lay below him, covered with a blanket of moon-lit snow. The admiral couldn't decide if the scene reminded him more of cloud cover as seen from above or of a calm, strangely gold-white night at sea. It was an Olympian view, he decided, although he didn't feel very divine. Just old and irritated. Maybe that's how *they* felt, he mused. Old and irritated.

Could this be it? The big one? The attack he'd been preparing for, and dreading, all his adult life? No, this wasn't it. The news had been so encouraging lately. Not unless something else happened within the next few minutes. If this were it, SOSUS wouldn't be the target.

He hoped he was right. He couldn't afford a war; not that anyone else could either. He had a wife he loved, and children and grandchildren. He also had his own retirement to think about. He would buy a sailboat. Then he and Kate would spend their last days cruising the Chesapeake, a nutty, overweight old admiral who never quite got his sails trimmed and his ever-patient wife. The vision was overpoweringly seductive; that he might move at his own pace and pursue his own whims, freed from the tyranny of gigabytes, nanoseconds, and systems for this and that.

There would be no consulting jobs or meaningless boards or commissions for him. Perhaps it was all a dream, an illusion of escape as heady and, ultimately, as futile as heroin, but he couldn't wait to find out.

Admiral Williams looked at the remains of his cereal. I'm going to have a real breakfast this morning, he decided. I'm going to make a meal of the moron who allowed that worksub to be dropped from the display. He then realized, with regret, that it was Sunday. The culprit would probably be at home.

Moments later, his phone rang again.

"Admiral, this is Pendleton again. ComSubLant is worried about Zebra 403. He's issued an alert and is redeploying some of his units."

"Are any of their missile boats moving?"

"Not so far, Admiral."

"Very well. Has that follow-up message gone out to Cabot about its worksubs?"

"Yes it has, Admiral."

"Very well. I'm on my way."

As he spoke, Admiral Williams tasted his half-digested, late-night snack.

FIVE

LION FISH—DAY ONE

Sam Peacock had been awake for almost twenty-four hours and had loved every second of it.

Smoking a cigar and drinking his umpteenth cup of coffee, *Lion Fish*'s commanding officer studied the tactical plot in his control room. Eighty miles to the east, two Soviet attack boats were approaching; three miles to port of him, a third was escorting *Lion Fish* north. They were all heading for the same point, a small dot along the northern edge of Zebra 403.

Peacock's orders were to investigate the bottomed sub located at that small dot. But what kept him interested was the prospect of out-thinking and out-maneuvering not one but three Soviet boats.

For almost twenty years, all of his naval career, he had practiced hunting and killing other submarines. It was the sort of occupation one had to love to excel at. Although he didn't believe the Age of Aquarius had arrived, he doubted the occasion would ever arise for him to actually sink another sub. He had no compunctions about doing so but it didn't seem likely. In his opinion, there would be no direct, open conflict between the powers. All the players were being too careful for that. The struggle would continue as it had for decades—a peace of feints, bluster and harassment; of maneuver, intrigue, and deception; of propaganda; of love, kisses, and stilettos. There would be painful, bloody skirmishes, which would be denied by everybody, but no general conflagration unless one player panicked or gained a clear advantage over the others.

Peace was the "war" to which Peacock was accustomed. The thrill was in the hunt, the maneuver, the feeling of near omnipotence that surged through him every time seven thousand tons of high strength steel and delicate electronics meshed and jumped in response to his slightest utterance. He honestly never expected to execute a kill.

The drill with the Soviet boat now to port had been a good exercise but the Russian, and his boat, simply weren't in the same league as Peacock and *Lion Fish*. Maybe the three of them together would be more of a challenge.

"Captain, you realize those two will reach that sub before we do, don't you?"

Peacock looked at his navigator. "They won't be ahead of us by much. They'll still be there when we arrive."

Two hours later, sonar reported that the two Soviet interlopers had commenced using very high frequency sonar.

"That'll be their high resolution scanners, Captain. They must have arrived," remarked the XO.

"How are they maneuvering?"

"They're in column, one behind the other, making box turns around that sub, or whatever it is."

"Let's chase them away . . ."

"Captain," said the Sonarman, "The two Russians have secured their high freq gear. They're also increasing speed.

"Captain, they're leaving. They're heading east at high speed."

"Shit! We'll never catch them. What about our friend to port?"

"He's still with us."

"Very well. Light off the scanning sonar. I suppose we ought to know what they know."

Lion Fish slowed and circled the bottomed submarine.

"It's a small sub," reported the Sonarman. "Probably a worksub of some sort. A hundred feet long. No emissions, no nothing."

"All right. Now the TV monitor." Peacock turned his submarine until her bow pointed at the target and then brought her to a stop. He ordered the external flood light turned on and examined the hazy view on the monitor. "Doesn't look like one of ours . . . at least not Navy. No markings.

"XO. Try the hydrophone. See if there's any response."

The XO nodded and the Sonarman started to transmit. Sonar pulses, modulated into International Morse signals asked, "What ship is that? Do you require assistance?"

Over and over, the message repeated, with no reply.

"What's our friend doing?" asked Peacock.

"The Russian's about a thousand yards to port, Captain. He's just sitting there, probably listening to us."

"Very well. We're going to bottom and go quiet. If anybody's alive in that worksub they must have heard us by now. But just to make sure, I want a signaling charge detonated."

A small explosive charge was shot out one of the forward torpedo tubes and detonated. Then *Lion Fish* settled to the bottom and full Quiet Ship procedures were executed.

Peacock listened for forty minutes and heard absolutely nothing: no answering signals, no pounding on the little sub's hull.

"There may still be somebody there, XO, but we've got no way of knowing."

ComConDefServCom replied to his report an hour-and-a-half later. Peacock yawned, and said to his XO, "We're supposed to sit here a few days, watch this thing and keep the Russians from snatching it until the Bubbleheads from Cabot can get here."

"At least we'll have company," replied the XO.

"Yeh, but he's no fun. I'm hitting the rack."

Lion Fish resumed cruising in a box pattern around the bottomed submarine, continuing to listen as she went. The Russian took station astern and duplicated her every maneuver.

SIX

CABOT STATION—DAY ONE

Madeira encountered his Executive Officer in the passageway outside the cafeteria. "Good morning, Captain."

"Morning, XO. You trying to take my job?" He didn't like having to chew out a man whose main offense had been simple consideration. Just the same, it had to be done.

"Captain?"

"Number two compressor. Why didn't Mr. Sonneberg call me?"

"That's my fault, Captain. I thought Sonneberg and I could handle it without bothering you."

"You could. Obviously. But I'm paid to be bothered. If you were me, and you *will* have your own command soon, you wouldn't tolerate that sort of thing."

As he spoke, Madeira reversed the question in his mind. When he was an XO would he have called the captain? Probably not, especially if he liked him. He caught himself. If he had done so, he would have been wrong, just as his XO was wrong now.

"No, sir. I doubt I would. It won't happen again."

"Very well. Can I buy you a cup of coffee?"

"You have a deal, Captain."

"You have any guesses about what's going on in Zebra 403?" asked Madeira after they had collected food. As the two men settled at a table behind the curtain that defined what passed for a wardroom, he added, "and how it got there?"

"It doesn't look like an attack to me, but I wouldn't be surprised if they're trying to screw up SOSUS somehow."

"I'd love to catch them red-handed—if the attack boats will let us."

"Maybe *Lion Fish* will learn something."

"I doubt it. They're not equipped to. They'll probably just end up tangling with the Russians."

"Do you think they'd risk a serious incident?"

"They might. Getting caught in other people's harbors never seems to bother them. Why should this?"

"What about the crew, Captain?"

"You've got me. I suppose they're dead. Otherwise, somebody would be doing something, or asking us to."

"If the sub is theirs, it'll be a race between us and their salvage people. How will we get past their attack boats?"

"They'll have the same problem if *Lion Fish* stays. I don't know the answer, but I'm sure Admiral Williams will expect us to try."

The phone buzzed. Madeira answered.

"This is Mr. Merrill, sir. We've got an answer for that second message from the admiral. *Molly* reports that she ain't it, and she don't know nothing about it."

"Is that exactly what she said or did you paraphrase? Please read it to me exactly as we received it. . . . Very well. Forward it to ComConDefSurvCom. . . . No, you go ahead and release it yourself, if you can resist the temptation to improve on it."

"Well," continued the XO, "by tomorrow we'll have both worksubs."

"Whichever is ready first."

"Who do you want to send? Chief Mackinaw or Mr. Frazier?"

"Frazier. He's more experienced."

"He'll be tired when he and *Molly* get back."

Madeira paused. "He probably will be shot. Tell Hammerstein to go himself."

"Aye, aye, sir."

"Is there anything new on the Blue Crew?" asked Madeira, changing the subject.

"Same as before. Personnel says it's seriously under-strength but they plan to get it back up and send them out fairly soon. It seems they had to fill higher priority needs before getting to us. In the meantime, a few people may be on *Procyon* when she arrives next week, thanks to Captain Robertson."

There was a loud crash on the other side of the curtain.

"Watch where you're going, you stupid asshole!"

"Screw off, Pettit."

Madeira looked out the curtain just as Pettit, covered with coffee, stood up and grabbed Dumont who was holding an empty mess tray in his hands. The tray's contents were scattered across the mess table and around the deck.

"I'm going to beat the crap out of you, you clumsy shit!"

"Oh, really?"

The man seated next to Pettit stood up and placed himself between the two antagonists. "Hold it, Pettit. Cool off! It was an accident."

"Knock it off!"

Madeira craned his neck to watch Chief Mackinaw, the station's Chief Master at Arms, approaching the impending battle. "Sit down, Pettit! You too," he added, glaring at Dumont.

After Pettit had been sent off to change his uniform, the XO said, "It's surprising we haven't had more of that, Captain."

Madeira turned to his Executive Officer. "We've been lucky." He wondered uneasily if the fight might have anything to do with Dumont's and Jamison's romance. As far as he could tell, they'd heeded the XO's instructions to keep it cool, but Madeira also knew jealousy often blooms in fields fertilized with fatigue and fear.

The XO yawned. "Captain, if you'll excuse me, I'd like to have a word with Chief Mackinaw about that little drama. Then, I'd like to take a short nap. I had a long night last night."

Madeira studied the now almost empty cafeteria. The black and white tiles on the deck showed their years of service, as did the plastic tables and chairs. The white bulkheads looked faintly green, the fake wood paneling drab. Only the gleaming, stainless steel serving line looked as it had when new.

The space was clean but badly worn. Why the hell wouldn't they let him have the resources to refurbish it?

Shit! He didn't have the manpower to do it anyway.

The curtain parted and Susan Constantine walked in carrying juice, coffee and three English muffins. Although freshly showered she did not appear refreshed.

"Good morning, Professor," said Madeira as he stood up. "How are you finding life at Cabot?"

"A little trying, Captain, but I'm up to it." She smiled briefly as she sat down to eat.

Madeira found himself looking closely at Susan as he sipped his coffee. Straining not to stare, he examined her long dark hair, his glance returning repeatedly to her astonishingly green eyes. But there was more to her eyes than just green; there was also a sense of depth which hinted at either a great and complex pain, or great understanding, or both. And there was more to her than just her eyes; there was also her slender, but most unboyish, body.

He'd been as aware as anybody of her attractions the minute she'd arrived, but he'd forced himself not to think about them. She was a visiting academic on business. Just as he didn't want his men distracted by her, neither could he afford to be. There was too much work to be done.

Oh hell, he thought. It won't hurt to be polite.

"Ms. Constantine, I hope you realize just how much we all appreciate your pitching in the way you have. I wish there were some way we could pay you back."

Susan munched on that for a minute, aware and slightly surprised that he had been studying her. She wondered if it would be too much to ask him to redecorate the Porpoise Section. "I'm glad I can help. Anyway, you and your people have helped me a lot with my project."

Her project, thought Madeira. Another example of the "Cabot Touch." Another job gone wrong, or so his porpoise handlers seemed to feel. He asked her about it.

Is he really interested in my work, she thought, or is he just making polite conversation; not that she'd seen him shoot the breeze much until now.

"As you know, I developed certain hypotheses concerning how porpoises have changed as a result of associating with humans. Unfortunately, I can't seem to prove or disprove any of them."

"Maybe you'll get the data you need at Kam Station. They should be able to be of much more assistance than we've been."

"I'm afraid not. The data's not the problem. For the most part, I've collected exactly the type I expected to get. The problem is, the whole project was ill-conceived. I've bitten off more than I can chew."

"Do you mean that we don't have the background necessary to interpret the data?"

Susan was genuinely surprised at Madeira's perception. Could it be that he was something more than the zombie she'd seen up 'til now?

"Would another head be of any use? I might spot something too obvious and simpleminded for you to have noticed."

She laughed. "All help gratefully accepted. Are you sure you want to go into all the gory details? You have quite a few of your own to worry about."

Madeira assured her that he really did want to hear about the project. As she described it, Cabot Station and Zebra 403 drifted out of his mind. The project was interesting but she was more interesting. She looked so young, younger than her twenty-eight years. Despite his preoccupations, he noticed a warmth about her.

Following the path of her words, his eyes settled on her lips, so smooth and full. His thoughts returned to the sunlit meadow. Was she the girl on the blanket?

Sitting, staring at her, he realized that he had isolated himself from much of that which gave life meaning. A reasonable ambition to get the job done had become a consuming obsession.

Where did he stand now? Thirty-seven years old, trapped in a rotting steel can on the bottom of the Atlantic, enmeshed in problems that appeared to be way beyond his abilities to solve, feeling very much alone. Susan Constantine would leave eventually and he would stay. It seemed as if he would stay forever.

"Captain, am I losing you?"

"No, Ms. Constantine. Just the opposite, I'm afraid."

"Pardon me?"

"You were saying about the difficulties of defining 'culture' in terms of porpoises?"

Susan continued. It hurt, this recognition of himself and his future. He could see no escape, not while he was at Cabot.

SEVEN

CABOT STATION—DAY ONE

Madeira walked along the narrow corridor from the cafeteria to Central Command, his thoughts straying from the heavy, slow-moving images that had dominated them for months. The dark kaleidoscope of disassembled machinery and abyssal ooze was pushed far into the background by brilliant visions of green eyes and dark hair. A thousand old dreams came and went, the fantasies of a sailor too long at sea—or in his case, under it.

His wandering mind snapped back to Cabot Station when he entered Central Command. He greeted Ensign Ryan, the OOD, and then walked over to the display of the North Atlantic.

Even though it was Sunday, Central Command was becoming busy. At Cabot, every day was a workday. One of the phones buzzed and was answered by the Petty Officer of the Watch.

"Ms. Ryan, Mr. Hammerstein requests permission to open the watertight door between the Submarine Section tunnel and Central Section."

"For how long?"

"Ten minutes, ma'am."

"Permission granted."

Most of the requests and information which were now flowing through Central Command were routine. A few, if disregarded, misunderstood, or handled stupidly, contained the seeds of disaster. Sonneberg, the Engineering and Life Support Systems Officer, wanted permission to secure the electrolysis unit, the device which supplied Cabot with oxygen by breaking down seawater into its component gases, while his people did preventative maintenance on the compressors. The Porpoise Section wanted permission to send two unsaturated porpoises on patrol and to start decompressing two currently saturated porpoises.

Madeira watched and listened as Ryan responded to each request or report. She was the junior officer aboard the station. She had only recently been qualified to stand watch as OOD, but was handling everything crisply and correctly.

He stopped his pacing at one of the vacant consoles and switched on a TV monitor, the camera of which was mounted on a surface monster buoy. The buoy, which supported various radio and radar antennae in addition to the TV camera, was rolling so violently that it was difficult to determine if he was seeing gray sea or gray sky.

There's ice out there too, Madeira thought. He couldn't see it, but he knew it was there. Pack ice. Forty, fifty miles to the northwest. One year the ice had even torn the monster buoy away.

Transfixed by the storm for several minutes, Madeira's thoughts continued to wander. He wondered if the storm, and the mystery in Zebra 403, were bringing war with them. Today? Tomorrow? Next month?

If there was to be a nuclear war, he mused, he would be nothing more than a spectator. "Look at the bright side," he told himself. "At least we'll survive the initial exchange."

Madeira departed Central Command for his office, where he wedged himself in behind his tiny desk and looked at his "In" box. It had been filled to overflowing by the yeoman.

He grabbed a handful of paper. On top was a recommendation of promotion for one of the divers. He read the letter over and started to sign but found his pen dry. Throwing the useless pen in the wastebasket, he searched his desk for a fresh one. As he did, his mind wandered yet again.

He'd almost married once. Years ago. A few years after he'd graduated from the Academy, when he was still young, when he still enjoyed shouting at the wind and waves.

He'd loved her. He'd ached for her. She, however, had second thoughts. Just as well, he decided. His would undoubtedly have been one of the fifty percent of marriages that fall apart.

Anyway, she wasn't the girl on the blanket.

Madeira returned distractedly to the pile of papers before him, reading and signing mechanically while his mind roamed everywhere and nowhere.

At 1125 the messenger brought him an incoming message:

```
FROM: COMCONDEFSURVCOM
  TO: CO CABSTA
INFO: CONCLANT
      CINCLANTFLEET
      COMSUBLANT
      LION FISH
      DIRECTOR CENTRAL INTELLIGENCE
      DIRECTOR DEFENSE INTELLIGENCE


      LION FISH REPORTS SUBMARINE REPORTED ZEBRA
FOUR-ZERO-THREE APPEARS TO BE WORKSUB
APPROX LENGTH ONE-ZERO-ZERO FEET/NO
INDICATION OF LIFE ABOARD/WHEN READY FOR SEA
DISPATCH CABOT WORKSUB TO INVESTIGATE AND
BOARD IF POSSIBLE/MISSION TO BE CONSIDERED
HIGHEST PRIORITY AND UNUSUALLY HAZARDOUS/
ONE SOVIET SSN REMAINS VICINITY/LION FISH TO
REMAIN VICINITY AND PROVIDE PROTECTION CABOT
WORKSUB/RULES OF ENGAGEMENT TO BE
SCRUPULOUSLY OBSERVED/ADVISE ETD CABOT AND
ETA ZEBRA FOUR-ZERO-THREE/BT
```

Madeira tapped his pen on the desk, then reached for the phone and buzzed the Submarine Section.

"This is the Captain. Is Mr. Hammerstein there?"

There was a pause.

"Bob. We've just received orders to send a worksub to board that whatever-it-is in Zebra 403. Is tomorrow afternoon still the best we can do?"

"Yes, Captain, and that'll take some luck."

"Very well."

Madeira hung up and drafted a reply to ComConDef-SurvCom, which he dropped off in Central Command on his way to lunch.

When he arrived at the table, Susan was already there talking with, or rather listening to, Merrill. Madeira smiled at her, sat, and turned to his Executive Officer, also at the table.

"XO, about Zebra 403. How many trawlers have been in the area recently?"

"Not many, Captain, 'though they have a lot of trouble keeping track of them, especially in weather like this. They've probably all run for cover by now."

"It's hard to tell the difference between a trawler and an intelligence ship, except for the smell," replied Madeira, smiling as he thought of the summer vacations he'd spent working on his uncle's trawler.

The XO also smiled. He remembered Madeira's stories about his brief career as a fisherman. "I can't believe anybody's out doing much sniffing around right now. Even in good weather there's no way to check on all of them."

The phone buzzed. "Captain, this is Communications. Admiral Williams is on the secure phone for you."

"I'll take it here."

Madeira heard several clicks.

"Madeira? This is Admiral Williams. Do you read me?"

"Yes, Admiral. I read you fine."

"Very well. Is tomorrow afternoon the absolute earliest you can get a worksub underway?"

Madeira squirmed. "Yes it is, Admiral."

"I had hoped you'd be able to respond more quickly, but tomorrow will have to do. I have nothing else to send that will arrive before your sub. For that matter, you and your worksubs are about all we have that can handle this at all. The damn thing seems to be under near-solid ice. It's about five miles inside the current ice line and we have to get a man aboard."

Madeira couldn't help wondering if he really wanted Cabot to be the only facility that could handle the problem.

"Madeira," Williams continued. "I cannot stress strongly enough how serious and sensitive this affair may prove to be."

"I understand, Admiral."

"This may be the first phase of something big, although I doubt it's an attack."

Madeira decided the admiral had also been thinking of Pearl. He was almost old enough to have been there. "I'm inclined to think it's some sort of test or probe, Admiral, or maybe they're trying to screw with SOSUS."

"Those are all possibilities."

The admiral paused, then continued, "I'm personally inclined to think it's the Russians but I have no idea what they're doing and, to be honest, we have no intelligence, hard or soft, which indicates that it really is them. It seems Russia has gone a little murky lately. We're having trouble getting reliable information out."

"You feel it could be anybody, then?"

"Yes, although I still favor the Russians. They appear to have known about it as soon as we did, if not sooner. Two of their attack boats did lope in, sniff around, and then amble off before *Lion Fish* arrived."

"*Lion Fish* may have been their initial objective and they stumbled on it. Or maybe they've been reading our mail again."

Admiral Williams sighed. "Yes, both of those are very real possibilities, Madeira, especially the latter. But I'm not interested in possibilities. I want answers and you're going to get them for me.

"Now please listen carefully because there are several complications which make this whole affair even more delicate and important."

"Yes, Admiral?"

"First, the Canadians. As you know, they are extremely sensitive about people intruding on their Arctic domains. . . ."

"Didn't they almost declare war on us a few years ago for sending a ship through the Northwest Passage without their permission?"

"Exactly. It's damn difficult for them to exercise effective sovereignty over that huge land area of theirs. There's just not enough of them. The President doesn't want them, or anybody else, to know about what's going on for the time being."

"Why? Because they might think the sub is ours?"

"They might very well. In this regard, they really don't trust us much. But that's not the main reason. The main

[32]

reason is that he wants to keep it out of the papers. He doesn't want to be forced into accusing the Russians of anything until he's sure it's them and until he knows what they're doing. If we tell the Canadians, or more than two or three people in Congress, it'll get out and his hands will be tied.

"Remember, he's scheduled to sign Phase Five of the Conventional Arms Reduction Agreement in May."

"I'd forgotten about that. This could make a difference, couldn't it."

"Yes, of course. Depending on whose it is and what it was doing, it might be unwise for us to sign any further agreements, no matter what the media says.

"To be honest, I suspect he's wondering if he's dealing with the right people . . . if they'll still be around in six months." The admiral cleared his throat. "Madeira, whoever you send must have his head well screwed on. In the unlikely event he does stumble into an attack force, or if he is attacked, he's to alert us at all costs. This is his highest priority, higher than his own self-preservation. Otherwise, he is to get aboard that sub and determine whose it is, what it's doing there and, if possible, how it got there undetected."

While Admiral Williams paused again, Madeira looked around the table at the others. They were all looking at him with expressions ranging from fascination to amazement, saying nothing. It was obvious that they'd all been listening to his side of the conversation.

"*Lion Fish*," continued Williams, "will be there to protect your people but she may have her hands full with that one remaining Soviet. Should they decide to concentrate their forces then both your man and *Lion Fish* may be in trouble. CincLant has redeployed to protect against something major. He can't reinforce *Lion Fish*.

"I'm very much aware that getting a man aboard the sub at that depth will be very dangerous, even if they don't harass your sub, but it must be done! Your man is to avoid creating any unnecessary incident but, at the same time, he is not to let himself be pushed around. Can you trust your skipper with this sort of responsibility? There may not be time for him to contact you, or for you to contact me."

"Yes, I can, Admiral. I'm sending Lieutenant Hammerstein, my Submarines Officer. He's the most senior worksub skipper and has excellent judgement."

"Captain, this is Ms. Ryan, the OOD. I'm sorry to cut in but we've just received a transmission from Mr. Frazier in *Molly* reporting that they've suffered an engineering casualty and are reducing speed to six knots."

"What's down and how far out are they?"

"One of the main propulsion motors, sir. They're about three hundred miles out." She sounded out of breath.

"Do they have any other damage? What about their life support systems?"

"The only damage he's reported so far is to the one motor. There was a fire but he thinks it's out now."

"Very well. I'm on my way to Central Command."

"Madeira!"

Oh shit! Admiral Williams was still on the line.

"I apologize for the interruption, Admiral."

"Quite all right. Your OOD did the right thing, don't you think? Reflects well on her CO."

"Yes, Admiral. Thank you."

"And what are you going to do now? Save *Molly* and her crew or carry out my order as expeditiously as possible?"

Madeira clutched the phone so hard his knuckles cracked. After taking a moment to collect his thoughts, he replied, "Admiral, unless otherwise directed and unless new information comes to light, I will recover *Molly* and then investigate Zebra 403. If a Soviet attack force *is* headed our way, the war will be over before *Patty* ever leaves Cabot. I seriously doubt the Russians can remove that submarine before we get there, assuming *Lion Fish* is on the ball. I'm also sure that if they choose to mass their forces they will do so long before we can reach Zebra 403. However, the loss of one of my two worksubs *will* make a big difference in SOSUS' long term effectiveness."

"What is your estimation of their intentions?"

"That is irrelevant, Admiral. My decision is based on their capabilities, as I understand them, and ours."

"What about *Molly's* crew, Madeira? You know them all personally. Probably like them. Is your friendship influencing your decision?"

Exasperated, Madeira replied, "Yes, Admiral, I'm sure it is. My motivations are mixed. I realize that!"

"What about the crew of the mystery sub, whoever they are? Don't they deserve to live?"

"There is no indication that they are still alive and every indication that warrant officer Frazier and his crew are."

"Very well, Madeira. Carry on."

The line went dead.

Madeira excused himself and headed for Central Command. When he arrived, he noted a new undercurrent of tension at Central Command. He looked at the status board and at the display. *Molly* was three hundred miles out and two hundred feet down. In this weather, surfacing was not an option. One more major casualty would kill Frazier and his crew—and casualties always seemed to come several at a time. The old warrant officer, like Admiral Williams, was due to retire soon. Madeira clenched his teeth.

He crossed to the XO, who was standing behind Ryan. "Tell Hammerstein to shake a leg. He's going to take *Patty* and go get Frazier. We'll worry about Zebra 403 after we get *Molly* back."

Aboard *Molly*, Warrant Officer First Class Jack Frazier, coughing from the acrid fumes left by the electrical fire in the motor, was interrogating the sailor sitting at the control console. "Tell me again just how it happened."

"It was so quick, Mr. Frazier. There was a surge on the ammeter and then a loud bang. I secured power right away and called you."

"That was it? You had no other warning?"

"No, sir."

"Okay. Sounds like you did everything right, son."

"This motor's finished," said a voice over the intercom. "It's completely burned out, boss."

Frazier turned to the bulkhead-mounted speaker. "Roger, Arnold."

Just then, there was a "pop." *Molly* veered sharply to port.

"I thought you secured power to that motor!"

"I did, sir. That was in the console."

"Shift to manual override!" ordered Frazier, as he grabbed

[35]

a fire extinguisher and shot it into the smoking console. The console clicked a few times as the smoke dissipated.

"I have her under control, Mr. Frazier, although the steering and trim are sloppy."

"Do the best you can."

The warrant officer then spoke into the intercom. "Arnold. Finish securing that motor and come forward. You and I have to tear this fucking console apart again."

"Roger, boss."

"Mr. Frazier, we're in deep shit, aren't we?" asked the sailor at the console.

Frazier looked at him. One of the youngest at the station. This was his first real trip in a worksub.

"Yes, we are, son. But don't worry. We'll get out of it. There's nothing I can't handle, except for my ex-wives."

EIGHT

PEPPERMINT PATTY— DAY TWO

Bob Hammerstein was even more "career" than Madeira. Hammerstein was a mustang. Raised in Iowa, he had enlisted at an illegally early age, risen to second class petty officer, been sent to college at the Navy's expense and then commissioned an ensign.

Now, after eight years of commissioned service and the original six of enlisted service, the rigors of his chosen life fazed him little. All the same, he was worried about *Molly*. It was obvious to him that her overworked electrical system was self-destructing component by component. He knew that he had to reach her before the degeneration got too far; before she killed Frazier and the rest of his crew.

As soon as Hammerstein learned of the emergency, he had accelerated *Peppermint Patty's* overhaul by a few precious hours, achieving this feat the only way possible, by taking even more shortcuts.

Sitting at *Patty's* control console as she raced away from Cabot, he wondered about the wisdom of his actions. He may well have condemned two crews in a misguided effort to save one. It was a race with time but the race was rigged against them. *Molly* and her crew could be snuffed out at any time, no matter what he did.

He shifted in his seat. My God, he was tired! He ached all over. He wondered if fatigue had clouded his judgment.

Hammerstein looked over at Pettit sitting behind the port conning console. A good man, although high strung. He racked his brain for some way to start a conversation. It would help keep them both awake. Unfortunately, everybody at Cabot knew everybody else's life history by now.

It didn't matter. Hammerstein was sure Pettit would stay awake. Pettit knew he could just as easily be aboard *Molly* as *Patty*.

During the first hour after her departure, *Patty* scooted along at a depth of two hundred feet, about a hundred feet above Flemish Cap's surface, as she headed just east of north, almost into the southeasterly flowing remnants of the Labrador Current. Despite the current's drift, which was slowing *Patty*'s advance, the little submarine was making good time.

As she approached the Cap's edge, the bottom started to drop away rapidly. When the fathometer indicated one thousand feet of water below the sub's keel, Hammerstein dove to eight hundred feet, a comfortable cruising depth below the level of the current's maximum velocity.

Patty was now making eighteen knots but there was virtually no sensation of movement. The worksub's motors, powered by fuel cells, whirred almost imperceptibly. Hammerstein looked out one of the viewing ports and saw very little. One high-powered flood light, pointed directly ahead, revealed a perpetually ill-defined green room with dark walls. Reference to the TV monitors showed the same unending scene. *Patty*, surrounded by a dim ball of green light, was racing out of darkness into darkness.

Rarely, a speck of detritus, plummeting to the ocean's ever-receding bottom far below, would appear like a star in the flood's beam. Then and only then, could Hammerstein's brain perceive or imagine motion. Once the speck disappeared from the light's limited sphere, all became as before.

His thoughts drifted to other times and places. A summer evening on an Iowa farm, the wind gently ruffling the endless acres of corn. A beach in Hawaii. His mind began to separate itself from his body. A sense of warmth and relaxed comfort settled over and through him.

"Mr. Hammerstein. It's 1900 hours and *Molly* just reported in."

Pettit's voice dragged Hammerstein back. "What did they say?"

"Everything's okay except they're still having trouble clearing the foul air. The scrubbers aren't operating up to capacity."

God damn Frazier and his ironman act! thought Hammerstein. The old bastard could be choking to death but he'd never admit it.

Nine hours after they had left Cabot, the bottom dropped to almost twelve thousand feet, more than two miles below *Patty*. Hammerstein called all hands to recheck every system and piece of equipment and ascended to two hundred feet.

Two hours later, guided by Sonar homing signals, the two sisters emerged from the cold darkness into the dim glow of each other's lights. Despite the vagueness of the green glow, Hammerstein could see *Molly* was wobbling as she went. Fourteen thousand feet below the rendezvous point, the last of the continental slope was merging with the Atlantic's abyssal plain.

Hammerstein reported the rendezvous to Madeira and established voice contact with Frazier using the digital encoder.

"Good to see you, Fraz. We were all worried."

"Welcome, Bob. There's nothing to worry about. We've got everything under control."

"How's your air? Would you like a shot of fresh O2? We'll trail an air line with a drogue."

"I don't think we can do it. Our steering and trim control are too sloppy. We'll just tear the hose to pieces—if we catch it at all."

"We could bottom and do it there."

"I'd rather not. Can't trust my trim controls at that depth."

"Very well. We'll escort you back to Cabot."

"Roger. Glad to have you along."

Hammerstein guided *Patty* around her slow-moving sister, looking for external signs of damage. There were none. Satisfied, he turned to parallel *Molly*'s wobbly southwesterly course and took station fifty yards abeam.

Making six knots, the two worksubs commenced the return trip, aided now by the Labrador Current. As they crept through the barren waters back along the Continental Slope, Hammerstein cursed the repair parts that never arrived. If they had sent him what he needed, he wouldn't have had to jury-rig and rework so much and *Molly* wouldn't be limping along now.

One hundred sixty miles to go. With the help of the current, a little over twenty hours. He started counting the minutes.

Three hours after rendezvous, *Molly* wobbled violently and plunged into the darker waters below.

"*Molly*. This is *Patty*. Over!"

Nothing.

"*Molly*. This is *Patty*. Do you require assistance?"

Silence.

Hammerstein tried again and again to contact Frazier as he drove *Patty* ever deeper in pursuit of her crippled sister.

PATTY TO CABSTA/ MOLLY DIVING RAPIDLY/ APPEARS
OUT OF CONTROL/ UNABLE TO RE-ESTABLISH
CONTACT/ AM PURSUING/ BT

"Oh Christ!" mumbled Madeira as he read Hammerstein's transmission. The pencil in one of his hands snapped.

There was near silence at Central Command as *Patty*'s reports continued.

PASSING ONE-FIVE-ZERO-ZERO FEET. NO CHANGE.
PASSING TWO-ZERO-ZERO-ZERO FEET. NO CHANGE.
PASSING TWO-FIVE-ZERO-ZERO FEET. NO CHANGE.

Down went *Molly* with *Patty* plummeting behind her. Down toward the ooze.

Madeira stared at the communications console, almost unable to move. He felt like screaming in frustration. There wasn't a single useful thing he could do at the moment. He could, of course, transmit all the bad, irrelevant advice he wished to—he *was* the captain—but that would be childish.

[40]

He wasn't on the scene and he possessed no relevant information that Frazier and Hammerstein lacked.

Despite years of service, at times like this he still had to force himself to recognize that his was an authority designed to be delegated. It was his responsibility to establish policy and to select others to make most of the decisions and issue the orders. To the extent that they succeeded or failed, he succeeded or failed.

CABSTA THIS IS PATTY/ MOLLY NO LONGER DIVING/
APPEARS UNDER CONTROL/ AM ATTEMPTING TO
REESTABLISH CONTACT/ BT

Madeira took a deep breath and found himself holding it, waiting to hear that *Molly* had lurched out of control again and was headed for oblivion.

CABSTA FROM MOLLY/ REGRET RECENT
PERFORMANCE/ CO2 LEVEL BUILDUP/ HELMSMAN
PASSED OUT/ EVERYTHING UNDER CONTROL NOW/ AM
BLEEDING IN LAST O2 RESERVE/ ESTIMATE FOUR
HOURS BREATHABLE AIR/ AM ASCENDING TO EIGHT-
ZERO-ZERO FEET AND CONTINUING TRANSIT/ BT

Four hours of air left in *Molly*, thought Madeira, and at least that long until she reached Cabot. It was going to be tight, especially if Frazier was overestimating his air supply.

A few minutes later, the two worksubs appeared on Cabot's long-range Sonar display. As Madeira watched the faint, seemingly stationary blips, he mulled the next move, which in this case was his to make.

"Cabsta, this is *Patty*. Over." Voice communications had been established.

"*Patty*, this is Cabot. I read you faint but clear."

"Roger, Cabot. Approaching edge of Flemcap. Commencing ascent to two-five-zero feet."

"*Molly*, *Patty*, this is Cabot. Immediately upon arrival Flemcap, bottom and transfer O2 to *Molly*. Upon completion transfer, proceed home. Upon arrival Cabot, *Molly* to go dead in water. *Patty* to warp *Molly* onto lock number one, I say again, one. Upon completion warping *Molly*, *Patty* to lock onto lock three, I say again, three, and commence reprovisioning."

While the XO headed for lock three to assemble the provisions for *Patty*, Madeira watched the Sonar display as the two blips crept over the edge of the submarine plateau.

"Cabsta, this is *Patty*. Have bottomed at three-six-seven feet. Am commencing O2 transfer. Unless otherwise directed, will use divers to save time."

One more damn risk, thought Madeira.

Two of *Patty*'s crew in diving dress emerged from her escape trunk into the sub-freezing waters. They swam the twenty yards to *Molly*, dragging behind them a light span wire with a thin, high pressure air hose lashed to it. After securing the wire to *Molly*, they secured the hose to her O2 supply cock.

"*Patty*, this is *Molly*. Connection complete. Ready to commence transfer."

"Roger, *Molly*. Commencing O2 transfer."

The hose, lashed every ten feet to the span wire, jumped slightly as the first charge of oxygen passed through it, then settled into a slight pulsing.

"*Patty*, this is *Molly*. Main flasks show two-zero-zero-zero pounds pressure. More than enough to get home. Recommend securing transfer."

"Roger, *Molly*. Securing transfer."

Aboard *Patty*, the O2 supply was secured. Then Frazier tripped the hose, which was reeled back to *Patty* and, within a few minutes, the two worksubs were underway again.

The last fifteen miles were no easier on anybody's nerves than had been the preceding three hundred. To fail now, so close to success, was unthinkable.

When *Molly* was one hundred yards from Cabot's lock number one, Frazier cut power.

"*Molly* to Cabsta. Request permission to complete this job under our own power."

"Cabot to *Molly*. Negative. Not with that sloppy steering. *Patty* to warp you in. Stand by for linehandlers."

As Madeira spoke, two porpoises appeared, each with a warping line. The trained cetaceans dropped the ends of their lines with eyes spliced into them over cleats located along *Molly's* sides. Then they pulled the other ends over to *Patty* where they inserted them into self-tailing warping winches.

As Hammerstein gently nuzzled *Patty's* bow into *Molly's* side and took the slack out of the warps that now joined the two sisters, the porpoises shot off, grinning and squeaking to each other, to grab a breath of fresh air at one of the air bells.

When *Molly* was about ten yards from the lock, the porpoises reappeared with lines running from Cabot's warping winches. These were secured to *Molly*. After collecting the warps running between the two worksubs, the porpoises disappeared again into the green murk.

In the Submarine Section, Chief Mackinaw peered intently at the TV monitor as he powered the warping winches. Slowly, gently, *Molly* was dragged toward the lock.

The screech of *Molly's* hull scraping against the lock immediately caused Mackinaw to slack off one winch while heaving around on the other.

There was a clunk that he both felt and heard. He pressed the LOCK MATE switch. *Molly's* main hatch was now safely secured to the lock.

When Madeira, in Central Command, saw the green light flash on the console, he leaned back and took his first deep breath in hours.

NINE

COLORADO—DAY FOUR

"Goddamnit, Jim, this is it! The last straw!"

Admiral Williams, his shirt rumpled, his tie loosened, and his heart assaulted by alternating stabs of fear, guilt, and anger, leaned forward in his chair and came very close to pounding on his desk as he glowered at his Chief of Staff, Captain James Ring, who was seated on the admiral's black leather couch.

"They made it back safely this time. But they won't the next. Cabot is disintegrating and it's not their fault, it's mine. We're not giving them the support they need to survive."

"I agree, Admiral. I've spent a great deal of time recently on Cabot's problems."

Williams examined his Chief of Staff. Trim, fit, efficient, always alert, and unlike the admiral, unfailingly diplomatic, Ring was the epitome of the modern naval officer. Definitely on the fast track.

So why, Williams wondered, not for the first time, was Ring assigned to me? This billet is a dead end as far as his career is concerned. Maybe to keep me under control? To soften my rough edges? Maybe just because he was so junior—he'd just gained his fourth stripe a few weeks before reporting to Colorado. It would be several years before he would be considered for further promotion. He'll spend a year or so here, just long enough to break in my relief, and then they'll move him on to something more glamorous.

"I know you have, Jim, but we have to do better. Squaring Cabot away is now our highest priority project."

"I'll lead the attack, Admiral, although I'm not sure exactly what we can do that hasn't already been tried. I've pushed every button I can think of."

There it was, thought Admiral Williams. If Ring did have a shortcoming, and maybe it really wasn't one, it was an excessive respect for the system. He didn't really understand irregular warfare, not in his gut, anyway. But he'd soon learn. Maybe that's why he'd been sent to Colorado, although such reasoning didn't seem likely for the powers that be.

"I'll lead the attack personally, Jim. We're going to terrorize some and distract and confuse the others if necessary. I'm going directly to the CNO. Then I'm going to personally make sure that his wishes are carried out."

"Shouldn't you go through Admiral Barnes? Are you sure the CNO will back us?"

"We don't have time to romance Barnes. Don't worry, the CNO will take my call and he *will* back us."

The admiral paused, a smile spreading across his big, weathered face.

"He used to work for me, you know. Years ago, when he was a jaygee. In fact, I got him out of a little difficulty he got himself into. He made the mistake of attempting to execute an illogical order logically. We had a CO who wasn't always logical."

Ring smiled to himself. Admiral Williams never failed to amaze him.

"You know, I've never even tried to collect on that little chit, and it really won't be necessary this time either. He's a good man but he's got a thousand problems to worry about. Once I bring Cabot to his attention, forcefully, he'll give us a license to kick butts, and he'll do some kicking for us."

Ring, thought the admiral, looked a little skeptical.

"I've been around a long time, Jim. I've got a lot of uncollected chits stowed away. I've made a point over the years of never trying to collect on them—it always struck me as a dirty way of doing things. I'd planned to have them buried with me but, under the circumstances, I'm going to use some after all."

Ring couldn't keep from smiling outright now. The admiral was a bull, although a clever one. He'd never see his third star but he was a pleasure to watch in action. Every navy needed a few bulls.

"What's the plan, Admiral?"

"You and I are going to sit down with Cabot's personnel records, both crews, and see what sort of bodies they really need. Then I'm going to get on the phone and get them. On her next supply run, *Procyon's* going to have enough passengers to get the Gold Crew up to allowance. And, the Blue Crew's going to be on its way shortly thereafter. This business of the crews relieving each other five or six weeks late is intolerable!"

The admiral heaved himself out of his chair and started pacing.

"For that matter, Madeira's overdue for a good assignment. He's a fine officer. The son of a bitch deserves a decent job, one that'll help him get his third full stripe."

"I couldn't agree with you more, Admiral."

"I want a print-out of the status of all critical repair parts that Cabot has on order. You and I are going to pick up our telephones again and get those parts. I'll call whoever's necessary. I'll go visit whoever's necessary. If we have to steal the stuff, I'll drive the truck. I'll blind 'em with my stars. I'll hang out in sailor bars and shanghai qualified personnel . . ."

"We'll have competition, Admiral. Everybody's screaming for personnel, and everything else."

"We'll win, Jim, because we're more desperate."

"We'll have to start by getting our budget increased so we can increase Cabot's. Between the custom equipment they have on order and some defective items they've rejected but are still being charged for, they're way over right now."

"I'll clear all that up immediately. And I will get more money."

Williams continued pacing. "Jim, let's do this right. After we've gone over the data, I want you to fly to Portsmouth and meet with Ozawa, the Blue Crew CO, and Madeira, too. Have him return in *Procyon* next trip. His XO can run the station for a couple of weeks.

"I want you to go over the records with them. Make sure we understand the situation as well as they do, if that's possible."

"What about the sub in Zebra 403?"

"That's top priority too. Can't separate Cabot and that sub. Madeira should have time to finish taking a look before *Procyon* reaches Cabot. If not, she can wait a day or two for him to finish."

"I got another call today from Courtney, that deputy undersecretary of state, reminding us not to create an incident."

The deputy undersecretary ought to explain all of that to the President, thought Williams.

"I don't want an incident any more than he does. All they have to do is pick up the phone and tell us it's theirs and to keep our hands off . . . whoever "they" are. Until they do, it's up for grabs."

This thing could really turn into a diplomatic horror show, thought the admiral as he spoke. If the Russians wanted that new agreement as much as they said they did, why didn't they try to grab the evidence and make it disappear? If they did, then it would be their word against ours. They'd stand an even chance of pulling it off.

They can't, he answered himself. It's under pack ice, and they probably don't have a submarine based–heavy/deep lift capability. They can snoop around and probably get a man aboard but they can't lift it from that depth under ice. Cabot's worksubs are probably the only vessels in the Atlantic capable of doing the job—unless they have something we don't know about.

Or, he continued to himself, it may be a political matter. Perhaps the old line Communists, the Neo-Communists, and all the other factions are so busy trying to send each other to Siberia that nobody has time to clean up the evidence. Then again, it might not be political at all. It might be ethnic.

"If they do tell us to keep our hands off," observed Ring, "they'll have to explain what it's doing there."

"I should think so," replied Williams.

Tiring of fruitless conjecture, the admiral returned to the facts. "As it stands, Jim, the President and the CNO both want to know why that sub's there, the Agency claims to want to know why it's there and, most importantly to you, *I* want to know why it's there—and how it got there!"

"Aye, aye, Admiral."

TEN

CABOT STATION—
DAY FOUR

When he emerged from lock number one, Frazier was still coughing and his eyes were such a hideous, flaming red that Madeira feared for a moment that it was blood oozing out of them.

"I've got one hell of a crew, Captain," he croaked. He rubbed cold sweat from his almost bald head.

Trying to look stern, Madeira replied, "You and your hellish crew have screwed up our schedule." Then to the surprise of Susan, who was one of many spectators, Madeira put his arm around Frazier's shoulders and hugged him briefly.

"I think the irresponsible old son of a bitch should be court-martialed," growled Hammerstein as he walked out of lock number three. "I'll write him up myself."

"Well done, Bob," said Madeira, beaming. "Well done."

"Not bad for a college boy," added Frazier, who looked happy to be alive.

Madeira's smile faded. "Bob, you and your people deserve a rest but I can't give it to you."

"I understand, Captain. We'll see if we can catch them in the act."

"Who?" asked Susan.

"Whoever it is," replied Hammerstein. "Probably the Russians."

"You really think it's them?"

"I really don't know, but who else? If it were the Brits or the Scandinavians we'd know about it by now. Even the French would contact us, once they'd figured out they couldn't handle it themselves."

"So what if it is the Russians? They're probably just doing research."

"I doubt that. The whole area's pretty boring, except for the fish. They seem to like it but there aren't any volcanos or rifts or anything that might interest humans. Anyway, they'd have notified us. . . ."

"Enough!" snapped Madeira, the euphoria over *Molly's* safe return already wearing off. "We've got work to do. Chief Mackinaw's ready to top off your fuel and O2, and don't forget to transfer your divers to the chamber. Mackinaw's got replacements for them."

He paused, looking at Frazier, who was slumping slightly and, for the first time in Madeira's memory, showing his age.

"Mr. Frazier, I want you and your crew to report to sick bay right now!"

The stench of *Molly's* charred guts was beginning to permeate the Submarine Section.

"XO, I want *Molly* and the SubSection vented."

He paused again, his eyes settling on Susan's angry face, as he tried to think if there was anything else to be done. Had she been starting a political argument? Does she really think we're—I'm—some sort of Cold War fanatic itching for a fight?

"Bob, if there's anything *Patty* needs, installed equipment or spares, that you can get from *Molly*, take it. Cannibalize her if necessary. Mackinaw'll have to rebuild what's left as best he can."

"Aye, aye, Captain," said Hammerstein, "we're hot to trot."

After watching the Submarines Officer disappear back into the airlock, and the rest return to their various duties, Madeira walked over to Susan, who was still wearing an offended look.

"I'm sorry for cutting you off but it didn't seem the time for a political discussion. I apologize for being so sharp."

She looked at him, her anger ebbing somewhat. "I really wasn't trying to start an argument—although I do think you people are a little quick to blame everything on the Russians. Hammerstein was probably right, though. They would have notified us if they were doing legitimate research. Apology accepted," she concluded, trying to smile.

Three hours later, *Patty* pulled away from Cabot at eighteen knots and headed northwest, directly into the bitterly cold Labrador Current.

During the first twenty hours of the trip, *Patty* bustled along at a depth of about five hundred feet, a depth sufficient to avoid the maximum velocity of the current. By the end of the first day, the depth of the bottom had dropped away from several thousand feet to almost 15,000 as they passed into the Labrador Basin, along whose western edge they continued.

Whenever possible, *Patty* communicated with Cabot. This was usually accomplished by means of very low frequency radio ground wave transmissions sent to special land-based receiving stations and forwarded to Cabot.

Much as a telephone lineman perched atop a pole can call in to the central office, *Patty* could also communicate with Cabot by means of low-power Sonar transmissions aimed at SOSUS sensors. These messages were received at SOSUS Atlantic and forwarded to Cabot. When communicating thus, *Patty* depended on small transducers sprinkled here and there among the sensors to receive messages. Whenever she passed near one, *Patty* transmitted a short, low-power coded signal. In return, she received any traffic directed to her.

Radio communication was, by far, the more convenient of the two methods but it was not always dependable and was subject to eavesdropping. Thus, when unable to establish radio contact, which was a far-from-rare occurrence, or for especially sensitive messages, SOSUS was used.

Patty churned purposefully through the heavy waters, an insignificant speck in the ocean's immensity. Within her plastic and steel hull her crew, when not standing their four hour watches, performed maintenance work, sat in her small lounge and played cards, looked at video cassettes, or lay in their crowded bunks, surrounded by pipes and provisions, sleeping, daydreaming, or worrying about mothers, fathers, wives, children, and girlfriends.

Fifty hours later, *Patty* was in the Davis Strait, roughly two hundred miles east of the mouth of the Hudson Strait. Further to the northwest was Baffin Island while Greenland, not at all green, lay some three hundred miles to the east. Now close to the boundry of Zebra 403, Pettit, who was on watch, called Hammerstein from his bunk.

"Slow to eight knots," the Submarines Officer ordered as he took his seat at the control console. "Come left to two-nine-zero degrees and dive to two-zero-zero-zero feet."

As *Patty's* track on the inertial navigation display crossed the red-dashed line marking the southern edge of Zebra 403 and the bottom approached three thousand feet, Hammerstein called all hands to their stations.

"Mr. Hammerstein," said Pettit. "That damn sub's been damn quiet for too long. Do you think it's a robot?"

"It might be, Pettit."

"Do you think it's armed?"

"It might be." As he replied Hammerstein wondered if Pettit remembered that a Soviet SSN was also waiting for them.

Although no member of *Patty's* crew would admit aloud that this mission was more dangerous than any other in which they had participated, there had been little skylarking from the time they had entered the zone. The near-silence was broken only by the gentle whirring of the sub's electric motors.

"I think I have them," said the Sonarman. "Two attack boats, about eight miles north, bearing approximately zero-two-five."

Hammerstein glanced at the navigational computor. It indicated that the bottomed sub was just under fifteen miles ahead, bearing zero-one-six.

"Can you tell which is which?"

"No, sir. One is closer than the other but I can't tell which is which. This ain't attack boat gear we've got here."

Hammerstein looked at *Patty's* navigational sonar. The man was right, of course. The gear was fine for everyday navigation but almost useless when it came to identifying distant subs or any other combat application.

Hammerstein reduced speed again and edged north.

"They're pinging, sir. They're both pinging us."

"Very well."

"One's signalling now . . . Sierra . . . Quebec . . . Uniform . . . India . . . Shit! Now the other's signalling, too . . . Tango, I think . . . Sierra . . . Oscar . . . I really can't tell, both are using the same frequency."

"Keep trying. That Russian's trying to jam *Lion Fish*."

"Hotel, sir . . . and Alpha. Only one's signalling now . . . Delta . . . That's it. Both are silent now."

"Very well. One of them is definitely *Lion Fish*. They were to challenge us with 'squish'. It must have been the Russian who sent 'toad'."

"Squish? Toad?"

"They're trying to insult us. Signal 'Tango, Oscar, Whiskey, Echo, Romeo.' "

"Aye, aye, sir."

The Sonarman started to key the reply. "There they go again . . . Okay, it's all out. I'm sure *Lion Fish* got it. With their gear they could pick it out no matter what the Russian did."

"Well done."

"Oh no! Here we go, Mr. Hammerstein. One of them is putting on turns and heading directly for us."

"Which?"

"The farther one . . . now the other's doing the same . . . They're both heading right at us."

"I hate this 'chicken' shit," Pettit mumbled.

ELEVEN

LION FISH—DAY EIGHT

"Toad! Is that what they sent? Toad?"

"Yes, Captain, toad," said the Sonarman to Peacock.

"Do you think they knew we were sending 'squish'? Could they have read our mail?" asked the XO.

"I hope not. They probably know what those worksubs look like," replied Peacock.

The XO chuckled.

"XO, they're strange, you know. Strange."

"The worksubs, Captain?"

"No. The Bubbleheads, the divers."

The XO looked at him, questioningly, while he thought "look who's talking."

"I can see putting on a SCUBA tank and looking at the pretty fishes in the Bahamas but not what they do. They usually end up working in muck . . . in shit . . . and they're always alone when they're doing it. Even when a bunch of them are working each is in his own little suit. When something goes wrong, each dies by himself."

"Isn't it always that way, Captain? For all of us? What difference does it make if somebody else dies at the same time you do?"

"It does, XO, it does. Loneliness is a terrible thing."

"Captain, the Russian is cranking up and heading south."

"The son of a bitch! He's trying to rattle the Toad . . . All ahead flank! I want an intercept for the Russian!"

The navigator tapped the keys of the tactical computer.

"Two-zero-three, Captain. Thirty knots. Six minutes. He's faster than we are but we're closer to the worksub."

"Come right to two-zero-three. I want thirty knots!"

Lion Fish's screw spun furiously as the supply of super-heated steam to her turbine increased.

"Coming right to two-zero-three. Speed three-zero."

"Very well. How close will the Toad be to the intersect?"

"Toad, Captain?"

"The Bubbleheads. It *does* fit."

"One hundred yards, Captain, if they hold course and speed. If they turn or increase speed, there could be a monumental three way collision." As he spoke, the navigator wondered how his wife would bear up at the memorial service.

Peacock, his eyes gleaming again, watched the chronometer. 1524 . . . . . 1525 . . . . . 1526 . . . . . 1527 . . . . .

"Range to the Russian?"

"Two thousand yards, Captain."

"To the Toad?"

"Ninety-five hundred, sir."

"Captain, we're being set a little to port. Recommend two-one-zero."

"Come right to two-one-zero."

The XO looked at the gleam in Peacock's eyes and decided he really was a little insane.

"Right to two-one-zero, sir . . . Steady on two-one-zero."

"Very well."

1528 . . . . . 1529 . . . . .

"What's the Toad doing?"

"Holding course and speed, Captain. This is going to be closer than I thought. The Toad will be about fifty yards from the intercept." The navigator prayed that the Russian captain was giving serious consideration to the future of his own family.

"They're probably a little nervous by now," observed the XO.

"Aren't we all, XO. Aren't we all."

"Captain, I think the Russian is turning right."

"Are you sure?"

"Yes, sir. It looks like he's turning west."

"Right to two-four-five! We've got him now!

"Signal the Bubbleheads—'Proceed on mission assigned, Toad. Good luck'."

"Aye, aye, sir."

"He's still turning right, Captain."

"No he's not! Right to two-five-five."

One after the other, the two attack boats thundered across *Patty's* bow, at almost thirty knots, missing her by less than two hundred feet.

"He's stopped turning now, Captain. I think he's started to turn left."

"Shift your rudder! He's not going to turn anywhere until I let him. He already knows I'm a mean bastard. . . ."

"Are we going to chase him all the way to New York, Captain?"

"No. I don't want to be drawn too far west, he may have a friend someplace. We're going to chase him about fifteen miles west and then keep between him and the Toad. With our maneuverability and the inside position we'll be able to keep him away long enough for the Bubbleheads to do their job."

"He's turning right again, Captain."

"So are we. Commence pinging him."

As the two sleek, steel *Orcas* performed a mad ballet, twisting and turning at high speed through the dark waters, *Patty* plodded on toward the mystery that had brought her north.

TWELVE

PEPPERMINT PATTY—
DAY EIGHT

"Mr. Hammerstein, they're getting damn close," mumbled the sonarman nervously. "I hope *Lion Fish* knows what she's doing."

"So do I."

All hands in *Patty's* control room watched the sonar display wide-eyed as the two giant submarines hurtled at them. The seconds ticked by, collision becoming more and more imminent.

"Range 5000 yards. Bearing constant," chanted the sonarman.

"Range 3000 yards. Bearing constant."

"Range 2000 yards. Bearing constant."

"Shit! Shit! Shit!" groaned Pettit under his breath.

"Hold course and speed," commanded Hammerstein unnecessarily, half mesmerized by the sonarman's chant. This is insane, he thought, a coldness settling over him. At one thousand yards, I'm going to turn away.

"Sound the collision alarm, Pettit."

The terrifying shriek of the alarm almost drowned out the next report, "Range 1000 yards. Bearing constant."

I'll turn at five hundred yards . . . there'll still be time.

"Tell me when they're six hundred yards away and stand

by for a sharp turn to starboard." It'll be quick, anyway, he thought without enthusiasm, if I've waited too long.

"Thank God!" cried the sonarman. "One is turning away, I think . . . Yes, the nearer one is turning right."

"Range?"

"Six hundred yards, sir."

"Very well."

"Now the other is turning after him."

"The second must be *Lion Fish*."

"They're still going to cross our bows pretty close, sir."

"How close?"

"Hundred yards, maybe."

Hammerstein passed the word for all hands to hang on, an awful fear growing that the sonarman might be wrong, or that one of the attack boats might turn again.

"There goes the Russian, sir. He's past."

Hammerstein, sitting tensed in his command chair, realized with a start that the collar of his coveralls was soaking wet. So was his back.

"*Lion Fish's* past now."

"How close did she pass?"

"Sixty yards, sir."

The Submarines Officer started to slump in relief, then tensed again. "Hang on!"

A few seconds later, *Patty* shuddered, then started to pitch and roll violently as she slammed into the subsurface waves left by the two racing attack boats.

"Mind your helm and trim, Pettit," snapped Hammerstein, thinking of all the jury-rigged and marginal parts he'd used in overhauling the control systems.

"Mr. Hammerstein. *Lion Fish* is signalling . . . Proceed on mission assigned, Toad. Good luck."

"Are you sure that was *Lion Fish*? They're a lot of smart-asses in the Soviet Navy."

"Yes, sir. It has to be *Lion Fish*. She's directly between us and the Russian. She'd mask any transmission from him."

"Damn submariners are arrogant pricks, aren't they," he remarked to no one in particular.

When *Patty* was well clear of the turbulence, Hammerstein reduced speed and edged north. They were getting close. He nodded to the sonarman to keep a close eye on the high resolution sonar.

"Do you think they'll be back, Mr. Hammerstein?" asked Pettit.

"Not if *Lion Fish* knows her job; and she certainly seems to."

"We have it, Mr. Hammerstein. Bearing zero-one-three, range six thousand yards."

"Very well." Hammerstein commenced steering based on *Patty's* sonar plot.

When the little dot glowing on the sonar display was one mile away, Hammerstein, fearful that the little submarine might be booby-trapped with an explosive charge, stopped motors and allowed *Patty* to settle to the bottom. He then launched one of her unmanned work vehicles.

As the remote unit churned its way toward the mystery sub, Hammerstein watched its TV transmission intently. For some time the scene was identical to that generated by *Patty's* own monitors, a small empty area of gray-green surrounded by darkness. Then, directly ahead of the work vehicle, a more substantial darkness appeared. Within a few minutes, the sea bed was clearly defined. At the far edge, the rounded lines of a small submarine could be seen.

"Mr. Hammerstein, that's a God damn Siren!" shouted Pettit.

The work vehicle's operator guided the fishy robot to examine the unidentified submarine from all sides. Pettit was correct. It was a standard Mitsubishi *Siren*, one of the most widely used commercial survey and general work submersibles.

The robot's monitor showed that the Siren had a slight list to starboard.

"What's that?" demanded Pettit, pointing at the video display.

"What?" asked Hammerstein.

"There's something under the Siren. It looks like a long cylinder or something . . . see? Here." Pettit tapped the display as he spoke.

"Yes, I see it. I wonder what the hell it is. Take the vehicle in closer . . . try to get under the Siren."

All hands waited in silence as the robot crept under the Siren.

"Can't get in any closer, sir," reported the operator. "The vehicle's almost stuck between the Siren and the bottom." The video showed the hazy outline of what appeared to be a large cylinder, partially lost in the ooze, mounted on the Siren's bottom.

"Very well," sighed Hammerstein. "I guess that's the best we're going to be able to do for now. Do we have a good videotape of all this?"

"Yes, sir," replied Pettit.

"Get the remote out of there before we lose it. Take it all around the Siren one more time . . . just to make sure we've got everything on tape."

Once it was clear of the Siren's overhang, the remote vehicle circled the mystery sub, videotaping it in as much detail as possible. Then, Hammerstein had the vehicle nuzzle the Siren here and there—the escape hatch, the other through-deck hatches, along the sides.

No reaction, except that the noise generated by the contact hinted, surprisingly, that only the escape trunk was flooded. The sub's interior sounded dry.

"Where are *Lion Fish* and her friend?"

"About fifteen miles due west, sir."

Hammerstein sat back in his chair and immediately sprang upright again. The clammy back of his coveralls was icy cold.

He was to board the Siren at all costs and as quickly as possible, but, if at all possible, he was to avoid hazarding *Patty*. There was no evidence of an external booby trap but the possibility of an internal one remained. He had no choice but to use an APTC. However, a remote work vehicle with an Accessory Personnel Transfer Capsule mounted on it was very difficult to maneuver. It might not be possible to mate.

Oh shit! If necessary, he'd use a diver in a semi-armored deepsea dress. It wasn't recommended at three thousand feet but it had been done before. It'd be okay if the diver was only exposed a few minutes. Anyway, luck seemed to be with them. *Patty* had performed perfectly so far, despite all the jury-rigged controls. He ordered the two-man APTC mounted on the second work vehicle.

"Dobieski! Pettit! You're going for a ride."

THIRTEEN

THE SIREN—DAY EIGHT

The Accessory Personnel Transfer Capsule was a typical naval afterthought. Five years after the Mark 15 Unmanned Work Vehicle had been put into service, somebody had spotted a means of saving a little money. If a method could be found to use the Mark 15 to transport personnel at one atmosphere on relatively short projects, the cost of additional manned minisubs would be saved.

The result was a twelve foot cylinder that could carry and support two men for ten hours. Riding in the capsule was pure torture, especially if the passengers were fully dressed in semi-armored ultra-deep sea units. During the transit they had to lie prone in a space slightly larger than the combined diameters of their bodies plus equipment. The cylinder's passengers conned the composite unit by means of a small joy stick and prayed that the television monitor didn't crap out and blind them.

To get out, the divers had to slither backwards, snakelike, until their legs dropped down the angled access trunk. Those experienced with the capsule felt the exercise bore an unpleasant similarity to being born. Re-entering was only slightly less inconvenient.

While Dobieski piloted the composite, struggling to keep it from being driven off course or from bouncing and grating along the ocean floor, Pettit and he talked.

"I don't like this one damn bit, Dobie. You and me cooped up in this damn capsule, going in almost blind against who knows what. Why doesn't Hammerstein just take *Patty* in and get it over with?"

"What's your problem, Pettit? You some sort of closet claustrophobic that they missed in diving school?"

"No, I ain't no claustrophobic and I do more than my share, but I like things to have an end. Around here nothing ever ends. Everything just drags on and on."

"Don't let it get to you. Mr. Hammerstein's right being careful and we're going to be cool and careful, too."

"What's so fucking careful about a guaranteed case of the bends? Ain't Hammerstein ever heard of what happens to you if you come from ninety A's too quickly?"

"Chances are that you'll never leave one A. We'll mate with the Siren, look around and be back in time for chow. Anyway, even if you do have to go outside it shouldn't be much of a problem with that ultra-deep dress."

"Right! I'll only be squeezed by 11 A's instead of 90, if everything works right—which it usually doesn't."

"You're in good shape, Goddamnit. You concentrate on doing your job correctly and we'll both be in good shape."

"You already sound like a chief."

"Pettit!"

"Okay, okay. Do you think there'll be bodies?"

"Pettit!"

When the composite was about fifty yards from the white Siren, Dobieski slowed to a crawl to avoid creating a large pressure signature, the one external means of triggering a booby trap that the first work vehicle had not been capable of simulating. He then turned the composite into the slight current and slowed further, almost to a stop, thereby positioning the lower hatch of the capsule's access trunk about five feet above the Siren's escape hatch. Using the vehicle's water jet thrusters, he edged the hatches closer until, with a grating sound, the capsule's hatch slid over the Siren's. As the hatches continued to slide together, Dobieski pressed his LOCK MATE switch. The composite rose slightly and tilted. There was a shudder. The hatches would not mate.

"Damn!" he mumbled.

Dobieski lifted the composite and tried again. This time, just as the mate was about to be effected, the composite yawed slightly and was spun gently to port by the current. Again the mate failed.

He tried for the next hour to join the hatches, to no avail. As time passed he lost more and more of his finesse as fatigue overcame adrenalin. Each succeeding attempt was less accurate than its predecessor. His maneuvers became cruder, less precise. Finally, realizing Dobieski was too exhausted to complete the maneuver, Hammerstein lost his patience and told him that one of them would have to go outside after all. "Roger," had been Dobieski's reply.

"Okay, Pettit. Here we go. We're going to have to do it the hard way."

Dobieski rolled over on his right side and started to unharness his backpack. With Pettit's help he finally succeeded. Pettit then grabbed his own helmet and started worming his way aft.

"Shit!"

"What now, Pettit?"

"I hit my fucking head."

"Other than that, are you okay?"

"Yeah, I'm okay."

"Good. Put on your helmet and get down that hatch."

As soon as Pettit's helmeted head disappeared into the trunk, Dobieski slithered aft until he was scrunched up against the cylinder's aft bulkhead. Bent over, half-sitting and half-lying, he helped Pettit secure his helmet and inflate his ultra deep dress. He then closed the trunk's upper hatch and returned with difficulty to the prone position. "Pettit. You can flood the trunk whenever you're ready."

"Roger, Dobie."

As the water entered the trunk, Dobieski compensated so that the lower hatch was still only about ten feet from the Siren's when it dropped open beneath Pettit's feet.

Pettit slid down and out. His head emerged from the capsule. He looked around and got his first glimpse of the Siren, illuminated by the work vehicle's flood lights. He already felt better. He could at least see now, although there wasn't much to look at.

"Dobie, this looks like a normal Siren, except it's got no markings and it's got that thing underneath."

"Can you see it?"

"No. It's under the Siren."

"Want to go take a look?"

"Shit no! I ain't staying out any longer than necessary. Hammerstein didn't say to go look at it, did he?"

"No."

While he talked, Pettit checked the cylinder's lower hatch. It had swung up into the recess in the cylinder's bottom. He then reached up and grabbed one of the six hooks hanging in a circle around the lower hatch. He dragged the hook and the wire rope to which it was connected down to the deck of the Siren where he hooked it on to one of the six eyes surrounding the escape hatch.

He worked his way back up the wire rope, grabbed the next hook, dropped down to the Siren and secured it to another eye. After he had repeated the process six times in all, the two vessels were securely moored to each other.

Pettit re-entered the capsule's access trunk, feet first. "Okay, Dobie, the hooks are all in place. Heave around when ready!"

"Roger. Here goes."

Pettit held himself suspended, face down, waiting, while Dobieski heaved around on the six wires. The white Siren slowly approached. The submarine's escape hatch, sticking straight up from its slightly listing deck, grated across the access trunk's face and then entered the trunk itself.

"Looks good, Dobie. We've almost got it."

"What's the distance?"

"A few inches."

"Centered?"

"Very close. Best we can do for now."

There was a bump, then a rasping sound, then silence. Dobieski put ten pounds of tension on each capsule and wiggled the capsule very gently. The composite rocked slightly forward, then side to side, as he activated alternate pairs of thrusters.

With a clunk, the two hatches slid into position. Dobieski hit the LOCK MATE switch and a band in the capsule's hatch locked into a bevel that ran around the collar of the Siren's escape hatch.

"We have a seal, Pettit."

Three hours had passed since the capsule had left *Patty*. Now came the tricky part. The inside of the capsule was at one atmosphere. So, probably, was the inside of the submarine. Pettit, however, had been under eleven atmospheres pressure for almost a half-hour and would require extensive decompression prior to being able to return to a one atmosphere environment.

Dobieski tapped the data into the decompression calculator and noted the result for Pettit.

Pressurizing the capsule was easy enough but there wasn't enough gas to pressurize the whole Siren. Pettit had to get back into the capsule and pressurize it while Dobieski slipped down into the submarine and explored it at one or two atmospheres.

"You ready for phase two of this drill, Pettit?"

"I guess so, but I don't like it. If we fuck up, even a little, we're both dead. You sound awfully fucking confident."

"I'm as scared as you are, but the decision's been made. Use the schedule I've noted for you."

"Okay. Let's do it and hope it works."

Dobieski started dewatering the access trunk, thereby lowering its pressure, while Pettit turned on his back so that he was facing aft. At the same time, Dobieski increased the pressure inside the capsule to three atmospheres while he struggled into a small, self-contained breathing and communications unit. The unit was just large enough to hold him if the submarine was filled with noxious fumes. It might also give him a very slight chance of surviving should the Siren flood while he was in it.

When the pressure in the trunk had dropped to three atmospheres, the hatch into the capsule dropped open. Pettit, who had been struggling to breathe calmly, immediately forced himself up. As his legs started to clear the hatch, he jacknifed at the waist, forcing his legs into the aft section of the capsule.

"Give me a hand, Dobie! I don't want to explode."

"I'm pulling, damnit."

With a few more rapid acrobatics, and some tugging by Dobieski, Pettit was out of the trunk.

"Dobie. I think I'm bent! My shoulder hurts like hell."

Although it was possible, Dobieski doubted that Pettit was suffering from decompression sickness. "Can't be. It usually takes more time for the symptoms to appear."

"Maybe it's not my shoulder. I think it's my chest. My God! I've got an embolism. That's even worse."

"I doubt that too, but just to make sure get the capsule down to five A's as soon as I secure the trunk hatch and follow the treatment schedule instead of the normal one I worked out."

Dobieski slipped aft and down into the trunk before Pettit could answer. Between them, they got the hatch closed.

Even before the hatch was secured, the gases which had dissolved in Pettit's blood under the pressure of eleven atmospheres began to expand and creep out of solution. Without recompression and then controlled decompression, they would soon coalesce into bubbles, causing decompression sickness and probably death.

Well aware of the facts, Pettit was certain he could feel the bubbles already forming and his blood beginning to froth.

Panting, he squirmed forward and started pressurizing the capsule. While the capsule's pressure increased, he continued depressurizing the trunk. "Who the hell ever heard of treating yourself for an embolism! he said to himself. "It ain't allowed. It's nuts."

The whole procedure *was* incredibly dangerous. It was so dangerous, in fact, that no responsible authority had ever considered it necessary to forbid.

A wave of nausea passed over Pettit.

After a few minutes, he became calmer. He was still alive and his eyeballs hadn't exploded or anything, although his shoulder still hurt. He remembered Dobieski, who had been waiting quietly, and called him. Dobieski reported that he was fine.

The pressure in the trunk read one atmosphere when Dobieski tried to lift the Siren's hatch. "Pettit, this hatch won't budge. What pressure do you have on your gauge?"

"I've got you right at one atmosphere and me at five. Do you think it's jammed? Booby-trapped, maybe?"

"I don't know. Maybe one of the dogs is bent. I'm going to try securing it and then undogging it again. Hold on a minute."

Dobieski spun the steel wheel on the hatch, dogging it shut. It spun smoothly. He then spun it in the opposite direction, freeing the hatch again. "Pettit? The hatch seems okay. I could feel the dogs locking and unlocking."

Jesus Christ! thought Pettit. There must be a partial vacuum in the sub. It must be at less than one atmosphere! "Okay, Dobie. Do you want me to drop you below one A?"

"Might as well try. It's going to be hell if we have to cut our way in."

Pettit cut in the capsule's small evacuating pump. The trunk's pressure dropped very slowly. At .77 atmospheres, Dobieski, sounding a little strange, reported that he thought he could force the hatch open. He cracked it and air hissed through the opening until the trunk and the sub were equalized. At his request, Pettit bled in additional air until the sub was up to one atmosphere.

Dobieski shone his light into the darkness below and felt a little sick himself. He was no happier with the situation than Pettit.

"Okay, I'm going in."

"Roger."

He started down the ladder into the still, dark Siren. With his breathing gear on standby, he noticed the distinctive, acrid tang of an electrical fire in the recent past.

"Pettit. There's been a fire here. I can smell it. That's where the air went."

"Is it still burning?"

"I don't know."

Part way down the ladder he felt the sub shudder and move. He pressed himself to the ladder, almost dropping the light in the process, and prayed. In a few minutes, the motion stopped and all was silent again.

"You okay, Dobie?"

"Yeah."

"Any sign of the crew?"

"Not yet. You be sure to relay my reports to Hammerstein."

"Roger."

Dobieski thought he understood what had happened. The work vehicle and capsule, attached to the Siren near its stern, had acted like a sail, forcing the sub to swing into the slight current. He also realized that the sub must be light to swing that much. Some of its ballast tanks must still have air in them.

He descended the ladder and shone his light around what appeared to be the control room of a standard, nondescript Siren.

Because the Sirens were designed to carry a crew of six for fairly short jobs, no longer than a week or so, they contained very little storage space. This made the search easier.

The Siren shuddered and groaned. He was tempted to make a quick search and get the hell out but decided not to. If he wasn't thorough he might end up doing it again.

"Pettit. There's nothing that tells us anything in the control room. There are no logs and all the record cassettes have been removed."

"All of them?"

"There may still be one in the internal communications recorder but I don't think I can get at it without more tools. The main switchboard burned out and fell on it. Even if there is one there it's probably melted."

"What about bodies. Have you found any bodies?"

"No bodies either, Pettit."

He moved aft into the second of the Siren's three pitch dark compartments, which contained a decompression chamber, several pipe berths, and the sub's limited sanitary facilities. Much to his surprise, he found no personal effects or other evidence of the crew. He did, however, find something else.

"Pettit. They've got some extra air flasks or something here . . . they're huge, mounted in the berthing space . . . and some humungous batteries . . ."

"What're they for?"

"Don't have any idea but I don't think there was a crew aboard. There's no food, no clothing, nothing."

"Must have been a fucking ghost ship."

Disregarding Pettit's last remark, Dobieski shone his torch on the sub's main beam, confident it would tell him something. It did. The vessel's registration number, engraved into the thick beam when the sub was built, had been burned out with a cutting torch.

The Siren groaned and moved again. He hung on to a stanchion. Her liveliness was getting on his nerves. He thought about flooding all of the ballast tanks and rejected the plan. He couldn't be sure about the controls or the condition of the tanks.

Ducking into the propulsion machinery space he found the major source of the all-pervading acrid aroma.

"Pettit. Both main propulsion motors have burned out. That's why the air is so foul."

Throughout Dobieski's explorations, Pettit had been forwarding his reports to *Patty*. Dobieski had finished re-examining the motor room and was in the process of doing the same to the midships space when Pettit called him.

"Dobie, Mr. Hammerstein wants you to check out the internal communications recorder again and I wish you'd shake a leg. I still don't feel right."

Neither did Dobieski. He was developing a headache and still felt vaguely sick. He attributed both symptoms to the foul air. He spent a minute poking around the extra, and unexplained, gas cylinders and batteries and returned to the control room. The internal communications recorder was still there, under the tangled wreckage of the roasted switchboard. He tinkered idly with the wreckage, expecting to find it immovable. Much to his surprise, the wreckage easily lifted off the recorder, which was only slightly charred.

"I was wrong, Pettit. The switchboard lifted right off the recorder and that doesn't look as bad as I thought it would."

"What about the cassette?"

"Just a minute . . . I'll be damned! It's here. It looks okay."

"Grab it and let's get the hell out of here! What's on it?"

"How the hell should I know?"

He removed the cassette, made another fruitless inspection of the control area and then decided to take another look at the mysterious gas flasks and batteries.

"Hey, Pettit! I found 'em."

"What, Dobie? What did you find?"

"The scuttling charges."

"Shit! Are they booby-trapped?"

"Don't think so . . . but I can't be sure. It looks to me like they're rigged the same way we do it. There are two blocks of TNT with blasting caps inserted. The wires run . . . they seem to run into the control room . . . I think it's a remote system."

"You mean there's some fucking Ruskie sitting somewhere with his finger about to push a fucking button?"

"Nobody's pushed anything yet. It may be on a timer, or the system isn't working . . . but I'm going to pull the caps out just to make sure. You relaying all this to *Patty*?"

"Yes, I'm relaying. Let's get the fuck out of here."

"Okay. The caps are out. I'm not going to screw with the rest because I don't understand how it works. If somebody tries to detonate it now all they'll do is make a little noise."

With the cassette in one hand and the flashlight in the other, Dobieski took one more look around and checked once again to insure the caps could do no damage if detonated. He then re-entered the Siren's escape trunk, dogging the lower hatch behind him and climbed through to the APTC's access trunk where he reached down and closed the upper hatch of the Siren's escape trunk.

"Pressurize the trunk, Pettit."

Pettit pressurized the access trunk to the capsule's pressure and opened the hatch. After Dobieski had re-entered the capsule and secured the inner hatch, Pettit pressurized the trunk to ninety atmospheres and lifted the capsule ten feet above the Siren. As the capsule rose, he tripped the six hooks that had been secured to the Siren and closed the outer hatch.

The composite returned to *Patty* with an hour to spare. Dobieski and Pettit were transferred to *Patty's* decompression chamber and the cassette was locked out to Hammerstein, who looked it over carefully and played it immediately.

A nerve-rattling cacophony of screeches, squeeks, and beeps attacked his ears, forcing him to turn down the volume.

"Dobieski," growled the Submarines Officer into the decompression chamber intercom, "I thought you said this is from the internal communications recorder."

"It is, Mr. Hammerstein. At least I think it was. It looked like one but I'm not all that familiar with Sirens."

"If it is, that Siren had a crew of aliens."

"I don't think it had a crew at all."

"What about those flasks and batteries you found in the berthing space?"

"All I know is that they were about ten feet long and four in diameter, the flasks, that is. Don't know what's in them, 'though I'm willing to bet they have something to do with that thing on the Siren's bottom."

Now what to do? thought Hammerstein. Send Dobieski and Pettit back? Send a fresh crew? Who? He didn't have a fresh crew. Use *Patty* to nudge the Siren over on its side so the work vehicle could look more closely under it? That would be pushing their luck and they probably wouldn't learn anything more, anyway.

He pulled the cassette out of the player and looked it over carefully. Maybe the heat from the fire had made the noises. No, the cassette showed no signs of heat damage and, anyway, the squawks and screetches sounded more purposeful. Dobieski might have mistaken the external communications recorder for the internal one but he doubted it. He wouldn't have made that obvious a mistake. Most likely, the internal system was being used for something other than talking, but to determine exactly what would require a thorough examination of the Siren by experts.

"Where are *Lion Fish* and her friend?"

"Still about fifteen miles west, Mr. Hammerstein."

"Very well. Steer zero-nine-zero, speed twenty, and start looking for a transducer. I want to try to fax some shots from the videocassette . . . and we'll also try to send them part of that cassette."

Six hours later, *Patty* settled to the bottom beside a transducer. Having assured himself that the Russian attack boat, now over a hundred miles to the west, was too far away to be able to pinpoint *Patty's* location, Hammerstein commenced the long transmission.

Three hours later, he received a reply.

"Ascend to 2000 feet and steer two-three-zero. We're going home."

FOURTEEN

COLORADO—DAY EIGHT

Admiral Williams, in shirtsleeves, was standing in his conference room studying a map of the North Atlantic when Ring entered.

"You sent for me, Admiral?"

"Yes, Jim. Take a seat. Did you see the traffic that just came in from Cabot's worksub?"

"Yes, I did, Admiral, although the fax wasn't very clear."

"Their description was."

"Yes, it was . . . but a Mitsubishi! Do you still think it's Soviet?"

"I know it is! Within the last few hours they've suggested to the President—informally, quietly—that 'whatever it is' should be left alone, that it would be best for everybody if it wasn't picked at."

"But they didn't actually admit it's theirs?"

"No. They admitted nothing and told us nothing about it."

"What's the President going to do?"

"He still wants to know what it is."

"Do you have any idea what the special gear Cabot reported is? And what's on that cassette?"

"From what Cabot reports, the Siren appears to be a drone. That means they needed some sort of control system. Perhaps they were using the IC system as part of the control system, although it's equally possible, when we analyze it, we'll find it contains some sort of data they were collecting."

"SOSUS?"

"Somehow related to it," replied the admiral as he lowered himself into one of the chairs lined up precisely along the wall.

"You think they were charting the SOSUS sensors?"

"They may have been. They already know where some of them are."

The admiral was on his feet again, pacing. He's a bull, thought Ring. A nervous one, pitted against a bear he can't yet see but can smell. "Knowing where more are would make their life easier. But that's not what's really worrying me. I'm afraid they were testing something and it worked."

"The special gear, whatever it is?"

"Jim, that Siren just appeared! We should have detected it hours before we did."

"Jesus! You think they've developed an effective masking device of some sort?"

"Yes. I think they have more respect for SOSUS than some of us do."

"Then we'd damn well better get our hands on it. Why haven't they?"

"The weather? The ice? Maybe because we knew where she was before they did? If my guesses are correct, the Siren had an engineering casualty and they lost control of it."

"I'd think they would've prevented Cabot's worksub from boarding it."

"They tried. They couldn't very well sink them with *Lion Fish* there."

"We're guessing, Admiral."

"Yes, we are, but we've got to act on these guesses. Cinc-LantFleet has already agreed to keep *Lion Fish* there and I've spoken with the Supervisor of Salvage. He feels that it would be possible for two worksubs and an attack boat to do the job but he doesn't like the idea of towing the Siren underwater. He prefers to employ worksubs and a surface ship. Unfortunately, he's only got two in the Atlantic and one's undergoing overhaul. He's promised to send *Falcon* in about two weeks to work with Cabot's worksubs, if Madeira can get them both operating at the same time."

"What about the weather?"

"Of course. We'll have to wait for it to settle down somewhat, but so will the Soviets."

"You want me to start preparing an Operations Order?"

"Yes. The CO of *Falcon* will be Officer in Tactical Command and Madeira will be salvage master. When he gets to Portsmouth, keep him there to make his preparations. We'll helo him out to *Falcon* as she heads north."

"SupSalv isn't sending his own man?"

"Madeira *is* his man. He may work for me but he's a Bubblehead, and SupSalv is their spiritual leader, whoever they may work for.

"Now," demanded the admiral, changing the subject, "how are we doing on Supply?"

"Your chat with the CNO has helped but it's still heavy going in a couple of places."

"Where?"

"Ship's Parts Control Center, for one. I'm beginning to believe that they really don't know what the hell they have in their own warehouses. Every time I try to get the true story from them they just repeat what the print-out says. The computer seems to be the highest authority they recognize."

"We'll see about that! Any other problem areas?"

"There seem to be funding and political problems with several of the orders for custom parts for obsolete equipment. They're arguing about which contractors, in which Congressional Districts, should get the jobs."

"I want names and numbers on those."

"I've got them right here, Admiral."

Ring passed a handful of papers to Williams, who looked them over quickly. "I'll take care of these," he mumbled, and dropped them on his desk.

"For your information, Jim, I called Admiral Hodges and got twelve bodies for the Gold Crew. They'll be in Portsmouth in time for *Procyon's* departure in . . . what is it? Two days?"

Hell! thought Ring. I worked on Hodges' deputy for three months and got nowhere!

"Should I alert Portsmouth?"

"Yes. I want special handling for those people. Tell the

Commander there, Captain Robertson, to send a limo to the airport if necessary to get them there on time."

"What about the Blue Crew?"

"He said he'd work on it personally. Oh, yes, and tell Madeira to bring that cassette from the Siren with him. The Agency wants to take a look at it."

FIFTEEN

CABOT STATION—
DAY EIGHT

"I see we're getting some new bodies," said Merrill to Madeira at dinner.

"Twelve, if we can believe them."

"And you're going on vacation, Captain."

Madeira smiled at Merrill's seemingly never-ending cheerfulness. "Yes, Mr. Merrill, beautiful Portsmouth in March."

Despite the sarcasm, Madeira was very much looking forward to the meeting—Ring would be there and it was clear that the admiral himself intended to take a hand in getting action—and was especially excited about recovering the Siren. Not only would the task be a challenge to Madeira's ingenuity, but also an opportunity to solve a mystery he found both fascinating and troubling.

"At least we're not going to have a nuclear exchange tomorrow," observed the XO.

"Not yet, anyway. But what the hell are they doing there? What's all that extra crap they've loaded into the Siren?"

After maintaining a thoughtful silence for some time, Susan suddenly spoke up; "Has Zebra 403 ever been commercially surveyed?"

"For minerals?" replied Madeira. "I doubt it. It would have to have been done years ago, before SOSUS was installed. We'd never allow a mining operation there." Madeira paused, looking at Susan.

"But it's possible there *are* mineral deposits there, especially oil," she continued.

"We're listening," answered Madeira, leaning forward.

"From what I hear, there's talk of closing SOSUS down in a few years. If that happens, we'd have to permit drilling . . ."

"And you're suggesting the Soviets might be trying to get a head start?"

"Assuming it's them. It could be almost anybody, even American companies," concluded Susan, brightly.

Madeira reached into his pocket and took out a pen, which he played with as he thought.

"You may have something there," he said, mostly to himself. "The extra gear on the bottom may be some sort of magnetometer." He paused. "What about the big flasks and the batteries?"

He tapped his pen rapidly on the table. "Could that thing underneath be a shock-wave generator? Could they be using bursts of air, or some other gas, instead of explosives to produce the waves for a seismic survey? If so, those flasks must be under tremendous pressure."

"That's how they do it now," said Susan, clearly relieved that she'd been able to offer a plausible explanation other than yet more Cold War skulduggery.

Madeira stopped tapping. "If we're correct, they must not have had a chance to use it. Otherwise, SOSUS would have picked it up."

"Would they have recognized it?" asked Susan. "I'm sure they pick up all sorts of strange booms and burps from time to time."

Madeira smiled at her. "Very scientifically phrased. We'll suggest ComConDefSurvCom check to see if there were any unexplained booms or burps."

He turned to Merrill. "Are you going to be free tomorrow afternoon?"

"Yes, sir. The quarterly hull inspection?"

"Yes. Let's get it done. Right after lunch."

"Aye, aye, Captain."

After dinner, Susan and Madeira were left alone in the

wardroom, sipping coffee with the muted clatter of the galley in the background.

"Then all your relatives are fishermen?" she asked after a while.

Madeira considered the question, and his situation. The growing attraction he felt toward Susan made him uneasy. He didn't need any distractions now and he certainly didn't need another romance at Cabot—Jamison and Dumont were enough, not that they'd caused any problems so far.

He leaned back in his chair, taking a deep breath. He did, after all, have rights, even though they might be restricted somewhat by Navy Regs.

"No. My grandfather was, and so are my uncle and one of his sons, but my father is a CPA. He was the first Madeira to go to college."

"But you must like ships and the sea. Why didn't you go into fishing too?"

"I didn't see much of a future in it. Even then, when I was in high school, it was obvious that mariculture was going to change it all. Fish were going to be a commodity, not a specialty item. I figured old-time fishing was doomed."

"People are still doing it."

"I know. My uncle's one of them, remember? Somehow he earns a living but it's harder than ever. Most people think he's nuts."

"Because he's still fishing?"

"Partially." Madeira found himself laughing at the thought of Uncle Carlos' madness. "Mainly because he acts that way. He tells the most outrageous sea stories. Nobody who lives in Gloucester believes him but the summer people sometimes do. He tells them with such a straight face and with such detail that I think he sometimes believes them himself."

"You like your uncle, don't you?"

"I like and respect him."

Susan was smiling along with him now. "Why didn't you go into mariculture?"

"I don't know. I guess it seemed too tame, like farming. There was no romance to it. I wanted to see the world and I had the opportunity, so I went to the Academy."

"Then diving school?"

"No. First, two years on a destroyer. Then diving school. When I was in high school, the Navy's Man in the Sea Program was still running. Even though they killed it before I got to the Academy, the vision stayed with me. It was a whole new world to be explored."

As he concluded, Madeira realized with surprise that he had said more about himself to Susan than he had to anyone else in years—and that he was enjoying doing it.

"Should I ask about you?"

"You can. I've wanted to be a marine biologist ever since high school." She laughed. "I think I spent too much time looking at National Geographic Specials, and PBS."

"You glad you did?"

"I think so, though this project's got me a little discouraged."

"It'll work out."

"I hope so."

Madeira, more relaxed than he had been in some time, allowed himself to be further drawn out by Susan as the watch changed. When he mentioned that photography had been his only real hobby since high school, Susan asked to see some of his work. No longer surprised at his own openness, Madeira obliged.

While he was off getting his slides and a projector, Susan started to wonder if she had made a mistake. Was she going to have to sit through hours of ships, old shipmates, and common tourist attractions, all slightly out of focus?

What Madeira showed her surprised her. Spotlighted sea anemones that appeared to be lunging at her. Stark compositions of snow, rock, and winter-naked trees which chilled and intrigued at the same time. Soaring, rolling, sleeping landscapes that made her yearn for the real world; and some amazing close-up studies that made even the most common objects seem wonderful and totally new.

"How did you ever get that perspective on this rock?" she asked at one point.

Madeira leaned forward to examine the slide more closely. "You know, it's been almost two years since I picked up a camera. I think I must have used a telephoto lens and a polarizing filter, but I'm not sure now."

"Al, is that your Uncle Carlos?"

"You mean with the live cod in his mouth? Yes, I'm afraid it is. I included this slide so you'd see the sort of mind it takes to be in the fishing business today."

"Who are the others? They look normal."

"One is my brother. He sells computers now. The rest are cousins."

"You could make a living from these; from some of them, anyway."

"I've sold one or two but I could never make a living at it. For every slide I've shown you, I've thrown away thousands."

"Just the same, I like them. Every time I try to take a picture, as opposed to a technical photograph of a fish parasite or something, it ends up looking like a technical photograph of a fish parasite."

During most of the slide show, Madeira had been looking at Susan more than at the slides. When he did drag his glance away from her, he found himself unsettled and almost distressed by what he saw on the screen.

Did I really take these? he asked himself as he studied his own slides. Technically, and artistically, they were fine. He was proud of them. But many, despite their color, exuded a coldness, an almost Scandinavian air of bleakness and melancholy. I was once attracted to that look, he thought. But now? Maybe that's why I haven't looked at them in so long.

SIXTEEN

CABOT STATION—DAY NINE

Following the noon meal, Madeira returned to his cabin and lay down for a few minutes.

Despite the distractions, Cabot never totally left his thoughts. Closing his eyes, he breathed deeply and willed his body to relax. He wanted to concentrate on the job at hand. He tried to wipe his mind blank. *Molly*, *Patty* and Zebra 403 kept forcing their way in.

He then tried, with better success, to concentrate on Susan.

Feeling better, he got up and put on his heavy woolen diving underwear. The bottoms were, as always, tight around his ankles and calves. He knew that when he removed them, the skin and hairs in those areas would ache. He hitched the bottoms up to his waist and threw on the top with its tight wrist cuffs. Finally he put on a heavy blue robe and lined slippers and headed for the primary diving station located in Central Section's lower level.

When Madeira arrived at the diving station, Merrill was already there, chatting with Chief Mackinaw. Also present were three tenders and a stand-by diver, already partially dressed. The two Mark 19 self-contained diving systems with variable volume suits were all laid out, ready to go.

"Mr. Merrill, where's the Doomsday Book? I want to review it before we go out."

"Here it is, Captain," replied Merrill. He stooped over and picked it up from the deck.

Madeira and Merrill reviewed the loose-leaf notebook, filled with plastic-laminated plans of the station. On these were marked a number of fittings and features which were prone to failure. In addition, Merrill had marked various things that he wanted to check, along with the location of every discrepancy noted by Madeira during his last structural inspection.

Shit! thought Madeira as they completed the review. It would take us six months to correct what we already know about. How much more will we find today?

"Let's suit up," he said to Merrill, a note of urgency in his voice.

After inspecting their suits, backpacks, helmets, and communicators, the divers climbed into the fabric-covered neoprene dry suits with the tenders' assistance, using soap to lubricate their hands and wrists as they slipped them through the watertight sleeve seals, and zipped them shut. Next came the backpacks, which contained the helium-oxygen breathing mixture and mixing equipment. Since they would not be using umbilicals, Mark 37 digital sonar communicators had been secured to the backpacks. With the addition of their weight-belts and gloves, they were ready to enter the access trunk.

"All set, Mr. Merrill?"

"Yes, sir. We're on our way."

"Okay, Chief. Let's get on with it."

Chief Mackinaw lifted the thick round hatch and helped the two divers down the short ladder to the small deck in the trunk. There they hooked up their buddy line and tested all their equipment again. While the chief was closing and dogging the hatch, Madeira and Merrill sat on the edge of the deck and put on their short swim fins. They let their legs hang down the short, vertical tunnel and started to breathe the heliox mixture. Mackinaw ordered the trunk flooding valves opened.

Madeira heard the water rush into the tunnel, and felt a brief twinge in his guts as the cold and darkness rushed at him. When the water reached the deck on which they were sitting, it stopped. The air around them, tinged with the bluish haze of rapid compression, was now pressurized to eleven atmospheres, the same as the water outside.

Collecting their flashlights, chipping hammers and scrapers, the divers dropped one after the other into the tunnel and floated down. When they emerged from under the bottom of the station, Merrill did a summersault and shouted, "Wahoo! This is what it's all about, Captain. It's like being in outer space."

As the two divers swam up the side of Central Station, Madeira reported to Mackinaw, "Control, this is Red Diver. All okay."

"Roger, Red Diver," replied the Master Diver. "I assume from his last transmission that Yellow Diver's okay, too."

"That's correct, Control," reported Merrill. "What's that background static I'm picking up? Something wrong with our transceivers?"

The "static" sounded to Madeira like laughter. He had trouble keeping from laughing himself.

"That's nothing serious, Mr. Merrill. We'll have it under control in a minute. You, sir, are an inspiration to the troops."

"Kind of you, Chief. That's what the Navy pays me to do— lead and inspire."

About halfway up the side of Central Section they came to the jackstay, a one-inch diameter steel bar that ran the length of the section, and hooked their lifelines onto it. They hung on to the jackstay as they caught their breath and checked everything again.

The underwater floodlights illuminated a small portion of Central Section in a hazy, lifeless, green light. The large cylinder was covered with a thick layer of marine growth that made its lines indistinct. The only sharp features in their world were the jackstay, access trunks, airlocks, and water intakes. These were kept clear of all growth. The divers looked around in all directions. The feeble green light disappeared into the surrounding blackness within a few feet of the station, leaving the hilly, sand- and mud-covered surface of Flemish Cap invisible.

The water movement, a combination of current and a deep surge from the long-lived and ferocious storm above, was surprisingly violent. Both struggled to avoid being tossed against the sharp marine growth on the station's side.

Having caught their breath and regained their bearings, they reported to Mackinaw and then started the inspection. Guided by Merrill's notebook, they swam slowly along the side of Central Section, stopping to examine intakes, discharges, braces, and fittings. They frequently used their scrapers and hammers to get a good look at a fitting or to find the frame numbers that were welded, in two-inch relief, on the side of the station.

They kept up a running commentary as they went, all of which was recorded at Diving Control. For the most part, Madeira asked questions and Merrill answered them. "Why is this discrepancy still uncorrected?" How did Merrill anticipate repairing that corroded strut? It looked like the corrosion might be due to electrolysis. Here and there they found minor problems that would require attention, but nothing critical. The most potentially serious were several intakes which had not been cleaned recently.

As they were approaching the end of the Central Section a patrol porpoise shot by, turned on his side, and waved a flipper at them.

"Look at that, Captain. He's saluting you."

"Are you sure about that, Mr. Merrill? He could have been making an obscene gesture."

The porpoise continued on to one of the air-filled bells that were placed around the station at regular intervals.

When they reached the end of the Central Section, Merrill unhooked his lifeline and swam to the jackstay on the hemispherical Porpoise Section. Once Merrill was safely anchored, Madeira released himself, joined Merrill and hooked onto the stay. The inspection continued. Half the time they were fighting to hold themselves in closer to the station while the remainder was spent struggling to avoid being dashed against its abrasive sides.

They worked their way around the Porpoise Section and then down the other side of Central Section.

Another porpoise came by and inspected their work. As he watched the porpoise do a barrel roll and snatch one of the fish that had been attracted by the lights, Madeira realized he didn't

feel the joy of weightlessness, the sense of freedom and unique-
ness that had always made diving, under even the most impossible conditions, satisfying. He had too much on his mind.

When they reached the end of Central Section, both men
were beaten and bruised from being bounced off the station's
hull. Madeira was exhausted and a little discouraged. So far,
they had found no new critical problems but a host of small
ones. He knew that the way things were going he would never
get them all corrected.

"Yellow Diver, this is Red. Let's take a break before going
on to the Submarine Section."

"Roger, Red."

The two men wedged themselves between the braces
which supported the Central Section on its foundation and
rested. Despite their protective suits and heavy underwear,
both Madeira and Merrill were suffering from the heat-robbing
powers of the black-green waters and the heliox breathing
mixture.

"How are you feeling, Yellow Diver?"

"I'm okay, Captain, though I have a small leak at my left
cuff . . . my left arm's a little cold."

"How cold?" asked both Madeira and Mackinaw simulta-
neously.

"It'll be okay."

Madeira wondered if they were heading for trouble. Extreme hypothermia was fatal. Even if not allowed to go that far,
it could cause fatal lapses of coordination and judgement as
well as complications during decompression.

"This self-contained unit was a mistake. I apologize. We
should have used the hot water suits."

"We can make it, Captain. Let's get it over with. No
problem here."

After resting a few more moments they continued, working their way slowly along the exterior of the long tunnel
which connected the Central Section with the Submarine
Section. The latter was separated from the rest of the station
to insure that any damage done by a careless submarine skipper would not endanger the whole station.

Just before they reached the connection between the Submarine Section tunnel and Central Section, Merrill shone his

high-powered torch on a small, dark, colorless hydra growing on the station's side. When powerfully and closely illuminated, the drab, plant-like animal showed its true colors. Its stem and most of its "flower" were a brilliant red made all the more striking by the delicate pink of its gently waving tendrils. Merrill stopped to admire the little living flame.

"Look at that hydra, Captain. Isn't it beautiful? It looks like a tulip, or maybe a carnation."

Madeira's first thought was of a bloody toadstool oozing out of a pile of rotting mud. Then he thought of Frazier's bloodshot eyes.

At the end of their three hour inspection, both officers were totally exhausted. They floated up the access trunk and were helped onto the deck by the two tenders Chief Mackinaw had stationed there.

With the tenders' assistance, they shed their diving gear and crawled into the decompression chamber through the airlock in the side of the trunk. Each then received a brief physical from one of the tenders, a hospitalman, and lay down on the built-in cots. While one of the tenders helped them with blankets, the other secured the hatch and reported that the chamber was secured.

Chief Mackinaw told Hirsh, who was the outside tender manning the decompression console, to reduce the chamber's pressure to the first stop on the decompression schedule. He then had the access trunk dewatered, the pressure in it reduced to one atmosphere and the diving gear retrieved, cleaned, and restowed.

The Master Diver was worried about Madeira. He looked too cold, too tired. Merrill also looked cold but the Captain looked like death. Mackinaw knew that Madeira was especially susceptible to the bends. According to his records, he had been bent at least twice before. It could be a long night!

SEVENTEEN

THE DECOMPRESSION CHAMBER—DAY NINE

Once in the chamber and wrapped in a blanket, Madeira lay down on one of the cots. He was bone-tired and cold to the core, despite the heavy blanket. God! he thought as he shivered violently, I should have used the heated units.

Outside the white painted cylinder, Chief Mackinaw and Hirsh were seated behind the small console that controlled and monitored the chamber.

"What do you think, Chief?" asked Hirsh.

"Should be routine, although they're both bushed. We'll keep alert, won't we?"

Ten minutes after starting decompression, Hirsh reported that it was time to move to the next stop. Mackinaw nodded and Hirsh advised the tenders in the chamber. He then bled out air to reduce the pressure.

Mackinaw picked up the schedule he had worked up on the decompression calculator. He had supervised or participated in thousands of decompressions during his long career, and almost all of them had been routine. Almost all of them. Despite one hundred years of research, decompression was still not a cut-and-dried operation. The tables had been refined continuously, yet there were still accidents. Nobody knew for sure exactly why they failed when they did. In addition to the basic mysteries that still existed concerning the behavior of human bodies in general, there were too many variables involved in each dive, and each diver, for any one set of tables to cover them all. What had been the water temperature? How strenuously had the divers worked? How tired were they? How was fat distributed through their bodies? The list was endless and, many suspected, still incomplete.

Mackinaw glanced at the TV monitor. All appeared quiet in the chamber.

There were two prolonged hisses as fresh air was automatically bled into one end of the chamber while stale air was vented from the other end.

A brief physical examination indicated that both divers had sustained bruises and scrapes but nothing serious. As decompression proceeded, embolisms and related conditions were still possible, but the big danger was decompression sickness, the formation of bubbles in the divers' blood. The bubbles could cripple the divers for life or cause brain damage or even death.

The Master Diver looked around. A mess cook had arrived with six dinners in insulated containers.

"Over here, kid," said the chief as he walked to one end of the chamber. "Hirsh, tell them supper's on its way."

Mackinaw looked in the viewing port and saw the same scene he had seen on the monitor.

He checked a pressure gauge and opened a small round door on the end of the chamber. Inside the door was a small transfer chamber, three feet in diameter and three deep, which had a second round hatch into the main section of the chamber.

"Okay, kid. Put four of the meals in here." He then closed and secured the door.

"Pressurize the medical lock, Hirsh." There was a throaty hiss, then Hirsh told the inside tenders to open their door and retrieve their suppers.

About half-an-hour after they had finished the evening meal, Hirsh reported to Mackinaw that it was time to decompress to the next stop on the schedule. The chief nodded OK.

"Going to the next stop," said Hirsh into a microphone.

"Roger," replied one of the inside tenders.

A throaty hiss whispered through the compartment as Hirsh lowered the chamber's pressure. Mackinaw tensed. If there were going to be trouble it would probably appear while moving between stops or shortly after arriving at one.

The hiss died away. "Everything's OK here, Chief," reported an inside tender. Mackinaw waited another five minutes and then started to relax a little. It would be almost an hour before they moved to the next stop.

When Susan arrived she found Madeira and Merrill inside the chamber talking with Sonneberg. She listened as they discussed how, and if, they could correct the discrepancies found during the hull inspection.

Sonneberg informed Madeira that they had a visitor as he beckoned her to the microphone.

"How are you two?"

"We're steaming right along on all four," answered Merrill.

"And you, Captain?"

"As Mr. Merrill said."

"Say, Ms. Constantine," said Merrill. "Could you come up with a plan to get the porpoises to do a little more of the real work around here? We're falling behind."

"That's been tried," growled Madeira.

"I have a theory on that," replied Susan. "It's all in the motivation. I think they're just lazy. They're not interested in the work ethic. They're willing to do patrol and lifeguard duties. I don't know why, maybe it makes them feel good to be helpful as long as it doesn't take too much effort; but to get them to scrape barnacles, or whatever you have in mind, we're going to have to find some way of making it worth their while."

"How about sex?" suggested Merrill.

"They don't need us for that."

As she looked through the heavy glass observation port at Madeira, Susan couldn't help but observe how sad he looked. Tired and trapped in a steel cage, like an animal. And so am I, she thought. I'm trapped by my cells and by my mind, by my ambitions and preconceptions. I like this guy but somehow I can't convince myself I could become involved with him.

Shortly after Susan and the other visitors left, Mackinaw moved the divers up to another decompression stop. A few minutes later, Madeira suddenly sat up and grabbed his hip. Severe pain showed on his face.

Hirsh awakened Mackinaw, who was dozing. "Chief, the Captain reports a sharp pain in his right hip."

Alert almost instantly, the veteran chief asked, "Does he have any bruises there?"

Hirsh repeated the question into the microphone.

"No, Chief," replied the hospitalman in the chamber. "He does have several on his left side but the only visible injuries on his right are on his leg."

"Okay, Hirsh. Tell them to secure the hatch between the two halves of the chamber. We're going to take the Captain back to the last stop."

"Roger," replied the chamber.

After the hatch was closed, Mackinaw nodded and Hirsh cracked a valve. Compressed air hissed into Madeira's side of the chamber. Less than a minute after the air stopped hissing, Madeira reported that the pain was gone. Mackinaw wiped his brow and adjusted the treatment schedule. He then called the XO, who had been trying to get some sleep.

"This is Chief Mackinaw, XO. The captain got bent in his right hip. We've split them up, recompressed the captain, and added two hours to his time. The symptoms disappeared when we recompressed and he's comfortable now. There doesn't appear to be any permanent damage."

"Do you have him on oxygen?"

"No, sir, not yet. He's still below sixty feet."

"Very well, Chief, I'll get somebody and we'll spell you and Hirsh."

"Thanks, but no thanks, XO. You have other things to do. Hirsh and I will take care of the captain and Mr. Merrill."

"You sure?"

"Yes, sir. We've got everything under control. I'd like permission to contact the diving medical officers at New London about the treatment schedule."

"Go ahead, Chief."

Six hours later, new symptoms appeared, again shortly after reaching a new stop. This time Madeira reported that his shoulder felt as if it were on fire. Mackinaw recompressed them again, adjusted the schedule, put Madeira on oxygen and began to worry for real. The onset of symptoms twice, in a man with Madeira's history, was serious.

The captain was older than many divers and somewhat chunky. Treating people of his age and build could be tricky. Mackinaw didn't want to think about the possible outcomes of an error on his part. Crippled joints. Brain damage. Death. All he could do was cross his fingers and sweat it out, waiting for the excess dissolved gases to slowly work their way out of Madeira's blood.

EIGHTEEN

CABOT STATION—DAY TEN

Dressed in a wetsuit and standing navel-deep in the chilly water of the treatment tank, Susan cursed quietly as she watched two similarly dressed porpoise handlers help Melissa into the treatment sling. The poor animal was obviously sick. Usually playful and affectionate, Melissa now resembled little more than a lifeless, inflatable toy. Her breathing was ragged and the most she could do to help the handlers was to flutter her fins and tail ineffectually.

It was pneumonia, they'd decided. Susan would have felt more comfortable with the diagnosis if it had been made by a veterinarian, but Cabot was too small to rate a real doctor for either its human or cetacean crews. Life being what it was, they'd have to trust in their own judgement.

"Careful," said one handler to the other, "she's almost in."

Susan stepped over to the sling and reached in, guiding Melissa the last few feet.

"Okay, she's in now. Raise the sling a few inches."

"Roger, Dr. Constantine."

The sling rose slowly, lifting Melissa's charcoal gray back clear of the water. As it did, Susan kept her hands on the porpoise's sleek sides, partially to keep her from moving, although she showed no inclination to do so, and partially to comfort her.

She feels so hot, thought Susan, grimacing. Although she

knew that Melissa had a fever, she also knew that there was no way she could detect it with her bare hands under the circumstances. It was her sympathetic imagination at work again.

Susan took a deep breath as she examined the patient. Melissa had contracted pneumonia twice before. While porpoises in the wild were subject to the disease, as well as to others equally familiar to the human race, the repeated occurrences struck Susan as strange. Was Melissa especially susceptible to pneumonia? If so, she would have died in the wild from the first bout and there would have been nothing unusual about it. Perhaps human medicine had only allowed her to live on to exhibit her natural weakness.

But maybe she didn't have a natural weakness. She certainly didn't appear, usually, to be anything but a healthy, young female porpoise. Maybe it was life at Cabot, which must be as stressful for the porpoises as it was for the people. Neither were designed to live underwater this way. It was unnatural. It had a way of grinding them all down, of draining the life from them.

Susan thought of Madeira lying in the chamber. She'd known many divers who'd been bent. Some repeatedly. It wasn't all that uncommon among people who dove frequently and under less-than-ideal conditions. She also knew of at least one who hadn't survived the experience. She felt a tightness across her chest.

"Don't worry, Melissa," she whispered soothingly, "you'll get better. Everything's going to work out."

While the handlers waited, assuming Susan was still examining Melissa, Susan examined herself. What was the attraction she felt for Madeira? Was it the occasional sparks of humor and life, the long-suffering decency she sensed in him? Or was it the challenge of drawing him out from behind his official facade to see what he was really made of? Was she attracted to him, or to the prospect of examining an intriguing specimen?

Must you examine everything? she asked herself with a sigh. She turned and reached for the syringe of antibiotics. It's there, the feeling. It may be nothing or it may be something. Play it by ear and see what happens.

Melissa flicked her tail slightly and turned her head toward Susan, almost as if to say, "Let's get on with it."

"This won't hurt a bit," said Susan, trying to smile. "You'll feel much better in a while."

Melissa didn't flinch.

A few moments later, Susan was sitting on the edge of the deck watching one of the handlers walking slowly around the tank with Melissa.

Just the day before, when they'd learned of the new personnel headed for Cabot, everything had seemed so bright. With their arrival, she would feel free to leave . . . and Al would be going with her, freed from the immediate pressures of Cabot at least for a few days. She'd also managed to convince herself that once ashore, with time to think, she'd find something of value in her data, in all the work she'd done over the past eighteen months.

Her elation had lasted less than twenty-four hours, killed by Madeira's mishap and Melissa's infirmity. Relief might be on its way, but almost anything could happen in the meantime.

Continuing to watch Melissa, she swung her legs out of the water and started to stand. As she did, her personal sun suddenly burst through the dense clouds that had been concealing it—its brilliance igniting her to near euphoria.

Melissa. Pneumonia. Stress-related illness! It could be Susan's salvation.

The porpoises could fool her about their behavior, but not about their illnesses. To what extent they suffered from stress-related illness generated by close contact with humans and participation in human activities, would fit right into her project. And, all she would need to start was a bit more data from their medical records. That, combined with what she already had, would be more than enough to work with.

"Don't give up, Melissa," she called cheerfully over her shoulder as she walked into the control booth to change out of her wetsuit, "there's hope yet."

NINETEEN

LION FISH—DAY TEN

Peacock was sound asleep when the Officer of the Deck brusquely awakened him. "Captain, our friend is underway again, heading for the Siren."

Within thirty seconds, Peacock, rumpled and showing the strain of the last two weeks, was in the control room studying the sonar display.

"He's making eighteen knots now, Captain," reported the OOD. "Still headed for the Siren. He'll reach it in about twenty minutes."

"I can see that," snapped Peacock. At forty-five, he was only now beginning to suspect that he might be getting too old for this line of business. "What the hell is he up to now?"

"I dunno, Captain."

"Whatever it is, he's not going to get away with it. I won't let him. Can we intercept him before he reaches the Siren?"

The OOD queried the tactical computer for an intercept.

"We can, Captain. Zero-four-three. Thirty knots."

"Steer zero-four-three. Speed thirty. Sound General Quarters."

The rudder was put hard left and superheated steam screamed into the turbines, causing *Lion Fish's* twin counter-rotating propellers to spin in a frenzy as the U.S. attack sub turned in pursuit of her Soviet counterpart.

Ten minutes later, the Sonarman reported that the Russian had turned slightly north.

"Very well," replied Peacock, a fresh cigar in his mouth. "We're going to keep after him, but we want to stay between him and the Siren."

Lion Fish thundered northeast, passing almost directly over the Siren.

As far as the general public was concerned, the world was more at peace than it had been in decades. Despite the bitter, bloody little wars that raged incessantly in the mountains and jungles of the Americas and Asia and on the great plains and deserts of Africa, the superpowers appeared to be sincerely seeking cooperation and mutual benefit.

In distant dark corners however—the realms of spies and nuclear submarines—the continuing differences of interest, both political and economic, continued to engender violent expression.

Two hours, and almost twenty course changes later, the Russian turned sharply and steadied on a southeasterly course.

"All right," said Peacock as he bit through what was left of his cigar butt, "he goes southeast, we go southeast. But keep inside him."

For the next three hours, the duel continued with the Russian twisting and turning, drawing *Lion Fish* slowly southeast, away from the Siren and toward two new Soviet arrivals.

"Captain," shouted the Sonarman, "I've got two additional high speed targets approaching from the southeast. Must be attack boats."

"Where the hell did they come from?" Peacock's exhausted brain ground to a halt as he tried to shift gears and consider the new problem. For the first time in his career, he was befuddled. Briefly, but long enough.

Almost as if able to read Peacock's confusion, the captain of *Lion Fish's* dance partner stopped his engines at that moment and turned hard right. *Lion Fish* shot past her. The Russian was now between Peacock and the Siren.

"That son of a bitch!" screamed Peacock when he realized what had happened. "He's inside us now. Right full rudder. Dive! We'll cut under him."

It was not to be. The Soviet captain, of whom Peacock had been so scornful, repeatedly anticipated and outmaneuvered

Peacock, keeping his own vessel between *Lion Fish* and the Siren.

"Captain," reported the sonarman, "those two other Red boats are splitting up. One's headed for us, and the other's headed for the Siren."

Peacock studied the display and tried again to maneuver past *Lion Fish's* companion of weeks—to no avail. Within a few minutes, two Soviet attack boats were between him and his charge.

"Captain," reported the sonarman, "the third Red has stopped about one mile from the Siren."

"Very well," replied Peacock in a low voice, now reconciled to what was to follow.

"They've just launched a torpedo, Captain."

"Very well."

The XO looked nervously at Peacock, then relaxed somewhat after looking back at the sonar display and determining that the torpedo was not intended for them.

Peacock stood, slumping, in the quiet control room.

Boom! The Soviet torpedo smashed into the Siren and detonated.

Thump! The two highly charged gas flasks burst, releasing a huge air bubble and further mangling the Siren.

Then, as the bubble expanded and shot toward the surface, what was left of the Siren imploded, completing its destruction.

Lion Fish trembled as the shock waves from the Siren's destruction caressed her.

Peacock stared ahead with an expression bleaker than any the XO ever expected to see. "XO, I've just committed one of the classic unpardonable naval blunders. I let myself be distracted. It's the first thing they teach you—never let yourself be sucked off station unless there's someone else to keep an eye on the henhouse."

"It was two . . . three against one, Captain," replied the XO.

"Bullshit! Our friend has been setting me up for over a week. He did me in all by himself. He let me get cocky and wear myself out chasing him."

The XO stood mute, not sure what to say.

"Captain," said the sonarman, breaking the silence, "all three Reds have turned north and are pulling away."

"At least," observed the XO in a hopeful voice, "they haven't sent any cute little messages."

"They're probably laughing their asses off."

"Captain," barked the XO in an almost insubordinately sharp tone, "it will be a while before you're hung. In the meantime, what do you want done?"

Stung by the verbal slap, Peacock spun and glowered at his XO. "We're going to take a look at whatever's left of the Siren, report this fiasco to CincLantFleet and then guard the wreckage while we wait for further instructions."

Then he smiled bleakly, his expression a mixture of acceptance and almost fatherly pride in his second-in-command.

TWENTY

THE DECOMPRESSION CHAMBER—DAY TEN

Madeira was scared. He knew he was out of shape. He knew he was especially susceptible to decompression sickness and he knew the more times he got bent the more likely the chance of permanent damage. He feared death and, even more, he feared the development of a bubble in his brain—a bubble that would cut off the blood flow and turn him into a vegetable. He didn't want to spend the rest of his life as a blubbering, drooling basket case—poor old Madeira, pitied by the kindhearted and jeered at by children.

He was trapped. Trapped in the chamber by his defective body and trapped in Cabot by his own stupidity. He was caught between Admiral Williams' grim determination to keep Cabot going and the realities of domestic economics and politics.

The nightmare had started, and he now felt his career had ended, eighteen months ago, on a snappy October day when he had arrived at Portsmouth to assume command of Cabot's Gold Crew.

He remembered walking across the apron and into the terminal, excited at the prospect of his first command. It wasn't a ship but it was the next closest thing. When he reached the baggage claim area he stopped and looked around. He had expected to be met by the man he was relieving or by the Gold Crew's Executive Officer. He saw nobody who could be either.

Damn, he thought. Could they be so screwed up that they can't even meet an airplane?

Before he had time to consider the question further he spotted a figure he did recognize. Steaming into the concourse from a side door was a tall, older naval officer wearing a frown and a dark blue bridge coat with four gold stripes showing on each shoulder.

The instant Captain W.R. Robertson—Rob to his friends—Commander, Portsmouth Naval Shipyard, spotted Madeira, his frown changed into a broad smile. "Al. Welcome to Portsmouth. It's good to see you."

"I'm very glad to be here, Captain, although I hardly expected you to pick me up."

The tall, fair but graying captain and the stocky, dark-haired lieutenant commander shook hands warmly. Madeira had served under Robertson on two previous occasions. During those tours of duty a firm personal friendship had developed between them.

"Why shouldn't I be the one to welcome you? Allow me a few prerogatives. The officer you're relieving has already left. Your XO was planning to come but I asked him to let me do it. I think he was relieved to let me explain the local facts of life to you."

From Robertson's tone of voice, Madeira gathered that there must be something unpleasant about the "local facts of life." In retrospect, if he'd been smart, he would have turned and run right then. He was unable, however, to pursue the topic because his luggage arrived and Robertson immediately grabbed a suitcase and said, "Follow me." Madeira grabbed the other and followed the captain out to his ancient station wagon.

With Robertson driving, they headed for the shipyard. The conversation initially concerned old times and mutual friends. Then, at a stop light, Robertson turned to Madeira. "Al, you know I don't like vulgarities but there's only one way to describe what you're in for at Cabot. You're going to be sucking hind teat."

The light changed, Robertson shifted into gear and continued. "As you know, I hope, Cabot is old. It's also worn-out. Unfortunately, a lot of people have reason to consider it obsolete so they assign it little or no priority."

"It can't be all *that* bad! I met with Admiral Williams before coming here and he seems to feel SOSUS and Cabot are still very necessary."

"Yes, Williams is on your side, although he'll push you hard. This is his twilight tour and he's determined to prove that he can make ComConDefSurvCom run right—something it hasn't done for some time. You can be sure that he'll do everything he can to help, but there's only so much he can do from Colorado and Cabot's only one of his problems."

Robertson swerved to avoid a pothole, then continued. "The main problem is that the American people don't feel they can afford us . . . but they don't have the guts to come right out and fire us and see what happens. Instead, they just squeeze and squeeze.

"They're partly right, I suppose. The world *is* changing and the economy really can't support everything, not if they devote all their time to trying to pick each other's pockets . . . but the world hasn't changed *that* much and I don't think human nature's changed at all.

"As I said, Cabot's old. Much of its equipment's old too, or even worse, custom-made. Many of the repair parts you'll be ordering are not stock items, they have to be made-to-order. In some cases, they're not even manufactured in the United States any more.

"All this custom stuff costs money but support facilities like Cabot don't get much. They don't get headlines, or votes, the way some of the sexy new projects do.

"And then, there's the personnel problem. Both Blue and Gold Crews have been shorthanded for over a year and there's been so much turnover that they've been relieving late . . . but you know about personnel. Not enough young bodies and life's too good on the outside."

"Rob," interjected Madeira, "how do you feel personally about Cabot and SOSUS?"

"The same as Admiral Williams. . . . That they're old and tired but still necessary. There's a lot of junk sitting around that we should scrap, both ships and shore facilities, but for the time being, we need SOSUS. The satellites are just too fallible and vulnerable." Robertson paused. "Perhaps I'm being too cynical, perhaps not. Anyway, what I've just said is off the record."

Madeira found the conversation unsettling. He would never have imagined such an outburst from the normally placid captain.

"I'm painting a pretty bleak picture, aren't I? There are a few bright spots. You're going to have good people working for you, although you'll be shorthanded. Your counterpart, Ozawa, the Blue Crew CO, is a smart, hard-working guy like you. He'll hold up his end. Finally, you can count on a few of us here to do everything we can for you."

Madeira wondered whether he was expected to shoot himself right away or to wait for a while.

"Okay, Al, the lecture's almost over. In one way I'm glad you took this job. If Cabot's to make it, it needs people like you and Ozawa. For your sake, I'm not so glad. This job may turn out to be a nightmare."

Madeira asked about shooting himself. Robertson laughed. "Not until tomorrow morning at the earliest. Janet wants you to come to dinner tonight and so do I."

"You say your kids are all gone?"

"Yes. Jeff's a Marine pilot, Cindy's in Med School and Will's got an honest job. Ironically, now that the nest is empty, Janet's quit her job and is concentrating on being 'The Captain's Wife'. She's redecorating the house. You're going to love it. It was built by a nineteenth century clipper captain right on the ocean."

Lying in the decompression chamber, Madeira shuddered at the memory of the interview. He had realized then that he was headed for trouble, but he hadn't realized just how much. It didn't really matter, anyway. Nobody forces you to accept a command. You have to beg for one. But, once you have accepted, there's no turning back.

Three weeks after Madeira's arrival in Portsmouth, the Gold Crew's long overdue movement orders finally appeared along with the winter's first snow and slush storm. Despite the weather, Madeira's executive officer loaded supplies and records aboard *Procyon* with dispatch. One last liberty had followed and they were underway the next morning.

The voyage under the world's most disreputable ocean to Flemish Cap had been uneventful. Three days after leaving Portsmouth, *Procyon* had slowed to a crawl and, after some backing and filling, mated with Cabot's lock number one.

There to greet them had been a frowning Lieutenant Commander Ozawa.

"I'm sorry we're so late, Captain Ozawa," said Madeira.

"Don't mention it. It's not your fault, I'm sure. Staff seems to have made late reliefs standard operating procedure." His frown lessened but did not disappear. "Welcome to Cabot Station, Captain Madeira."

Madeira pulled the coarse blanket more tightly around him. When the time came, how would he greet Ozawa's relief? Probably the same way. By the time the guy arrived at Cabot it would be too late to warn him off.

TWENTY-ONE

COLORADO—DAY TEN

"Admiral," said Admiral Williams into the telephone, "I want *my* people to finish the job . . . to recover the wreckage."

Ring, seated on the admiral's couch, listened to Williams' side of the conversation with the CNO.

"I can well understand that the President is demanding answers and I'm going to get them for him. . . . The Supervisor of Salvage agrees with me. . . . He admits we're best equipped to handle it."

Williams sat up, tensing slightly.

"As far as I'm concerned that clinches it. Why else would they torpedo it?

"According to Madeira's people, the charges and caps appeared functionable. I assume whatever system they had to detonate them—remote or time—was damaged by the fire. . . .

"No. I understand that he needs more. We will get it for him. . . .

"No, nobody's contacted me yet. It looks like you've been successful so far at that. . . . They're going to be tremendously angry when it *does* come out. . . .

"SOSUS Atlantic has reviewed their tapes. Nothing unusual was picked up in the area during the six hours preceding the Siren's discovery. All they heard were two Soviet boomers. . . .

"That's what worries me too . . . They haven't finished

analyzing it yet but they say the tape sounds like a recording of what they would get from the net when a boomer passes near a sensor. . . .

"Yes, I agree. They may have been tapping the net. All they would need is an induction coil and a good computer . . . or they may have been recording one of their own subs directly.

"No. The Agency wants it but they want us to recover it. They say we can do it more quickly. I've already spoken with them. . . .

"Hell! If they can put an airplane together after it's smeared itself across the side of a mountain then we can put a Siren back together. . . .

"Same as before. I want *Falcon* to work with Cabot's worksubs. I want Lieutenant Commander Madeira, Cabot's Gold CO, to be Salvage Master. He'll ride *Falcon*. And, if at all possible, *Lion Fish* must stay on, just in case. Give her CO a chance to redeem himself. In fact, I'd feel more comfortable if you could provide a second attack boat. . . .

"I hope not. They could make it impossible if they want to, no matter how many attack boats we send.

"He said he can't spare another one right now, but . . .

"I understand. *Lion Fish* will have to do. How about a destroyer for *Falcon*?"

Williams laughed. "I understand."

"He's qualified. In fact, I feel he's done a superb job so far. I want him to finish it.

"I've already spoken with SupSalv about him. He's due in Portsmouth shortly for an administrative conference. . . .

"I'm sending Ring to Portsmouth. I'll have him brief Madeira in person before we helo him out to *Falcon*. . . .

"I'm sure his XO can handle Cabot in his absence.

"Thank you, sir. All we need now is a break in the weather.

"Hodges told you about my call? He got me twelve new people.

"I know he's doing the best he can for us but some of the supply people aren't . . .

"I understand there are complications, but this is a crisis! If you can't support me on this, I'll have to close Cabot down. I'll abandon it, evacuate all hands in *Procyon*.

"No. I don't want to but I will.

"Thank you."

As Williams hung up, Ring gave him a questioning look.

"It's go, Jim. We're going to do it." The admiral grinned grimly.

"Admiral, Madeira has decompression sickness. He's in Cabot's chamber."

"He'll soon be out. Almost as good as new."

"If he isn't?"

"Then Ozawa, although I really don't want to use him for this. I want him to concentrate on getting his crew pulled together to relieve the Gold Crew."

"What about the Soviets?"

"Let's hope they feel they've done enough already."

"They probably couldn't recover it anyway."

"Don't underrate them, Jim. That's what *Lion Fish* seems to have done. We really don't know what their deep salvage capabilities are. Just cross your fingers that they think we're wasting our time."

As he spoke, Williams was struck by the realization that he was enjoying himself. A mystery to be solved, and a good fight! What a way to end a career!

Oblivious to Ring's presence, Williams' smile turned into a frown as guilt and a nagging fear replaced grim satisfaction. He shouldn't be enjoying himself. There was too much at stake, too many lives. He almost wished he were Madeira.

"Jim," he said, returning to his hated, windowless office, "let's get that OpOrder out ASAP."

TWENTY-TWO

CABOT STATION—DAY TEN

"They did what?" demanded Madeira into the chamber inter-com.

"They got by *Lion Fish* somehow, Captain, and torpedoed the Siren. They say there's not much left of her," replied the XO, speaking into the outside intercom speaker. "I guess that's it."

"I'm afraid that's not it," answered Madeira as he sat down on a bunk. "The Siren's still there and we'll end up having to recover her piece by piece."

"Oh shit! That'll take forever."

"Yes, it will," sighed Madeira as he lay back on the bunk.

The following day, while Madeira was still in the chamber, the Operations Order arrived and was locked in to him. He read it with mixed, and confused emotions. Like Admiral Williams, he dearly wanted to know what the Siren was doing. Further-more, the recovery operation would be a refreshing challenge, one that would have a definite end and would offer the chance of a tangible and satisfying victory, so unlike the never-ending struggle to keep Cabot shuddering along. As Salvage Master he would be free of his administrative worries for a while anyway, and he would be breathing real air. He might even see the sun.

On the other hand, working on the surface of the North Atlantic in April wouldn't be much fun; and who knew what the Soviets might do to make it even more unpleasant.

Damn them! he thought. They'd done enough already. The XO was right, picking up the pieces would take forever. The whole affair was beginning to look like a fiasco.

Madeira felt an irrational anger growing within him. Not only was the recovery going to be a mess, but what about Cabot's logistical problems? Would there be time for them now? Would anybody be interested? And what about Susan? He'd assumed that, with the new personnel arriving, she'd go ashore with him. He'd hoped to spend some time with her before she moved on to Kam Station. Freed from the confines of Cabot, who knew what might have happened.

Damn it! He'd make time, at least for dinner, and he'd make sure something was done for Cabot, too.

That afternoon, Madeira was released from the chamber. When he arrived in the wardroom for dinner, he was still feeling stiff, sore, and glum. The decompression sickness and its treatment had taken a lot out of him. The hull inspection had also been discouraging. Cabot was still falling apart faster than he could fix it, and the prospect of recovering what was left of the Siren looked more formidable with every passing minute.

As he brooded, Madeira started to gobble his food and caught himself. That's all he needed, to be fatter than he already was. He started to fire a question at Frazier concerning the repairs to *Molly's* damaged motor and then stopped when he realized that Susan and Merrill had involved the whole wardroom in a discussion of the horror film they had seen the previous evening.

"As far as I'm concerned," Susan was saying, "horror flicks should be made in black and white. None of the ones in color are really very scary."

"Baloney," replied Merrill. "You don't like Techna-Terror? What about *Psycho*? Hitchcock made a lot of good color ones."

"*Psycho* was black and white."

"You're right, damn it. What about *The Birds*?"

"Excuse me, Captain," interjected Frazier. "I have to relieve Ms. Ryan. Anyway, this conversation's getting way too deep for me."

As the warrant officer left, Susan continued her assault.

"I'm not criticizing Hitchcock. I like a lot of his stuff, too. Especially the short black and white shows he made for TV."

"I've never seen them," persisted Merrill, "but are you telling me that you didn't like *The Birds*?"

Madeira found himself listening with fascination. He would never have guessed that Susan was interested in horror films, although her moodiness, he decided, might have been a tip-off.

"What do you think, Captain? You're into photography so you must like movies."

Madeira was startled when she brought him into the discussion. He had planned to remain a spectator. It took him a minute to reply.

"*Nosferatu*. The original one."

"*Nosferatu*?" asked Susan. "You mean the old, silent vampire story?"

"Yes. *Nosferatu* is the most frightening movie I've ever seen. Aside from the plot, I think it's the strangeness of it, the disorientation, the sense of visual wrongness, that made me edgy and frightened."

As he spoke, Madeira felt a chill run through him. He could see the count's carriage ghosting through the mist, rising and falling slowly as it went. Hazy, indistinct, ephemeral. It was almost as if the scene had been shot underwater.

Every time he had seen the old movie he'd felt as if he were having a bad dream; as if what was occurring on the screen was really happening in his mind. Thinking of it now, recalling the image of the count's victim emerging from the wrecked ship, his life and soul drained from him and replaced with a whining insanity, he could see himself. That's the way he would look, he felt, when and if he ever emerged from Cabot. Drained of life and spirit by his demon, the North Atlantic. Each leak, each failing servo-mechanism, each corroded fitting was a manifestation of the ocean's evil power. The threats were clearly visible yet whenever he tried to grab one, to correct it, it flowed away from him, changing form as it went and splitting into ten new problems, each of which had to be solved before the initial one could be corrected.

"I'm really surprised that you all know so much about old horror films," said Susan.

"That's just about all we have here to do for fun," replied Sonneberg. "Look at seaprints . . ."

"All of which are at least fifty years old," added Merrill before Sonneberg could finish.

Ryan came through the curtain and sat down. Before she could lift her fork, Merrill asked her opinion of the best horror film.

"I never watch them if I can help it," she replied. "I think they're all stupid."

"Well, Merrill?" said Sonneberg.

Merrill smiled as if to say, "You can't win 'em all."

"How are you feeling, Captain," asked Susan, turning toward him.

"Great!" lied Madeira. "I'm completely recovered."

"I hear you're going to recover what's left of the Siren. I guess you were right, it is Russian."

"Yes, to both," he replied absently, his mind already partially occupied with planning the task to come.

Turning to the XO, he said, "Frazier and Hammerstein are going to have to get *Molly* put together again, somehow."

"Yes, sir. Frazier's already working on it."

Madeira turned back to Susan, "Are you ready to wrap up your work here? *Procyon's* arriving in a few days."

"I think so. Though I've come up with a whole new line on it. Stress-related diseases."

"The porpoises'? You mean I'm working the silly beasts too hard?"

"That's not what I mean, although you probably are. I think they're suffering from the stress at this place just like the rest of you are. The idea's probably not original but I think I can come up with specifics that I haven't seen published anywhere before."

"You think we're all neurotic?" chimed in Merrill, grinning broadly.

"No, not everybody, Mr. Merrill. And I suspect you were long before you ever heard of Cabot Station."

As the laughter subsided, Madeira's thoughts returned to the Siren. He'd been involved in pick-up-the-pieces jobs before and they were always messes, even in only thirty feet of water. He shuddered to think what it would be in three thousand.

TWENTY-THREE

CABOT STATION—
DAY TWELVE

When *Procyon* arrived, on time for a change, with the twelve fresh additions to the station's weary crew, Madeira discovered the supply sub had a new skipper, a young lieutenant commander.

"Captain Madeira, my name's Pete Schwartz. I'm your new grocery boy."

"Welcome, Pete. Please call me Al. How was your trip?"

"Fairly routine, although we did almost cream an iceberg on the way."

"An iceberg! Where? A big berg could scrape Cabot up and spread the pieces all over the North Atlantic!"

"Newfoundland Bank. I was a little nervous about bottoming, this being my first trip, so I was running shallow. Too shallow. It gave us all a real scare."

"There aren't supposed to be bergs there. I haven't seen any satellite reports about it either."

"I know. That's why I wasn't more alert, I'm afraid. These storms have been breaking all the rules about where the ice goes and when. They've also been causing problems for the satellites' infra-red and visual sensors."

"What about their radar?"

"Somebody probably just screwed up."

"Which way was it headed?"

"South, although if the Gulf Stream gets hold of it, it may turn northeast and come visit you. But don't worry, it only draws about eighty feet. It'll pass right over."

"Spoken like a true submariner, Pete. You forget we have a monster buoy on the surface."

"The storm will probably get that long before the berg does."

"With that type of humor you're going to fit right in around here."

"I certainly hope so. I understand you're going back to Portsmouth with us."

"That's right."

"And then you go on to recover that Siren?"

"The what?"

"What's the real story on that? Captain Robertson only told me a little. Said it's as secret as hell."

"What did he tell you?"

"Just that it's a Soviet drone, that it suddenly appeared, that the Soviets torpedoed it and that ComConDefSurvCom wants to know more about it."

"You know almost as much as we do. All I can add is that it has some sort of special gear installed. That's why we're going to recover what's left. Does any of your crew know about it?"

"Only my XO. Will *Procyon* be involved?"

"I doubt it. You can't dive deep enough. Anyway, you're going to be busy, I hope, bringing the Blue Crew out in a couple of weeks."

"Oh," responded Schwartz, looking disappointed. "The salvage operation sounds interesting."

"Pete," said Madeira with a slight grin, "I'd like to ask you for a big favor. You can say no if you wish. . . ."

"Shoot," replied Schwartz, looking a little suspicious.

"Do you mind taking two defective watertight door assemblies back with us?"

"No problem. That's what I'm here for."

"But I want only one of them to appear on your manifest; and you may have to bring the off-manifest one back next trip, still undocumented."

Schwartz paused, looking around the Submarine Section at the work being done on *Molly*. "Okay. I doubt you plan to sell it to a scrap dealer and pocket the proceeds. You mind telling me what you *do* plan to do with it?"

"I'd prefer not to, until it's done."

"Does Captain Robertson know what you're doing?"

"He will—if it works."

"Will he approve?"

"Privately, yes."

"I'll do it then. He said to expect a few irregularities."

When Susan spotted the twelve new arrivals, she came to see Madeira. "So we really did get the new bodies."

"Hard to believe, isn't it? Now you can get on to Kam Station."

"Al . . . I don't want to overstay my welcome . . . but would it be all right if I stay at Cabot a little longer?"

Madeira's jaw started to drop. "You want to stay? What about Kam Station? We've shanghaied you long enough."

"I'll be going on to Kam Station but there's still more I need to do here. This 'stress' line is turning out to be a gold mine for me."

Madeira smiled, despite the jealousy building within him.

"I'm glad to hear that. I was afraid this project was going to drag you down."

"So was I. But now I know I'm going to knock 'em dead with it."

"I still think you should git while the gittin's good."

"*Procyon* will be back in two weeks, won't she?"

"She's supposed to be but I wouldn't count on it."

"I'm going to assume she will be. Then, when you've finished recovering the Siren you can take me out to dinner at a real restaurant, one where we can look out the windows." She noticed Madeira's look of skepticism. "The Blue Crew will have relieved them by then, won't they? You won't have to come back right away?"

"Susan, I'll probably still be trapped in the ice, between Greenland and Labrador. Picking up the pieces isn't as easy as it might sound. I may be there a month. Two months even, if the weather doesn't cooperate."

Now it was Susan's turn to feel distress. "I guess I wasn't thinking. I should have known it could take a long time."

Then, smiling again, she looked up. "Al, I'll make sure I'm in Portsmouth when you get back. I'll delay my trip to Kam Station if necessary. They don't care when I arrive."

"Okay," he replied, now smiling himself, "not that I have much choice."

"You can always order me to leave."

"That would be stupid of me."

When *Patty* and her haggard crew returned, Madeira was waiting at the lock.

"Congratulations, Bob, and thank you. Two good deeds in two weeks."

"My pleasure, Captain. I wish we'd been able to learn more about the Siren. I can't believe *Lion Fish* let them by. She almost didn't let us by."

"We're not giving up. Admiral Williams has ordered me to organize its salvage. I'll be Salvage Master in *Falcon* and you and Frazier will be doing most of the work. So you've got to get *Molly* and *Patty* back in service, ASAP."

Hammerstein rolled his eyes. "Aye, aye, Captain." Then, after a pause, he added, "Here's the cassette."

Madeira accepted the cassette and peered at it, turning it over slowly in his hand. "It's a Sony. I don't know if they'll learn anything more from it ashore but they might."

An hour after transmitting the cassette's complete contents to ComConDefSurvCom over the landline, Madeira was aboard *Procyon* and she was underway for Portsmouth.

The voyage was like a pleasure cruise for Madeira, a form of decompression. Although life aboard *Procyon* was not significantly different from life at Cabot, Madeira was free of responsibilities and found abundant time to catch up on his sleep and to spend long hours in the wardroom chatting with Schwartz and his officers.

At one point, when they were alone in the wardroom, Schwartz looked pointedly at Madeira. "Al, I don't want to pry but there's something that's been bothering me."

"Yes?"

[114]

"It's your career pattern. Where do you go next? How do Bubbleheads become admirals?"

"We don't. And I have no idea where I'm going next. I really haven't thought about it much recently. Been too busy. There are a few staff jobs available but if I want to make full captain some day I'm going to have to go back to surface ships for a while. I'm not considered a qualified submariner; ours don't have torpedoes, missiles, or reactors."

"Are any Bubbleheads submariners?"

"None that I know of."

"How did you get yourself into this position?"

"I originally thought the Undersea Program would be bigger than it's turned out to be. After that, inertia took over.

"What about you, Pete? If you don't mind my asking. Why aren't you at school learning to be XO of an attack boat?"

"Because I shot my mouth off one too many times to the wrong people."

"So you were sent to Purgatory? For rehabilitation?"

"I hope that rehabilitation is what they have in mind, but, to be honest, this job is turning out to be more interesting than I had expected. And, however humble she may be, *Procyon is* a ship—and she's mine."

TWENTY-FOUR

PORTSMOUTH NAVAL SHIPYARD—DAY SIXTEEN

While Madeira was catching his breath, a large warm-air mass had forced its way up the East Coast, driving a long-lasting chain of North Atlantic gales away from the New England shore and replacing them with an only slightly less violent frontal system.

Three days after leaving Cabot Station, *Procyon* surfaced at the mouth of the Piscataqua River and found herself enmeshed in the unpleasant combination of icy rain and gusty winds that often plagues the New England coast in March.

Wearing a borrowed slicker, Madeira stood jammed into the tiny bridge with Schwartz and the lookout as they slowly covered the last two miles to the piers. It was exhilarating to be on the bridge of a ship, even someone else's, returning to port after a long absence. He looked aft at the smooth, swirling wake engraved into the choppy, gray water. He looked through the dark air at the rocky, wave-battered shore and at the shoreline houses, safely perched above the flying spume. The houses, brightly lighted in the stormy dusk, looked warm and inviting. One of them, he thought, was Robertson's. Despite the cold, driving rain, Madeira was glad he had prevailed on Schwartz to let him kibitz on the cramped little bridge.

Shortly before the heavy dusk turned to dark, tumultuous night, the submarine slowed and turned toward her berth. Three sailors, enveloped in yellow life vests and exposure suits, appeared on the submarine's tiny decks. Ashore, line handlers could be seen pacing along the pier, hands in their pockets. Behind the line handlers, Madeira noticed the inevitable row of cars parked with headlights on and windshield wipers doing their best to dispel the freezing rain. He had never been aboard a returning ship that wasn't met by that fleet of cars filled with wives and girlfriends and flocks of children.

With the wind blowing obliquely up the river and the tide and current running in near opposite directions, the approach was tricky. Madeira admired Schwartz's sure commands as the sub cut across the waves and through eddies that grew like mushrooms in the vicinity of the pilings. It hadn't taken the new skipper long to learn the feel of his new ship and her home port.

As the submarine approached the pier, a whistle sounded from the foredeck. It was answered from the floodlit pier. One of the yellow-suited sailors swung a coiled heaving line over his shoulder and behind his back. Propelled by a final underarm snap, the monkey's paw shot over the pier, dragging the light line behind it. The line handlers pounced and hauled it in. Within seconds they had their hands on the heavier messenger spliced to the heaving line, then the mooring line, which was tied to the messenger.

While the line handlers worked, Schwartz had not been idle. Using wind, engines, rudder, current, and momentum, he positioned his ship parallel to and only a few yards from the pier.

The line handlers dragged the number one nylon mooring line along the pier. The instant its eye was dropped over one of the large black bollards another whistle sounded on the submarine.

The stern line, along with the two spring lines, were then passed and dropped over bollards. Schwartz ordered a brief spurt of power, the forward spring line took the strain and the submarine nestled comfortably next to the pier.

"Double up all lines," bellowed Schwartz to the deck hands.

"Finished with the engines," he said into the bridge communicator.

When his ship was secured, he went below, followed by Madeira. They reached the main passageway and found it filled with the few other passengers from Cabot and the sub's liberty section all bundled up and waiting to go ashore.

Madeira and Schwartz changed and talked while the passageway emptied.

"I'm glad you're Cabot's new contact with the outside world, Pete. You run a good ship."

"Thanks, Al. I'm looking forward to the next three years. I meant what I said about being your agent at Portsmouth. You tell me what you're not getting and I'll pound on some desks. I'm sure that between us, Captain Robertson and I can get you better service."

"You won't make any friends. Captain Robertson hasn't."

"Hell with 'em. Adds spice to life. I'm already dreading the day your orders come through."

Schwartz laughed as he continued. "If you have a few hours while you're here, give me a call. We'd love to have you over for a home-cooked meal."

Madeira meant it when he said he hoped he would have a chance to do so.

Madeira checked his briefcase.

"Pete, I can deliver the cassette to the Crypto Office."

"It's way out of your way. My Comm Officer has to go there tonight anyway so he might as well take it with him. He won't lose it.

"And don't worry about your travel bag. We'll drop it off at the TOQ. It'll probably get there before you do."

They ascended to the weather deck, saluted the petty officer standing the OOD watch and crossed to the slushy pier. Most of the cars had already gone, leaving the pier darker and colder. Suddenly, a three-foot high figure came rushing at them, glistening in the damp arc light and shouting, "Daaa-a-ddy!"

"That's Debby, my oldest," said Schwartz. "She's six," he

added as he scooped her up and hugged her, almost dropping his briefcase in the process.

Madeira spent the next ten minutes standing in the rain, meeting the Schwartz family. It was with mixed emotions that he declined a second offer of a home-cooked meal but he had a busy day ahead of him, fighting the supply system, and he was convinced that Schwartz wouldn't really want a guest his first night home.

Madeira said goodbye and set out, whistling, glad that he had decided to stretch his legs rather than having *Procyon's* jitney take him to his quarters. Despite the dismal weather, he was feeling good. Cabot Station and its problems, while still very much on his mind, didn't have the gnawing immediacy that had been wearing so harshly on him.

Walking between and around the old concrete and brick buildings, he breathed deeply and tasted the air. It was real air, cold and damp, with the flavor of snow and a touch of pollution—the air of home.

When he reached the TOQ, Madeira checked in. Captain Robertson, he learned, had gone home but was expecting his call there.

"Rob, this is Al."

"Hello, Al. I'm glad you made it in such good time. I'd expected you to arrive about zero-two-hundred. Are you at the TOQ?"

"Yes. I'll grab some dinner and hit the rack. What's on for tomorrow? Before getting too wrapped up on the Siren, I'd still like to go over some of our supply problems."

"So would we all. Tomorrow, you and I are going to go over them. Then on Thursday, Jim Ring arrives. He wants to go over them again with you and Ozawa. Then he'll brief you on Admiral Williams' wishes concerning the Siren."

"Anything new on that?"

"Nope. *Lion Fish's* still out there, playing the junkyard dog. Your people report they're making good progress getting *Molly* back in shape and Jim's supposed to have a list of *Falcon's* equipment and its status. After you see the list, you tell us what else you need. If I can't get it for you, I'm sure Admiral Williams will."

"Outstanding!" replied Madeira with an enthusiasm that surprised him.

"I'm glad to hear you're looking forward to it."

If only Susan were here, thought Madeira as he hung up.

TWENTY-FIVE

PORTSMOUTH NAVAL SHIPYARD— DAY SEVENTEEN

"Rob" Robertson looked at his soap-covered face in the mirror and grimaced. Was that a dewlap beginning to form?

He poked a finger under his chin.

Hell no! It was no such thing, just his imagination. He wasn't that old, yet.

Of course not, he told himself. It was just decades of long days, midnight alerts, and tension.

Turning thirty had, for Robertson, been a non-event. On his fortieth birthday, he had been much too busy keeping over three hundred sailors, thirty-two officers and one ship all moving in the same direction to worry about old age. It was his fiftieth that was the shocker, and his job at the time had allowed him the opportunity to dwell on it.

Shortly before 0600, while he was still telling himself that he was as young as ever, the phone rang.

"Captain Robertson speaking."

"Captain, this is the Comm Station. We've lost all communications with Cabot."

Robertson stopped worrying about his age.

"What, exactly, happened?"

"They were in the middle of a routine administrative message when the circuit went dead."

"Are you referring to the cable?"

"Yes, sir. The cable is dead. We haven't been able to reach them by radio or sonar, either."

"Very well. Keep trying to contact them."

Robertson wiped the soap off the telephone as he hung up and quickly finished shaving, wondering what had happened and what was to be done. He was headed for the phone when it rang again.

"Captain Robertson, this is the Comm Station again. We are picking up an automatic distress signal from Cabot's monster buoy."

"Have you contacted ComConDefSurvCom?"

"We're doing it now."

"Very well."

Robertson took a deep breath, adrenalin surging through his veins, then called the TOQ.

"Lieutenant Commander Madeira, please. This is Captain Robertson."

"Yes, sir."

The Captain passed his hand through his short-cropped gray hair as he listened to the extension ringing.

"There's no answer, sir. He doesn't appear to be in his room."

"Very well," snapped Robertson. "I want him paged. I want him located. He's to report to my office immediately. I'll be there in forty minutes."

"Yes, Captain. Will do."

"What's happening, Robbie?" asked Janet from the bed.

"I don't know, dear. We've just lost contact with Cabot Station. I'm going to the office. I'll call you later, when I know more."

"I'm so very glad you're here, and not there," she replied.

"So am I, dear," he answered, pleased that she'd said it. But, of course, Janet always said and did the right thing.

He felt a twinge of guilt, and sadness, at all the worrying she must have done over the years while he was off seeing the world and she was picking up after the kids.

After showering and dressing quickly, he found Janet up

and waiting for him in her bathrobe. "Good luck, Rob. I hope it works out."

"It will, Janet. One way or another."

He kissed her goodbye and galloped down the stairs. Once out the door, he paused next to his station wagon and noticed that another cold front had swept down from central Canada, bringing with it clear skies and a considerable drop in temperature.

He started the engine and turned on the headlights. The engine sounded rough. Well, no matter now, he thought as he headed down the driveway. The wagon skidded slightly as he stopped at the end of the driveway, before turning onto the street.

Driving fast, but carefully, along the deserted, shiny-slick roads, he prayed that nothing serious had happened, that it was all just one more minor screw-up.

He made good time and arrived at the administration building just after dawn. He checked in at the entrance and headed immediately for the duty officer's office.

"Anything new on Cabot?"

"Yes, Captain. Hydro Quebec has reported that Cabot's power line breakers have tripped. They think it's some sort of massive short. They want to know if they should keep trying to restore the load?"

Robertson had to stop a minute to think.

"Tell them to keep trying but with very low power. We don't want to fry them if they've got their feet wet," he finally replied.

After trudging up the stairs to his own chilly, dark office, Robertson turned on the lights and took off his bridge coat. He started to remove his double breasted blouse and then thought better of it. It would be hours before the heat came up to a comfortable level. It would also be hours before his immediate aide arrived and he didn't have any coffee, damnit!

There was a knock at the door. It was the duty officer's messenger with a thermos pitcher of coffee and a cup of cream. God bless the man!

Robertson thanked the messenger and filled his white porcelain mug, smoothing the dark acid with cream. He had no idea what was happening and no way of finding out quickly.

He hunched over his desk, tension and frustration churning the coffee in his otherwise empty stomach.

Could it be the Siren? Could they have moved to prevent its recovery? Could it be that important?

He didn't know. There was nothing he could do at the moment but wait.

There was something! He picked up the phone and called *Procyon's* duty section.

"This is Captain Robertson. You are to call your captain and initiate emergency recall of your crew. Make all preparations for getting underway and report back to me when ready for sea. Captain Schwartz is to report, in person, to my office at uhh . . . eleven-hundred."

"Aye, aye, sir." replied the petty officer at the other end of the line.

Mug in hand, Robertson walked to his window which looked out over the piers. The day was finally arriving. The sky to the east was a deep, clean blue, tinged with a rich gold. It almost matched his uniform.

One of the moored vessels had steam up. It was an old amphibious assault ship that had made an unscheduled stop at Portsmouth to recover from an exceptionally rough passage from Europe. She was scheduled, he remembered, to sail at first light.

He returned to his desk. The thought of *Procyon*, alone and unarmed, swimming through the dark waters toward who knows what flashed through his mind and gave him pause. He grabbed the phone. "Give me ComConDefSurvCom, A.S.A.P."

He sipped his coffee and shivered while waiting for the connection to be completed.

"ComConDefSurvCom, Naval Section. Commander Pendleton speaking."

"Commander, this is Captain Robertson at Portsmouth. I assume you know contact's been lost with Cabot Station and they're transmitting a distress signal."

"Yes, we do, Captain. We knew as soon as you did and have been wondering what's happening. All appropriate parties have been notified. I'm confident you'll be receiving instructions shortly."

That Pendleton's a snide bastard, thought Robertson.

"Did you know their power cable's shorted out? They're not getting or drawing any juice."

"No, Captain. That's something you'd have to tell us. I'll notify Admiral Williams right away."

Again, that note of detached condescension in his voice. The bastard didn't really care, although he probably would deny the fact.

"Pendleton, are there any subs in the area?"

"A few surface ships but no subs within eight hundred miles."

"Then you don't think it's been attacked?"

"If we did we'd have taken action by now."

"Thank you, Commander. About the surface ships. How close is the nearest?"

"Roughly three hundred miles. We've already asked the Coast Guard to divert her."

"Thank you again, Commander."

Robertson hung up and decided to get a head start on what he suspected was going to be a long day by getting rid of some of yesterday's unfinished paperwork.

At 0705, Robertson walked over to his window again.

He watched the amphib steam down the channel. The gray ship sparkled against the brown-gold background of the leafless trees on the river's far shore. He could imagine being on the ship's bridge. He could smell the steaming mugs of coffee, the pungent snap of burning tobacco, and the indescribable tang of steel long exposed to salt. He could hear the rudder commands and the controlled flow of reports to the conning officer. He could feel the strange mixture of drowsiness and anticipation that accompanies an early underway. He could savor the sense of power as the big ship rounded a buoy precisely and steadied up on the final leg of the channel, bound for the wind-chopped Atlantic swells. He wanted to be there. That was the Navy. That was why he'd joined and that was why he'd stayed.

His thoughts were broken by the arrival of his personal aide, a lieutenant, bearing pastries. "I thought you might want some of these, Captain. They say you arrived early this morning."

"Yes, Henry, thank you. I'm famished."

"So I thought. There's more where these came from. I hear there may be trouble at Cabot."

"We don't know what's happening there yet."

"What can I do?"

"Stand by, Henry, stand by."

The lieutenant left and Robertson sat down to eat. He hadn't been joking about being famished.

At 0750, Robertson walked across the corridor to Henry's office, which faced out the front of the building, to watch the execution of morning colors.

At 0800, a bugle sounded for the second time and 'Prep' was executed. Throughout the shipyard, and on the ships moored to the piers, red, white, and blue bunting exploded in the gusting winds. As usual, several of the minehunters were laggards.

Since little was ever gained by chewing on the mineforce about colors, Robertson spent an unwanted half hour listening to Henry's accounts of various personal misadventures of the previous evening. All the while, as he waited for Al Madeira to reappear, he hoped for a call notifying him that contact with Cabot had been reestablished, that all was well.

Where the hell was Madeira?

TWENTY-SIX

PORTSMOUTH NAVAL SHIPYARD— DAY SEVENTEEN

Madeira had retired planning to sleep a little late the following morning. His meeting with Rob wasn't until ten and he felt he deserved a break.

Either because his internal clock was still in synch with the little travel alarm he had left at Cabot, or because his need for sleep had been satisfied by the three lazy days in *Procyon*, his body did not cooperate. He was awake at 0430, and even more so at 0500.

As he lay in the dark, silent room, bemoaning the loss of his luxury, he became aware of a dull cramp-ache in his legs, and especially in his calves. A brisk walk, he decided, would cure many of his problems. He jumped out of bed and picked his way carefully across the pitch black room to the window. Looking out, he could see stars, burning blue-white and unfiltered by three hundred feet of water. They were the first he'd seen in over four months. He felt an overpowering desire to walk beneath them, to bask in their sharp, cool light, and to force the natural, unreconstituted air through which they sparkled into his lungs.

Dressed in a jogging outfit, he was out the door in a few

minutes and walking rapidly toward the river. The air, colder than the night of his arrival, was invigorating. The outlines of the ships and buildings were as sharp as they might be in broad daylight.

His pace changed from a fast walk to a jog as muscles he hadn't used in months received unaccustomed supplies of blood.

He jogged along the river past several ships, still dark except for the red aircraft warning lights at their mastheads, occasional deck lights, and the pool of light that defined their quarterdecks. The sailors on watch all seemed alert as he passed them, although none challenged him.

After jogging about half a mile, he returned to a fast walk, not wanting to strain anything but not wanting to stop, either. He came to the big amphibious vessel and stopped for a minute, watching as her crew prepared to get underway.

He might have command of a ship like that someday, although not at the rate he was going. He paused to consider his career, taking up where he had left off with Schwartz two days ago. His decision to become a Bubblehead removed him from the running for command of a combatant but he could still eventually get an amphib or an auxiliary. If he stayed a diver, the best he could realistically hope for was a salvage ship and three stripes.

He started to walk again, the sweat on his face growing cold.

But, if he returned to surface ships for a while, his opportunities would increase dramatically. Freed of the confines of Cabot, he felt his horizons growing again. He'd still never make admiral, with one or two rare exceptions all the flags were going to submariners or aviators, but he might make captain.

As he continued to meander, alternately walking and jogging around dimly lit warehouses, machine shops, barracks, and other miscellaneous buildings, he wondered about his next billet. He was due for rotation soon. Presumably, his next assignment would be a diving-related shore billet, but did he want that? What about non-diving related shore duty, or even sea duty on a non-diving ship? He'd have to update his "dream sheet."

To the east he noticed the now-sharp, black outline of the

Kittery Bridge standing out against the brightening horizon. Time to head back to the TOQ.

He didn't want sea duty, not right away. If the past eighteen months had taught him anything, they had taught him that there was more to life than that. There was Susan Constantine, and all sorts of other, half-forgotten wonders.

Perhaps he should resign. There were jobs for men with his credentials in civilian life. The pay was better and so was the living.

Hell! If his relationship with Susan developed into anything, he'd have to resign. He didn't want to spend half his life at sea, away from her, and she probably wouldn't want him to.

But what about her? How many more years would she spend in the field? She'll eventually have to settle down to teaching, he decided, and her field work will become an occasional thing, summers and a sabbatical every now and then. She couldn't keep getting research grants forever. There might even be opportunities for them to work together.

He stopped, touched his toes a few times, then paused to watch the amphib steam down the river. As she passed, he found himself mentally following in her wake.

He wasn't, he realized, going to resign. There were civilian jobs for him, but not that many, and most amounted to little more than cleaning out sewers. If he wanted a job worth getting up for in the morning, he'd have to stay where he was, where he belonged. As for Susan, they'd just have to work it out, somehow. Rob and Janet had done it and so could he.

Although slightly winded when he got back to the TOQ, he felt good. Awake, alert, and ready for action. He also felt the press of time. He had a mission to accomplish before the meeting at Robertson's office.

He shaved, showered, and breakfasted quickly and, a few minutes past eight, was standing in the shipyard's cavernous Main Structural Fabrication Shop.

"Good morning," he said to the first person he saw. "Is the foreman around?"

"Over there," replied the man, pointing at an old, skinny Yankee in khaki pants and a checked wool shirt.

"Good morning," said Madeira as he offered his hand to

the foreman. "My name's Madeira, Al Madeira. I'm CO of Cabot Station's Gold Crew."

"Mawning, Cap'in. What kin ih do fer ya?"

Madeira found himself smiling at the man's nearly incomprehensible, almost sing-song accent, which reminded him of his youth, and marvelling at the man's age. He looked old enough to have served in the Great White Fleet.

"I've got a serious problem with a watertight door and the two replacements we've received are worse than the installed one. It's going to kill somebody some day."

"Saw 'em. Came through heya on the way ta ya. Junk! They weh junk. Don't undastand why they keep buyin' that crap from those people. Got 'nother on orda?'

"Yep," Madeira noticed himself slipping back into a pronounced accent, almost mimicking the foreman's. He struggled to stop, out of fear that he might offend the man. "But delivery time's six to nine months."

The old Yankee's eyes, as clear and sharp as the night stars had been, narrowed as he examined Madeira. "You from round heya?"

"Gloucester, originally. Been away a while."

"Understandable. Coffee, Cap'in? Come on inter my orface."

Madeira followed his guide across an immense assembly bay, under overhead cranes that dangled high over his head in the looming semi-darkness, and around and through a vast number of welding stations and other fabrication machinery, most of which was standing silent. Mixed with the damp, chill drafts whistling around the inside of the huge building was the sharp stink of oil and burnt steel.

The foreman opened the door to a glass cubicle in one corner of the shop and led Madeira in.

Stopping beside a coffee maker, the Yankee looked questioningly at Madeira.

"Cream only, please."

Mug in hand, the foreman settled himself behind his battered steel desk, pointing Madeira to an equally stark, and not particularly clean chair as he did.

"Ya want us ta fix er." It was a statement, not a question. " 'Xactly what's wrong?"

"The door itself's okay. The frame's warped."

"Have ta see er. Ya got er heya?"

"Aboard *Procyon*."

"Have 'em bring er heya."

"You think you can repair it?"

"Book says t'aint s'posed ta but yep, ih can . . . if it's no wors'n I 'memba. Can't certify er, 'though. Ain't 'sposed ta repair 'em. Don't want no paypawork."

"Won't be any."

"An ya keep that replacement on orda . . . an keep ordaing 'till ya get a new un, a certified un, that's good. Weya just making 'mergency repaya."

Shit, thought Madeira as he left the shop, headed for Robertson's office, if I can get that door repaired then I can sure as hell recover the Siren.

Piece of cake!

TWENTY-SEVEN

PORTSMOUTH NAVAL SHIPYARD— DAY SEVENTEEN

"Good morning, Pyle, is Captain Robertson in yet?" asked Madeira as he strode into Robertson's anteroom, still glowing from his success at the Structural Fabrication Shop.

"Good morning, Captain Madeira," replied Robertson's yeoman, her face revealing a mixture of distress and surprise. How could he be so cheerful at a time like this? "You're to go right in."

"Thank you," replied Madeira, beginning to realize, from Pyle's expression, that something was wrong.

"Where the hell have you been?" demanded the captain as Madeira stepped into his office.

"Up in the shipyard. Am I late? Is something wrong?"

"There sure as hell is. We've lost contact with Cabot and are receiving their distress signal. Their power line is also apparently shorted out."

Madeira, stunned, stood in the doorway. Jesus! he thought. It's finally happened. A numbness coupled with an almost extracorporeal sense of deju vu, settled over him. Over the past eighteen months, he had anticipated so many disasters in an effort to be prepared for, or to avoid them, that it really did feel as if he had been through them. At the same time, however, he felt as if he were not Al Madeira, but rather an observer reading and observing Madeira's mind.

"You have any idea what it might be?" asked Robertson.

Madeira could think of a hundred things it might be—parts that were ready to, or had already, failed, earth movement, catastrophic turbidity currents, Schwartz' iceberg or one of its siblings, sabotage, the Siren.

Could it possibly be the Siren? he wondered. There was a strong coincidence.

Then he thought again of his crew and of Susan. He *should* have ordered her to come ashore. She had no business being there at a time like this. She was a civilian!

"I can think of lots of things," he finally replied to Robertson," but nothing in particular, except possibly the Siren. What're we doing?"

"I've ordered *Procyon* to execute emergency recall and prepare for sea. Schwartz is to report here at 1100."

"ComConDefSurvCom?"

"They've been notified. They knew as soon as we did. All they've said is that there's nothing in the area. Neither ours nor theirs. They *have* asked the Coast Guard to reroute a merchant ship to take a look but she's several days away, in this weather."

"Then you don't think it's an attack?"

"No. We would have heard from somebody by now if it were. Do you have any suggestions?"

"The Blue Crew. Recall their divers. We may want to send some of them in *Procyon*."

"Pyle," said Robertson into his intercom, angry that he hadn't thought of it, "contact Captain Ozawa and have him recall his divers. He's to report here at 1100. And get hold of the meteorological officer ASAP."

"Aye, aye, sir."

As Robertson spoke, Madeira looked out the window, hoping for the best but expecting the worst, expecting now what he had feared for so long.

"Rob, what about *Falcon*?"

"She's still in the Caribbean."

"What about that frigate, *Purvis*, moored out there?"

"She came out of overhaul a few weeks ago and is part way through refresher training. What can she do for us?"

"There's a fly-away deep-diving rescue unit at Norfolk. We could get it here in a few hours and load it aboard *Purvis*. It's possible that she might reach Cabot before *Procyon*."

"Al, it's rough out there and nobody I know would ever describe a frigate as a 'stable platform.' Don't you need one for those diving units? She doesn't have much in the way of cranes or other lifting gear, either."

"I think she'll be stable enough and still fast enough to get out there in time, maybe. *Procyon's* so damn slow. As for lifting gear, we can drive a small mobile yard crane aboard and weld it to her fantail."

"Her captain will love that, but if you think it might work, it's worth a try."

Robertson's phone rang.

"Rob, this is Fred. What's up?" asked the meteorological officer.

"Fred. Something has happened to Cabot Station. That's not for publication. What's the weather situation out there?"

"Bad, Rob. It may be clear here, though that won't last long, but out there it's still a mess and I doubt it will clear up for some time. There's a very nasty anticyclone just sitting, south of Greenland."

"What about aircraft?"

"Not a chance, not for a while. They can fly over it, to take a look, but it would be near suicide for one to try to approach the surface. Even if a helo did survive it would be very difficult for them to find anything or anybody in that mess, if that's what you were thinking of."

"Okay, Fred, thank you."

As soon as Robertson hung up, the phone rang again.

"Captain Ring for you, sir."

"Thank you, Pyle."

"Rob, this is Jim Ring. Anything new?"

"Just the distress signal and the power line."

"Yes, I know about that. Do you have any guesses about what's happening?"

"No. I can't imagine anybody stupid enough to attack a

minor, unarmed maintenance station. Cabot has no tactical value at all. They must have had an accident."

"I concur. They could all be safe but angry—or dead."

"That's what we have to find out."

"It doesn't sound good."

"No. It doesn't."

"What have you done so far?"

"Al Madeira's here with me. We've recalled *Procyon's* crew and the Blue Crew divers. Al has also suggested that *Purvis*, she's here for RefTra, be used to carry a deep-diving fly-away unit. He feels she might be able to reach Cabot before *Procyon*."

"He thinks she can handle launching it in that weather?"

"He seems to feel it's worth a try, and so do I."

"What about her crew?"

"I saw her captain at the O Club a few nights ago. He seemed very pleased with how they were shaping up."

"Okay, get hold of her CO and brief him. We'll get some orders for him from Second Fleet. You go ahead and get that fly-away unit—and get *Procyon* underway ASAP."

"What about aircraft? My meteorologist doesn't feel they can operate effectively out there."

"Neither does mine. However, if they could get at their exposure suits or the escape capsules, aircraft might at least spot them. We've asked the Canadians to fly out and take a look."

"And if they find something?"

"Then whatever we do will have to be done by ship. Maybe that merchant ship will arrive in time. *Falcon's* been ordered to sea but it will take her a week to reach Cabot. *Procyon*, or *Purvis*, will, undoubtedly, get there first. Admiral Williams hasn't arrived here yet, we're having one hell of a blizzard, but he wants to retain overall command."

"What about the Canadians?"

"You mean ships? No, they don't have any deep-diving resources available. We're going to have to work with what *we* have."

"Jim. I suggest we send Al Madeira in *Purvis* as Salvage Master. Who's better qualified? They're his people."

"There's only one problem with that. If something serious

has happened, there'll be an inquiry and it may be very awkward since he'll undoubtedly be one of the respondents."

"Jim! Are we trying to save lives or our butts?"

The silence that followed at the other end of the line rang in Robertson's ear.

"Okay, Rob, send him," Ring finally replied. "In his present mood, Admiral Williams will undoubtedly agree with you. We'll originate the OpOrder for all units involved outlining what you and I have discussed."

"What about the press?"

"Don't say anything for the time being. We'll prepare something."

"And the families? Most of them live around here."

"That's always a tough one. It's too bad that neither Madeira nor his XO are married."

"Janet has taken it upon herself to fill in for the wives they don't have. Can she tell the families exactly what's happening?"

"Yes, okay. I would imagine they're pretty tight, those that live around Portsmouth, anyway. Ask her to make them understand it will be best for everybody if they don't broadcast the news. We should be ready to make an announcement soon."

"Roger, Jim."

"Captain Robertson," Pyle's voice came out of the intercom, "I've contacted the Blue Crew XO. Captain Ozawa left yesterday on emergency leave."

Shit! thought Robertson.

"The XO's recalling his divers and will be here at 1100."

"Very well. Contact Captain DeFranco of *Purvis*. Tell him to prepare for emergency underway and report here at 1100 for an explanation."

"Rob," asked Madeira, "what about me?"

Robertson looked up at Madeira, who was still standing next to the window, turning a pencil in his fingers like a twirler's baton.

"You heard what I said to Ring? You're going to ride *Purvis* as Salvage Master. Use that phone there to call SupSalv and ask him to load out that diving unit. Orders will follow shortly. Then make a list of everything else you'll need and start collecting it."

I wonder, thought Madeira glumly, who I call to requisition five hundred rations of luck.

"At 1100," continued Robertson, "you're going to tell us all what we're going to do."

TWENTY-EIGHT

CABOT STATION— DAY SEVENTEEN

Having prowled around the station half the night, the XO was up early, before 0500 local time. With Madeira gone, he had twice as much work to do but no more time in which to do it. His phone buzzed as he was zipping up his coveralls.

"XO, this is Hammerstein. We're almost finished with *Molly*. I'd like to send Frazier and Dobieski out on a trial run in about an hour."

"Roger, Bob. We can't get her back in service soon enough."

He thought for a moment about Frazier as he hung up. The warrant officer and Hammerstein had both been up all night. He wondered if Frazier was any more interested in retirement this morning than he had been two days before. Whether or not his feelings had changed, his orders would arrive any day now. Then he would be gone.

He'd miss the irascible old pirate. They weren't making any more of them.

He laughed to himself. They weren't making any more warrant officers. They were sending all the promising enlisted personnel to college and making them ensigns, but as for Fraziers, there were still a few around. Whatever their rank.

What the hell, he asked himself, would Frazier do with

himself after retirement? Sleep late a few mornings? Then what?

Before going to breakfast, the XO sat down to write a long overdue letter to his fiancée. He'd missed *Procyon's* last visit and wanted to be ready for the next one.

At 0603, when Frazier and Dobieski pulled away to test their work, Bob Hammerstein, slumped into a chair behind the small docking control console in the Submarine Section and listened to the short range voice communications between *Molly* and Cabot.

"Cabot," reported Frazier, "all systems okay. We're ready to commence steering and thruster tests."

Hammerstein glanced at the sonar display. *Molly* was about a mile east of Cabot. "Okay," he said to the sailor at the console.

"Roger, *Molly*. Commence steering and thruster tests."

Hammerstein continued to watch as the blip that was the worksub hovered, twisted, and turned over the surface of Flemish Cap.

0710.

"Cabot, this is *Molly*. Steering and thruster tests satisfactory. Intend to commence full power run."

"Roger, *Molly*. Commence full power run."

Molly started to move rapidly across the display, away from the station.

At 0735, Frazier reported that all was still okay and that he was heading back at two hundred feet. The blip raced toward Cabot.

As he approached the station and dove toward the Submarine Section, Frazier suddenly started shouting.

"Goddamnit, *Molly*, don't do this to me again!"

"What's up, Mr. Frazier," demanded a thoroughly startled Dobieski from his seat next to the warrant officer.

"This crazy, fucking bitch is doing it to me again! The steering controls are jammed. It must be those servos we overhauled."

"We going to cut power?"

"No, goddamit. Not yet. We're headed right for the Sub

Section so I'll try to bottom as close as possible. You check the servos and see if there's anything obvious."

"Roger."

"Cabot, this is *Molly*. We've lost steering and thruster control. Reason unknown. Intend to bottom as close to Sub-Section as possible."

"Roger, *Molly*."

Hammerstein sat up, tense but not really worried, waiting for Frazier to report either that he had regained control or had bottomed. At the same time, he dreaded the additional work required to retrieve *Molly*. They were under a tight schedule. The XO would not be pleased.

His tension grew as the sonar plot showed the submarine charging closer and closer, apparently determined to get home as quickly as possible.

"Cabot, this is *Molly*. We seem to have a bad case of gremlins here but don't worry—there's never been a gremlin born that Dobie and I couldn't subdue."

"Roger, *Molly*."

Hammerstein picked up the phone and buzzed Central Command.

"Ms. Ryan, this is Hammerstein. Mr. Frazier is having some trouble with *Molly's* controls."

"Yes, sir. We have been watching them here. Should I sound the collision alarm?"

"I would recommend it, just as a precaution, although I assume Frazier will cut power any time now."

"Roger."

Hammerstein turned and looked at the docking sonar display. Damn it! They were getting close.

"Cabot to *Molly*. Cut power. I say again, cut power!"

No reply.

"Cabot to *Molly*. I say again, cut power!"

"*Molly* to Cabot. Am attempting to cut power."

The collision alarm shrieked to life. Hammerstein glanced at the watertight door leading to the tunnel. It was closed and dogged. His eyes returned to the sonar display.

"Goddamnit, Dobie, this rheostat's fucked up too," said Frazier, his hand gripping the power control. "You get back to the motor room and hit the emergency trip switch."

Dobieski was out of his chair and headed aft before Frazier finished the sentence.

"Mr. Frazier," Dobieski's voice boomed over the intercom, "It's not just the servos. The panel board's arcing. I'm looking for some insulated pliers or wire cutters."

"Step on it! We're getting close."

Three precious minutes were lost before Dobieski found a pair of wire cutters. As he cut through the power cable, a shower of sparks erupted.

"Power's cut," he shouted, hopping back from the still-live end of the power cable.

"But we're still headed right for Cabot. I'm going to try to flood the tanks manually and bottom before we reach it. Hang on for a big bump."

As her ballast tanks filled with water, *Molly* slowed and started to descend, but not fast enough. While Hammerstein watched, the hundred-ton submarine, still making almost fifteen knots, rammed and crushed the escape pod located on top of the Central Section, tore away the communications cable running to shore, and then slammed into the Submarine Section, just where the tunnel to the Central Section joined it.

The XO was on his way to the wardroom for breakfast when he heard the collision alarm. A moment later he felt a slight shudder. He turned and ran to Central Command. The time was 0750.

The shock of the collision bloodied and dazed Frazier. Dobieski, securely strapped into his chair, had no such luck. He knew the console, and part of *Molly*'s bow, had been shoved into his lap. He was aware of the choking waters that rapidly filled the small compartment and understood what they portended. He was fully conscious right up to his last gurgling gasp.

In addition to killing Frazier and Dobieski almost instantly, *Molly*'s charge also crushed and broke through the walls of both the tunnel and the Submarine Section at their joint, a point weakened over the years as different parts of the station had shifted slightly or settled unevenly.

The rest of the worksub flooded almost immediately. When the water reached her motor room, the tiny space filled with crackling blue arcs. Then, silence and darkness.

The now-dead submarine dropped away from the lethal breach her madness had caused. The heavy waters of the deep Atlantic rushed in to take her place, quickly flooding the tunnel.

Jamison, who was walking down the tunnel, was seized by the fury and thrown against the door at the other end. She never got a chance to drown.

A rock-like stream of water, a foot in diameter, shot around the crushed watertight door into the Submarine Section as large quantities of air flowed out. Hammerstein stood up shakily and stumbled right into the stream. It slammed him unconscious to the deck. Like Dobieski, the sailor at the console lived long enough to know how he was to die.

By the time the XO reached Central Command, the Submarine Section was lost.

"What the hell happened?" he asked Ryan.

"*Molly* tore away the Comm Cable and rammed the Submarine Section. TV monitors are out and we can't raise anybody on the phone. The water level indicators show both the Submarine Section and the tunnel are flooding fast."

"How many people are there?"

"Mr. Hammerstein and one other. Jamison may also be there."

"What about *Molly?*"

"She not answering our calls. Sonar indicates that she's lying on the bottom. She's not visible on any of the operative monitors."

The XO crossed to Main Control, the engineering and life support systems console, and looked at the airflow gauges. Cabot was losing thousands of cubic feet of air every minute.

"We've almost emptied one emergency air flask, XO," said the sailor at Main Control.

The XO took a deep breath while around him a touch of fear crept into the pervading shock.

"Ms. Ryan. Secure all air lines and vents to the Submarine Section and the tunnel."

"Aye, aye, sir," she said, thinking about the living and the dead.

Mixed with the sounds of half-a-dozen alarms were the status reports that began to flow in from various living portions of Cabot.

"Porpoise Sections reports no damage."

"Lower level reports water leaking in from the tunnel."

"Ms. Ryan!"

"Sir?"

"Secure those damn flooding and collision alarms. I think we're all aware of the problem by now."

"Aye, aye, sir."

The station's condition would have stabilized if the long-warped door between the tunnel and Central Section hadn't been leaking so badly. Ryan had already lit off every available pump. The XO ordered all compressors lit off and the electrolytic unit turned up to capacity operation in an effort to hold the water at bay with increased air pressure.

Down in the compressor room, Pettit rushed to comply. There was no problem bringing all four compressors on line but the cooling water supply was dropping. He checked the pressure in the master air flasks. Almost empty! The water intake valve had to be closed! He tried to open it, only to find it was jammed, probably unseated by the shock of the collision. He grabbed a bar and wedged it between the spokes of the valve's handle. Even with the increased leverage he couldn't budge it. Driven to rage, he seized a sledge and swung at the bar. He missed and hit the age-weakened valve instead. A deadly stream of seawater shot out of the shattered fitting.

At Central Command, the XO ordered the patrol porpoises recalled and the air supply to the external air bells secured. Meanwhile, Merrill led a party to help Pettit while Sonneberg worked to plug and shore the leaking door.

A few minutes later, the XO called down to the handler standing watch in the Porpoise Section. "Drive all the porpoises out. We're going to flood the Porpoise Section to force its air into the Central Section."

"But that will kill them, sir. The saturated ones for sure."

"I'm well aware of that. Now carry out your orders and step on it."

Susan, who was in the control booth studying medical records, had heard the alarm and felt the tremor of the collision. By the time the XO's order arrived, she was standing next to the pool, wondering what was happening.

Damn him! she thought at first. He's going to kill them.

Then the obvious seriousness of the situation sank in. He must have a good reason for doing this. Oh my God! We're going to die, she realized with a shudder. You stupid bitch! You should have left when you could.

"Can you give me a hand, Dr. Constantine?" asked the handler as he ran along the side of the pool.

"Yes. Of course!" she replied, recovering from the shock. Most of the porpoises would survive, she decided, except for the saturated ones. In fact, she thought, even they probably stand a better chance than we do if whatever's going on is as serious as it sounds.

With some difficulty, they locked the unsaturated porpoises into the saturated tank. After giving them a minute or two to adjust, Susan signalled for them to swim out.

The porpoises, especially those that had just been recalled, knew that something was wrong. Instead of responding to the signal, they milled around the tank in confusion. The most confused stopped swimming and just floated, almost vertically, upset to the point of inaction.

Susan repeated the signal to no avail. She wondered again if it really mattered. If they stayed, they died. If they left, they died.

Not true! If they hurried, some of them, the ones that had not been under pressure until a few minutes ago, might live.

By dint of banging and threatening, Susan and the handler finally frightened the porpoises out into the cold ocean. The handler then opened the air exhaust valve on the saturation tank and they retreated into Central Section where they found Chief Mackinaw waiting for them. "Quick. I'll help you secure that door."

"What's happening, Chief?"

"They lost control of *Molly*. She smashed into the Sub

[144]

Section and the tunnel. Now stop talking and help me with this door!"

While the handler and Chief Mackinaw carefully closed and dogged the watertight door, the water rose in the saturation tank, driving air out into the Porpoise Section. As the section itself filled with water, the pressurized air was forced back into Central Section.

Within a few minutes, the Submarine and Porpoise Sections were totally flooded. Merrill had succeeded in stopping the leak in the compressor room but there was no hope of getting at or repairing the electrolysis unit.

Sonneberg had less success in stopping the leaks around the door. Temporary shoring and the increased air pressure slowed the leak, but water was still coming in, and air was still escaping. The lower level was waist deep in water and, with the exception of Sonneberg's party, all hands were crowded into the smaller upper level.

Working in the icy water, now up to their waists, Sonneberg's party attempted to weld plates over the door combing. In the process, the temporary shoring was loosened and then blasted apart by the water pressure. The resulting flood drove Sonneberg and his bruised, frozen crew into the upper level. It also drowned the main switchboards—cutting off all power and plunging the station into almost total darkness, punctuated only by the battery-powered emergency lights. However, with all hatches dogged, the fifty-nine survivors were safe for the time being.

Once Ryan had secured the alarms, the disaster was a surprisingly quiet one. There had, for a few minutes, been running, splashing, and shouting as Sonneberg attempted to close off the warped door, but other than that the dominant sounds had been the deceptively gentle ones of flowing fluids—of water tumbling into the station and air bubbling out.

The XO sat on the corner of a console surrounded by the silence that had come once the upper level was secured and the rest of the station totally flooded. He was exhausted and felt sick to his stomach. He looked out of it when Sonneberg walked up next to him.

"The escape pod's hopeless, XO, it's completely flooded . . . but we're okay for now. It could be worse. We've got the emergency lights working and enough air for a few days—if we're careful. We even have some food, although it's getting a little cold now."

"That's just it, the food's getting cold. So is everything else. It won't take long for the whole station to drop to ambient temperature. How long can we take that?"

"A day or two, I guess. I can't think of anything to do about it."

"Do we have any diving gear?"

"No, sir. Nobody was at the diving station when *Molly* hit and it was the first area to flood. I should have thought to have somebody get some gear but I didn't."

"I should have thought of it. You were busy."

The XO stood up and wandered off through the clammy, dimly-lit compartments, inspecting his crew. They were, for the most part, following his order to rest and talk quietly or not at all. Here and there he noticed shivering and the chattering of teeth. Everybody's coveralls were soaked.

Ensign Ryan appeared, followed by two sailors carrying something. Sheets? Blankets? Table cloths? It didn't matter. At least by directing their distribution to the worst cases she was doing something constructive. Nobody else was. What a gem she is turning out to be, he thought. Too bad her career will be cut short.

TWENTY-NINE

PORTSMOUTH NAVAL SHIPYARD— DAY SEVENTEEN

At 1045, Robertson called his wife.

"It's as bad as I thought, Janet, if not worse. Something's wrong with Cabot's power supply. They're not drawing any and they're not getting any. The station's dead, and so will its crew be if they can't fix it, or we don't get them out soon."

"Oh, no, Rob. What do you want me to do?"

"You know the officers' and chiefs' wives, don't you?"

"Yes. Do you want me to call them?"

"Yes. Tell them that we've lost all communications with Cabot and picked up their automatic distress signal. We hope to have several ships underway this evening and we will keep them posted. Tell them . . . tell them this may all turn out to be a false alarm. No! Don't tell them that. Tell them whatever you think best to keep their spirits up without raising false hopes."

"I understand."

As Robertson hung up, his stomach started to knot at the thought of what Janet would go through if he were trapped in Cabot.

Cabot's being strangled to death, he thought. God damn them! God damn *us!* I was part of it.

For the first time in years, he felt despair as he stared out the window.

He had no illusions about death and destruction. He fully accepted that he was in a dangerous business and that, in the end, he was paid to kill people. It gave him no pleasure but he accepted it as a necessary means to an end.

It was the unnecessary death and destruction that bothered, even infuriated, him. The death caused by mistakes, miscalculations, and negligence. The destruction resulting from indifference, carelessness, and inattention to duty.

What the hell was he doing, wallowing dead in the water! Thirty years at sea told him they would all die if he sat there feeling sorry for them, and for himself. He had work to do.

"How're we doing, Al?"

Madeira looked up from his furious writing on a pad of paper.

"SupSalv says he can get the diving unit here in five hours . . . along with several other things I'd like to have."

"Good. You have a plan?"

"A preliminary one. It's going to take some luck."

"They always do."

Just as Commander DeFranco, of *Purvis*, walked in, the phone rang again. It was Schwartz. "Where are you, Captain Schwartz?"

"Next door at the supply center, Captain. These pricks have an electronics module we need and they won't give it to me. I'm going to kill the bastard in a minute."

"Let me speak to him." There was muffled talking in the background.

"This is Mr. Wrinkler, Deputy Administrator of Electronics Supplies speaking."

"This is Captain Robertson. Why can't you give Captain Schwartz the part he needs?"

"We have only one on hand and Schwartz's command has a low priority. He's going to have to wait until the one he has on order arrives."

"Now listen here, Wrinkler. This is an emergency and Captain Schwartz has the highest priority. Give him the part!"

"It's a HIVAC item—paperwork is needed. I'll have to check with the Administrator."

"Like hell you will. You'll give him the part. If you don't, both you and your Administrator will wish you were never born. You have five minutes. Put Captain Schwartz on the line and you shake a leg."

After a pause he heard Schwartz's voice. "Son of a bitch."

"Enough of that, Schwartz. Has he gone to get the part?"

"Yes, sir."

"Did you think to bring one of your people with you or are you going to have to take it back yourself?"

"I brought an electronics technician with me, Captain."

"Very good, Schwartz. Have the ET take the part back to *Procyon* and you get over here. And get control of yourself!"

"Aye, aye, sir."

Robertson hung up, bowed his head and clenched his fists. After calming himself he looked up at DeFranco, who was still standing at his door.

"Come in, Captain. Take a seat. I'm sorry you see me this way."

"Thank you, Captain Robertson, and please don't apologize."

DeFranco wasn't smiling as he sat down.

"Coffee, Captain?"

"Again, thank you, sir."

"Do you and Captain Madeira know each other?"

"No, sir. Pleased to meet you." They exchanged greetings.

As Robertson poured coffee, Schwartz stormed in, followed by the Blue Crew XO. He looked closely at the two new arrivals. Schwartz was flushed, his eyes blazing, and the Blue Crew XO had a face the color of unsalted butter.

"Schwartz, you need to learn about self-control. As for you," he turned to the Blue Crew XO, "I think you need a doctor."

"I'm all right, Captain. It's just that it hit me while I was walking over to your office."

The two younger officers seated themselves as Robertson looked over his visitors. Schwartz was foaming at the mouth and, except for Madeira, the others were waiting for him to pull a rabbit out of a hat.

Well, that was Al's job. He was the expert.

Robertson took several deep breaths and sat down behind his desk, formulating words that he hoped would get the meeting moving smartly in the right direction.

"Gentlemen, as you all know, we're here because we've lost contact with Cabot Station and are also picking up their distress signal. The lives of Cabot's Gold Crew, over sixty people, may be at stake. They may all be dead, or they may be dying, one by one, right this very minute. Many of us have friends among them."

Madeira and the Blue Crew XO squirmed at Robertson's words.

"Obviously, we also must determine what happened. Does it represent a threat to two-hundred-fifty million Americans or was it an accident? Or is it nothing?

"What is not so obvious to some of you," continued Robertson, looking at DeFranco and the Blue Crew XO, "is that, at the moment, Cabot is especially important. A Siren, a small submarine, managed to penetrate SOSUS undetected and has been found, bottomed and abandoned in 3000 feet of water off Labrador. Although one of Al's men managed to get aboard her a week or so ago, before the Soviets torpedoed her, we still don't know what she was doing there and *how she avoided detection!*"

DeFranco, for whom most of this background information was being provided, sat forward, following every word.

"As you can see, we must recover what's left of this damn Siren, and to do that, we need Cabot. So that is the objective for now: to get out and down to Cabot."

Robertson paused, taking a deep breath as he looked around his office at each member of his audience.

"One final complication—and a warning. Everything about the Siren, its significance, its very existence, is classified and extremely sensitive. It is not to be mentioned to anyone for the time being."

Following his preamble, Robertson outlined what had been done so far. Then he asked Madeira to explain his plan.

For DeFranco's benefit, Madeira spent several minutes describing the station and its crew. He then went into the various options he saw, none of which were at all attractive, and indicated which were the most desirable and likely to work.

As he spoke, Madeira remained a being divided. It was the dispassionate, methodical, almost mechanical observer who spoke of schedules, priorities, speeds, distances, and depths; who schemed to bring the maximum weight of resources to bear in the minimum amount of time. The Al Madeira who saw Cabot as individual faces, and as one face in particular, remained separate and silent. Only later, when the time came to execute the most difficult portions of the plan would it be desirable to fuse the elements of calculation and despair so as to obtain the force necessary to overcome the possibly insurmountable obstacles.

During the ensuing conversation it became obvious that the Blue Crew could provide enough divers for both *Purvis* and *Procyon*.

Schwartz, now calmer, anticipated no major problems getting survivors out of the station if he was the first on the scene. He could either mate with the Submarine Section or with one of the access trunks, or, if that was impossible, send divers with spare diving gear. It was, logically enough, DeFranco who raised the question that had occurred to everybody when they heard the plan.

"Captain Robertson. If those people can get to their exposure suits or escape capsule, I can pick them up in almost any weather. Furthermore, under even halfway decent conditions I am confident that I can launch and retrieve the recovery vehicle. As we all know, however, the seas at Cabot are impossible. It's very possible that I will be unable to launch the vehicle. Even if I *can* launch it, it will take numerous trips to get them all. How will we get the passengers out of the vehicle without its being pounded to scrap by *Purvis* during the transfer?"

"I know the whole scheme is a desperate one," replied Madeira, "But something has to be done. Maybe the weather will moderate. Maybe we will find them in their suits or capsules. If you can't launch the vehicle we might still be able to send down divers or we might even have the survivors use non-buoyant ascent and hope you can get them out of the water before they freeze to death. I don't know what will happen, but I want everything we've got in position to take advantage of any lucky breaks."

"To be honest," said DeFranco slowly, after a long pause, "I'm also worried about running an air hose to the monster buoy."

"There may be no other choice, Captain," replied Madeira, fully understanding DeFranco's concern.

"In that case, I guess I'll just do it."

"Are there any other questions? Or suggestions?" asked Robertson.

He looked around the office.

"Very well. Let's get to work."

THIRTY

CABOT STATION—
DAY SEVENTEEN

The XO's hands and feet were freezing. His chest was tight. A mass of pain crept into it and stayed. Then it bloomed and grew into his left shoulder. He sat down and tried to rub it away. His first—and last—command, he thought. He felt sad, numb, and surprised that he felt no fear. His chest felt a little better so he got up and continued his rounds.

Dumont was lying on a cleaned table, suffering from a concussion received when the temporary shoring on the lower level had burst. Pettit and Chief Mackinaw were helping the corpsman calm him.

"Does he know about Jamison?"

"Yes, sir, he does. He was very upset a while ago. He's calmed down now."

The XO continued on. Many of his people were battered and bruised although none as seriously as Dumont.

"A cup of hot tea would taste very good now, XO." He looked at Ryan. They both knew there was no fresh water.

Returning to Central Command, he called the officers and senior petty officers together for a brainstorming session. Pale and feeling fragile, he sat on the edge of a desk. When they were all there, he asked, "Anybody have any good ideas?"

Silence. Then Ryan asked, "What about non-buoyant ascent, XO? We can still get to one escape trunk."

He smiled. "That's a start, Ms. Ryan. You had the watch, were there any ships or subs nearby? Do you think aircraft could pick us out of the water in this weather?"

The spark went out of her eyes. "No, sir. They all seem to have left us." She had realized that while most of them would have made it safely to the surface, and perhaps up on to the monster buoy, only the strongest would have lived even a few minutes more without exposure suits.

"Okay, then. For the time being non-buoyant ascent is out but it might be useful if conditions change." He looked around. "Ryan got the ball rolling. Now I want the rest of you to come up with some more ideas, even if they are a little far-fetched. Make believe you're Frazier. He has—had—a reputation for getting out of tight spots." He wished Frazier were there.

Merrill laughed. "XO. Half those stories about Frazier took place before he became an officer and they involved the Shore Patrol."

Nervous laughter but no new ideas.

"In that case," said the XO, trying to sound upbeat, "we're just going to have to take it easy and wait for somebody to come and get us."

After the meeting, he walked slowly to a corner of Central Command and sat on the deck with his back propped against the bulkhead. Susan sat down beside him.

"Are you okay, XO? You look terrible."

"I'm okay, Doctor, I'm just cold and tired like everybody else."

"You sure? I think the corpsman should take a look at you."

"I'm okay. He's got enough other work."

Shortly after noon, the XO rounded up all hands and herded them into Central Command. He hoped, by jamming them together, to preserve their body heat, even if the air did become a little thick. Within a short time, silence fell as each of the survivors concentrated on his own thoughts.

Susan looked around Central Command, at the silent bodies strewn around her, at the dark consoles, the lifeless gauges and indicators.

If the monitors aren't working, she wondered illogically, then how can we be alive?

Her eyes settled on the closed hatch to the lower level. Death, the killing water, was only an inch or two away. The North Atlantic wanted to regain the volume that had been stolen from it for so many years. She could almost feel it pushing against the deck, impatient to get on with it.

It's always been this way, she thought. The water's always been only an inch or two away—but now it's different. It's gotten in and is coming after us.

She caught her breath when she felt the deck shudder slightly. Then she heard the steel around her groan.

Was it giving way? Was this it?

She waited, holding her breath.

There were no more tremors, no more groans. It was just the casing, or something contracting as it cooled, she decided. It might come yet, but not right now.

Trying not to dwell on her fate, Susan crawled over to the XO.

"XO, do we have any books here? Novels or something? Somebody could read to the rest of us. I'll volunteer to start."

He looked at her, fatigue, pain, and fear now etching his face.

"That's an outstanding idea. I'm sure there's something lying around, although it may be a little pornographic."

At 2200 the reading stopped and some of the emergency lights were switched off to permit those who could to sleep.

Before dozing off, Susan looked around the jammed compartment and wondered how many, if any, porpoises had survived.

Some were bound to have made it!

Funny, she thought. We're trapped here and they're swimming around free.

She then started to shrink and fold into herself, becoming obsessed with her most central, vital flame and ignoring all else.

During that first evening, the XO had two more of the dreadful, numbing attacks, which he managed to conceal from

[155]

the others. Everybody was colorless and drawn by now. Some were coughing harshly. Nobody noticed his distress.

Shortly before midnight, Merrill went to ask him a question. He found the XO's body lying in a darkened corner, the deck beside it covered with vomit. He informed Sonneberg, who assumed command.

THIRTY-ONE

PORTSMOUTH NAVAL SHIPYARD— DAY SEVENTEEN

By dint of good luck and the merciless driving of his crew, Schwartz was ready for sea by late afternoon. The balance of his cargo, including the two watertight door assemblies, had been off-loaded and new provisions on-loaded in record time.

He was standing on his bridge, waiting, with lines singled up and motor tested, when ten Blue Crew divers and a doctor arrived. The instant the last of his passengers was below and all but one hatch secured, Schwartz got underway.

"Take in one, three, and four," he bellowed to the linehandlers on deck.

"Sound one long blast," he said into the intercom.

As *Procyon's* whistle sounded its long, almost mournful, warning, three of her four mooring lines were hauled aboard, leaving only her forward spring line, which ran from her bow aft to the pier.

"Right full rudder. All ahead one-third."

The submarine jumped forward, her bow nuzzling the pier as her stern swung clear.

"All stop. Rudder amidships. All back one-third. Sound three short. Take in number two."

The spring line, *Procyon's* last connection to the pier, was taken in as her single propeller dragged her out along a curving track into the channel.

"Left full rudder."

Once well into the fairway, he stopped his motor, then ordered, "Right standard rudder, all ahead flank." The small, fat submarine slid down the channel and dove as soon as free of land.

Purvis' orders had arrived, along with the fly-away unit, before Schwartz left the pier. Even earlier, two mobile diesel cranes had driven up on the pier. On DeFranco's return the larger of the cranes picked up the smaller one and placed it on the fantail where its tires and wheels were removed. A small army of yard welders then descended on the ship and, within minutes, the crane was surrounded by little sparking, snapping fires. Two hours later the crane was braced and welded securely to the ship.

With her powerful diesels warmed up and her high speed gas turbines whining softly, the frigate waited while DeFranco and Madeira had the fly-away unit loaded and secured. The boom was rigged down to the deck to reduce top hamper. From the distance it resembled a huge cannon.

The frigate then duplicated Schwartz's whistle signals and backed into the channel as the sun disappeared behind the hills to the west. Turning downstream she charged toward the open ocean, chasing the storm and starting a sure-to-be-bitter race that, for all her crew knew, was already lost.

When well past the piers and other waterfront structures, DeFranco rang up flank speed. The sound of the turbines rose from a whine to a sustained banshee shriek as the powerful warship cut her way into the dreadful night.

As *Purvis* battled east against the rapidly growing seas, the wind groaned, howled, and shrieked, louder than the turbines. It just keeps blowing, thought Madeira as he stood on the port wing of the bridge, next to DeFranco, holding on for dear life as the ship rolled violently. Harder and harder. It never lets up and you never get used to it. It just pounds you, keeping you from thinking, keeping you from doing anything but wanting to hide.

For *Purvis'* crew, even those not buffeted by the terrible

wind, the race soon turned into a nightmare. Decks, bulk-heads, bunks—everything that comprised their world rose and fell, canted and twisted, assuming angles and positions that their nervous systems, programmed for use on stable land, said simply couldn't be.

The fact that most of them had been through it before made no difference. During the ship's long overhaul, many had lost their sea legs. The result was inevitable. With stunning rapidity, thanks to tortured inner ears and the belly-blow like stomach knots that occurred every time the ship's violent pitching was brought up short by the next wave, sea sickness struck. Within three hours of leaving the pier, almost half of the crew was vomiting and many of those who weren't almost wished they were. Even Madeira, who had taken precautions before *Purvis* got underway, was not feeling at all well. Throughout the ship, tempers became shorter as faces became longer and the general discomfort increased.

Robertson had spent much of the day at his window, watching the frenzied activity aboard *Purvis*. He continued staring out the window until well after the frigate had left.

When the pier floodlights snapped on he realized it was dark outside and that he hadn't eaten since early morning. He walked out into the staff offices and discovered that nobody had gone home. Tracking down the Staff Operations Officer, he told her to divide key staff personnel into three sections to supplement the normal night duty section. One senior staff officer would be in charge of each watch. The rest of the staff were to go home but stay close to the phone. With *Purvis* and *Procyon* underway, there was nothing more he could do.

While walking back to his own office he found Henry, a bachelor, wandering around the offices. "Why haven't you gone home, Henry?"

"Captain, I don't have anything important to go home to."

"I thought you had a date."

"I cancelled it. I decided to hang around for a while to see if I can help."

Although Robertson did have somebody to go home to, his sentiments were similar to his aide's.

"If we're both going to hang around, let's get some dinner."

"The O Club, sir?"

"No. I need a change. Let's go to the TOQ. I'm going to call my wife and be right back."

Robertson returned to his office, picked up his phone and dialed his home. The line was busy. He hung up, tucked his shirt, which had worked its way loose, back into his trousers, straightened his tie and put on his blouse. Then he tried calling home once more, but again the line was busy. He grabbed his cover and rejoined Henry. They walked down the stairs and left word with the Duty Officer where they could be reached.

The walk to the TOQ was mercifully short, since neither officer was wearing an overcoat. Robertson tried his wife again on the TOQ lobby telephone and finally got through to her. She said that all the families had been contacted and she would wait up for him.

Instead of going directly into the dining room, they went to the bar, which was filled with its usual complement of junior officers, drinking, talking, and looking at television. Although one of the tables was somewhat loud, the bar was much quieter than usual. It was obvious that word about Cabot was already making its way around. Robertson selected an isolated table and sat down while his aide went to the bar to buy and collect the drinks. A number of eyes followed their entrance but none of the lesser mortals cared to approach the Shipyard Commander to ask questions.

Sipping their drinks, Robertson and his aide reviewed the situation. "There's one thing, Captain, that I've heard no mention of. What about civilian salvage resources?"

"ComConDefSurvCom checked that out. There are none available within five days of Cabot. It's been a rough winter."

"And on top of everything else, that civilian biologist's still there, isn't she?"

"Yes, Henry. Do you know her?"

"I wish I did. They say she's very pretty."

Robertson found himself chuckling. Life did go on, didn't it. "Thank you, Henry, I needed that."

He found the first round of drinks so therapeutic that he bought a second. Finishing that, they went to the dining room. Talking it out with Henry, one of whose major job qualifications was a good ability to listen, had made Robertson feel much better. After dessert and coffee, they returned to their offices, where they found no change.

At 2030, Ring called. "Rob, you've done a superb job in getting those ships equipped and underway so quickly."

"Thank you, Jim. I hope it was quickly enough."

"I hope so too. The Canadians finally got an aircraft out there. They found the monster buoy on station but saw nothing else."

"That's good news, in a way, I suppose."

"Yes, I think so. Admiral Williams and the PR types in Washington have finally come up with a statement they all like. We're transmitting it to you now. It's supposed to be released later tonight in Washington but if the press starts pressuring you, go ahead and let it out early."

"Surprisingly, we haven't heard a peep from them here."

"That won't last. As I said, the admiral is very pleased with what you've done. He's decided to keep me here for a while, but be sure to call if you need anything we can get for you."

"I will, Jim. Good night."

Robertson was tempted to spend the night on his office couch but knew that would do no good. He did, however, wait for the press release to arrive. After reading it, he glanced at the clock. It was almost midnight.

THIRTY-TWO

THE NORTH ATLANTIC—
DAY EIGHTEEN

While Robertson spent an almost sleepless night talking with Janet, *Procyon* and *Purvis* raced east. Far to the south, *Falcon* steamed north, laboring through heavy seas.

Aboard the supply sub, all was quiet as its electric motor drove it through the thick, unchanging depths. Quiet, but not calm. *Procyon*'s whole existence was tied to Cabot Station. Their crews worked, and often played together. More than friendship bound them. There was also the common enemy, the dark waters of the North Atlantic. If anybody could imagine, and feel, the terror of what might be happening at Cabot, it was *Procyon*'s people.

Purvis' night continued to worsen. The high pressure system that had been stalled south of Greenland had started to slowly edge north, while the wet low which had blown past Portsmouth was working its way along the coast. The result was large, confused seas and weather that grew even viler as time passed.

As *Purvis*' steel decks and bulkheads rose, rolled, and fell in dizzying jerks and slides, the heavy weight of fatigue was added to the existing burden of sea sickness. All hands, whether or not their stomachs were in their throats, had to maintain a tight hold on something solid at all times, even when asleep. It wasn't merely a matter of slipping and stumbling, it was a matter of being smashed violently against cold, unyielding steel. The reward for observing the rule was exhaustion, the penalty for failing to do so was painful bruises, broken bones, and even more exhaustion.

Every time Captain DeFranco felt the ship's bow lift over a wave, he dreaded what would follow—the rush down into the next trough and the collision with the next wave. Standing in the dim red-lit pilothouse, he resented the loss of momentum that occurred whenever *Purvis'* sharp thrust was blunted by the seas.

The rough seas weren't DeFranco's only worry. There were also *Purvis'* temperamental gas turbines. If they should act up, forcing reliance on the main diesels alone, the frigate's speed would be cut drastically. Throughout the night, he kept thinking he heard a hesitancy in the turbines' screams or that he felt unusual vibrations through the soles of his shoes. On several occasions, he called his Chief Engineer, who assured him, tactfully, that it was his imagination.

While DeFranco paced around his bridge, in his cabin, Madeira tried to concentrate on the rescue plan. If *Procyon* arrived first, then the operation would be relatively easy—assuming she arrived in time—but *Procyon* wouldn't arrive first, not the way DeFranco was driving *Purvis*. So, when they arrived, he'd have to establish contact from *Purvis*, a near impossibility in these seas. He went over each step, imagining the struggle involved, and looked for ways to lessen the seemingly certain prospect of failure.

Maybe none of them would get there in time. Maybe it was already too late.

His nerves ragged from worry combined with all the coffee he'd consumed, Madeira wandered up to the bridge.

DeFranco was standing in the pilothouse, talking with his XO.

"Under no circumstances is anybody, repeat, anybody, to set foot on the forecastle without my permission. I don't care what happens, ask me before sending anybody out."

"Permission to come on the bridge," said Madeira.

DeFranco, unsmiling, turned to him. The poor bastard! DeFranco thought. No matter how this turns out, he's lost his command. Even if there are no casualties, the station's obviously been damaged badly while he was CO. They've hanged men for less. It's too damn bad. He seems like a very capable guy.

"Permission granted. And don't ask again. I want you to consider this bridge your own for the duration of this operation."

When DeFranco returned to addressing his XO, Madeira stepped out to the wing of the bridge, hoping to benefit from the fresh air. Instead, he was assaulted and almost knocked to his knees by the howling, moaning, spray-solid wind.

Hanging on as *Purvis* rolled violently, he worked his way out to the end and looked down. He could barely see the mountainous, icy waves that surrounded the ship, towering over her. He could, however, feel them thrust themselves into her sides. Then he caught sight of one of the assailants, a huge, shadowy, black mass illuminated by the starboard running light, as it burst into a green-tinged white froth.

Would they arrive in time? Would they be able to get them out? Was Susan still alive? What the hell was she doing there, anyway? She should have gone to one of the civilian research stations.

What were any of them doing there? He should have reported the station unfit months ago and abandoned it. Admiral Williams would have backed him, once the situation was explained to him clearly. He was tough, but he was no executioner.

The sun rose over the North Atlantic, unseen, high above the storm, finding *Purvis* still racing and shuddering through heavy seas. Twenty miles to the south, Schwartz was willing *Procyon* to go faster through the dark waters. Still further south, *Falcon* struggled north.

Madeira, after forcing himself to swallow some toast, returned to the bridge. DeFranco was already there, studying the weather fax.

"How's it look?" asked Madeira.

"No real change," snorted DeFranco, reflexively clutching at a shelf as the ship rolled. "If anything, they anticipate more wind, sleet, and even higher seas the next few days. That damn system's just sitting, waiting for us."

The ship shuddered as another monstrous wave caught her off balance.

"How much more can *Purvis* take of this?"

"I stopped worrying about that a few hours ago," snapped DeFranco. "They didn't build her just so we can keep painting her."

DeFranco, Madeira noticed, was staring at the bulkhead, his eyes seemingly unfocused. Then he turned back to Madeira, blinking as he did.

"Sorry about that outburst. I try to reserve those for my XO. We'll get there, don't worry."

The three rescue ships continued another almost routine day at sea. Watch followed watch as the crews monitored gauges, wrote up logs, ate, talked, dreamed, and slept. Aboard *Purvis*, now enveloped in thick snow and sleet, DeFranco waited tensely for his turbines to fail him. Madeira spent the day reviewing the operation with the Blue Crew divers, the fly-away unit's operators, and *Purvis'* crew. There could be no mistakes and no delays.

Later, resting in his bunk, bone-tired but unable to sleep, Madeira felt the faint, complex symphony that was *Purvis*. The barely noticeable vibration of her engines and generators, of the wind tearing at her superstructure, and of the waves pounding against her hull; the quiet creaking, cracking, and groaning of stressed steel; the hum of air blowers; the almost silent roar of hot gases exhausting up her stack and of other fluids flowing through her piping. Although unable to hear a note of this music, he felt every beat of *Purvis'* song. Every subtle and elusive harmonic tapped at the edge of his consciousness.

Cabot had its own song, he thought. I wonder if it's still being played.

THIRTY-THREE

CABOT STATION—
DAY EIGHTEEN

"How's your bod, Ryan?" said Merrill, leering at her in the near darkness.

"Merrill!"

"I know. The Secretary of the Navy frowns on lieutenants propositioning his ensigns but he's not here, is he? And your little blue nose turns me on in a way I can't describe. We could just slip off to the captain's cabin and. . . ."

"Freeze to death in private." She started to laugh through her chattering teeth.

"All right! I tried," said Merrill, sitting on the deck next to her. "With Frazier gone it's getting harder and harder to get a chuckle out of anybody."

"But you'll keep trying?"

"Of course. That's my job."

They sat in silence, shivering almost in unison and looking around the chilled compartment.

With the exception of Sonneberg, who was perched on the corner of the communications console reading a clipboard, all hands were either sitting or lying on the deck. Some were wrapped in blankets or sheets but most had only their damp coveralls for protection and many were beginning to hack and cough non-stop, victims of the relentlessly dropping temperature and the growing stench of trapped human bodies. Because the fresh water supply was limited to any condensation and frost that could be carefully scraped off metallic surfaces, most chose not to talk. Those who did talked quietly of sports, families, the future, and the past.

Thirty-six hours after the initial disaster, much of the shock had worn off. Death having been delayed, most of the survivors had returned to a state of mind that almost resembled normality—a resigned acceptance of the need to wait, and hope. It was obvious that the station, or what was left of it, would hold together for a while. It was equally obvious that, within a day or two, the air would be unbreathable. What was not so obvious was whether they would, in fact, be asphyxiated or whether they would freeze to death first, the cold having changed during the past twelve hours from an irritating discomfort to a frighteningly palpable and painful assailant, one that was squeezing the life out of them.

"Merrill, have I been coming on too strong, too formal? I mean, this is a pretty casual place and sometimes I think. . . ."

"Don't worry about it. For a freshly minted ensign, you've been doing a super job ever since you arrived. I think everybody understands your position—the only female officer aboard, and the most junior, too."

"Do you think we'll get out of here alive?" she whispered.

"Of course! Right now, half the Atlantic Fleet is headed our way."

"How's Dumont?"

"Bad. The corpsman says he's been delirious most of the day."

"Merrill, how can we tell when the air starts to foul?"

Merrill tilted his head back and sniffed. "Right now, it stinks, but I don't think it's starting to foul, yet."

"How can you tell when it does?"

"You may start breathing faster, panting. Then you get drowsy as the carbon dioxide builds up."

"And then?"

"Supposedly you just drift off to sleep."

"They say freezing to death is like that, too."

"I really don't know. I've never done it and I don't intend to. Now look, Ryan . . ." he noticed that Sonneberg was beckoning him, "The boss is calling, he probably wants to organize some more exercises, something to get everybody's circulation going without using up too much air.

"Anyway, as I was saying, foul air and freezing to death are the least of your problems," he paused to wave at Sonneberg.

"See those emergency lights?" he pointed at the yellow, battery-powered lamps mounted on the bulkheads, "they'll go long before the air and when they go it'll be pitch black around here. I'll be back then, Ryan, and you'll be in real trouble!"

"Thanks for the warning. I'll have my hat pin ready."

Susan, slumped alone in a corner near Ryan, had been wracking her brain for hours in search of some brilliant, logical, immediate solution to their predicament.

There has to be something, she kept telling herself. Something we've overlooked. Some little something that can be used or done.

We can't just *sit* here! she almost screamed aloud.

Distracted from her futile search by Merrill's antics, she found herself smiling, wondering if he was just being his usual outrageous self, or if he had fallen in love with Ryan.

Wouldn't that be the damndest thing! she thought. What a couple. Total opposites.

She settled back in her corner and surrendered to the inevitable conclusion that her intellect was not going to save her this time. Her thoughts turned to Madeira.

We're really very much alike, she thought. Our temperaments and our interests, but that's not necessarily good. Unless we totally agree on our goals, we could both go flying off, on the same wavelength, but in opposite directions. I *could* put up with the military bit, I suppose, but. . . .

I wonder if I'd feel any better if he were here? Could he do anything that hasn't already been done? Probably not, but I still wish he were here. I'd feel much better. Not so damn lonely.

That's it! she thought with a very small and very brief smile. I can talk to him, tell him things, and he listens. His world is close enough to mine that he understands what I'm talking about but not so close that we're competitors.

Then for the first time since *Molly's* crazed attack, she thought of her project and, by doing so, totally depressed

[168]

herself. It was all gone, all her work, all her notes. Even if she was saved, the notes never would be. She'd have to start all over again.

That wasn't totally true, she consoled herself. It was really just a matter of reconstruction. She knew now where she was going with it and what to look for. It would all take time.

Suddenly, she sat bolt upright, the little hairs at the nape of her neck sticking straight out. She'd heard, or felt, something brushing against the outside of the station.

She turned around, placing both hands and her cheek gently against an uninsulated steel fitting.

Nothing.

She waited, barely breathing, her muscles bow-string tight.

Still nothing.

"Mr. Sonneberg," she called. "I think I just heard something brush against the casing—but I haven't heard it again."

Almost sixty pairs of eyes swiveled in her direction.

"Brown," said Sonneberg to a sailor sitting close to him, "grab a wrench or something and start banging on the external bulkhead."

All hands watched, with bated breath, as Brown pounded as hard as he could.

Susan, like everybody else, waited, even more confident than the others that an answering signal would be heard momentarily.

When, after twenty minutes, it still hadn't come, she began to doubt her sanity.

"I could have sworn I heard something," she remarked to no one in particular."

"You probably did," replied Sonneberg. "It could have been debris; it could have been a rescue party; it could have been almost anything. We'll keep signalling for a while, every couple of minutes."

Then he turned to Brown, "You don't have anything else planned for the next hour or so, do you?"

Brown smiled, despite the growing muscle-ache in his right arm.

Sonneberg flexed his hands, which now ached incessantly from the cold.

"Now listen up. I want everybody to huddle together. No more wallflowers. Make believe this is a slumber party."

Slumber party my butt, thought Susan crankily as she slid herself slowly toward Ryan and several others. I don't need this. I need a quiet corner where I can think.

Susan never got her quiet corner and soon forgot she'd ever cared about it as her mind, like those of the others, became incapable of holding more than one simple, obsessive thought—I'm so cold! I wish I could be warm.

THIRTY-FOUR

PURVIS—DAY TWENTY

Madeira found DeFranco on his bridge well before first light, which arrived late due to the heavy snow and sleet. After greeting DeFranco, he moved off into a corner of the pilot house where he concentrated on drinking coffee and trying to bring his brain up to speed.

The hooded red light over the navigator's station, the tiny green-white lights illuminating gyro repeaters and electronic indicators were clearly visible, yet the darkness seemed as total as if they weren't there at all.

The dark's better, he thought. When it's like this, it's better to be in the dark. You don't feel as sick because you can't see the insane motion. You aren't as scared because you can't see the mayhem and as long as your brain's only running at half speed you really can't imagine it any better than you can see it.

Purvis rolled violently to port as an unusually large wave slammed into her and Madeira, standing some forty feet above the North Atlantic's chaotic surface and using both hands to hold the cup of coffee, was catapulted through the air like a dart. There was a resounding "bang" as his head cracked into a bulkhead that had been about ten feet away only seconds before.

"Oh shit!" he mumbled as he rubbed his throbbing fore-head and looked for something to clean up the coffee he'd spilled on himself.

When the day finally dawned, *Purvis'* captain studied what he could see of the waters around him. Coming in from just off the starboard bow, rank upon rank of mountainous black waves hissed and roared down at them, in seemingly endless assault. The air was filled with snow, sleet, and solid, rock-hard spray cast up by the ship's bow every time it thrust itself into one of the black monsters or torn directly off the monsters' curling tops by the screaming wind.

"You think we can use the fly-away unit in this?" DeFranco asked Madeira skeptically.

"Not a chance. We're going to have to do it the hard way. I'll go with the diving team. Mr. Pierce, the Blue Crew XO, will stay with you."

DeFranco started to tell Madeira that his station, as Salvage Master, was aboard *Purvis*, supervising the operation. The awareness that they were there to rescue Madeira's people stopped him. Anyway, he wasn't sure exactly what his relationship with a Salvage Master should be. He'd never worked with one before.

"Okay, Al, but you be damn careful. It'll be sheer hell trying to pick up anybody in this weather."

At 0830, *Nordic Chieftain*, the merchant ship diverted to investigate, reported that she was still one hundred twenty miles east of Cabot and had found it necessary to reduce speed to seven knots.

"Do we still want her, Al?" asked DeFranco.

"She might be useful, though I'm not sure exactly how at the moment."

"Very well. I'll ask her to continue toward Cabot. We can always release her if we've got everything under control when she arrives."

At 1130, *Purvis'* radar picked up the monster buoy and DeFranco called Lieutenant Wolf, *Purvis'* First Lieutenant, to the bridge for a conference with Madeira.

"I think we have it," concluded Madeira after the twenty minute review. "Just make sure," he added, looking at Wolf, "that the snatch block and a shackle are in the boat. And four chipping hammers."

"Yes, sir."

"XO," said DeFranco, "I'm going to take the conn for the

[172]

approach and hook-up. You be ready to relieve me if we end up having to keep station until *Procyon* arrives. I'll never last ten hours."

"Aye, aye, Captain."

DeFranco then commenced transmitting Cabot's call sign by sonar, in the faint hope they would receive a reply.

Shortly after 1300, the frigate established visual contact with the wildly rolling buoy. Despite its great size—eighty feet in diameter at the waterline and an almost fifty-foot high antenna tower—the monster was frequently lost among the huge, breaking seas.

"This is the Captain," said DeFranco in a loud voice, "I have the conn."

"The Captain has the conn," echoed the Officer of the Deck.

As DeFranco approached the buoy, the Blue Crew XO appeared at Madeira's elbow.

"The buoy looks okay, Captain."

"Yes, it does," replied Madeira. "Not that it means anything."

"I don't see any porpoises. If something were wrong you'd think they'd have sent them out."

"If they could. If they had time," answered Madeira, his heart sinking yet farther.

"XO," called DeFranco, "are we ready for this exercise?"

"We're ready in all respects, Captain."

DeFranco slowed, allowing *Purvis* to drift slowly downwind from the buoy.

"Swing out the starboard whaleboat and load gear at the rail," he said to the phone talker. After the order had been repeated, DeFranco turned again to the talker.

"Put that extreme weather gear on. You and I are going out to the starboard wing. I can't see a damn thing from here."

While DeFranco, the talker, and Pierce donned the knee-length coats and insulated pants, Madeira and Wolf, the First Lieutenant, supervised the diving team as it loaded its gear into the boat, which was tightly gripped against the ship's side. *Purvis*, although maintaining steerage way, continued to drop slowly back from the heaving buoy.

All the while, DeFranco issued almost continuous rudder

and engine commands to keep his ship's bow into the wind and seas as she pitched and rolled.

"Crap," he mumbled, grabbing the gyrocompass repeater as the ship rolled and he slipped on the slick deck. "Can you hear me in there?"

"Yes, Captain, barely," replied his XO, who was standing just inside the pilot house door.

"Goddamnit!" said DeFranco, a buildup of ice already forming around the hood of his coat. "Send another talker out here, one plugged into a bridge circuit."

"Captain," said the first talker, "Mr. Wolf reports the gear's loaded."

When the buoy was about one hundred yards off the starboard bow, DeFranco turned ten degrees to starboard, creating something of a lee for the boat.

"Load personnel and prepare to lower," he bellowed at the talker.

When his talker repeated the order, Wolf nodded to Madeira, who jumped for the whaleboat just as it rolled against the fenders hung along *Purvis'* side. He landed on his knees and grabbed the gunnel barely in time to avoid being pitched overboard.

Looking up, he noticed the boat's coxwain, a young boatswain's mate of about twenty, staring out at the seas. Like the rest of them, he was dressed in an exposure suit, with only his face showing, and tethered to the boat by a lifeline.

As Madeira watched, the coxwain blinked, then quickly crossed himself. I wish, thought Madeira, I had his faith.

After the rest of the boat's crew and the diving team were aboard, Wolf reported the boat ready.

"Lower away," shouted DeFranco.

"Lower away," shouted Wolf to the Chief Boatswain's Mate standing next to him at the boat station. Within seconds, the boat's engine burst into life with a bang and a cloud of blue smoke.

"Lower away. On the painter, there!" shouted the Chief. "Keep a strain on that painter."

As the boat dropped, its passengers and crew held on to the monkey ropes that hung from the davits, and looked at the fury around them with dismay. The instant the boat hit the water, it surged forward, dragged by the taut painter, bobbing and bouncing a few feet from the high steel side of the pitching frigate.

"Cast off aft," bellowed the Chief down to the boat. The boat's engineer, kneeling, tripped the quick release hook and struggled to keep it from swinging and smashing the men's heads, while the hands on the frigate pulled it up.

"Cast off forward," bellowed the Chief and the bowhook repeated the engineer's act.

Even before the forward falls were aboard the frigate, the boat's coxswain put the engine in gear and shouted, "Cast off," to the bowhook who then freed the painter, which was immediately yanked aboard the ship. The motor whaleboat hopped forward and slid away from *Purvis*, surfing on the frigate's bow wave, as the coxswain turned slowly to starboard. When the boat was clear, the coxswain paralleled *Purvis'* course until they passed the frigate's bow. Then, exposed to the storm's full fury, he turned in the general direction of the buoy.

While the boat pitched wildly over and through the wind-ripped waves, DeFranco turned *Purvis* slightly to port, maneuvering into position one hundred yards downwind of the buoy. Standing with his binoculars hanging from a strap around his neck, the commander watched the little gray boat pound through the great, gray seas, throwing up sheets of icy spray as it went, and crossed his fingers.

The wind screamed with increased fury, tearing the tops off the already frothy waves.

"Captain," shouted *Purvis'* XO as he turned away from the anemometer, "that one just hit sixty knots."

"Very well," murmured DeFranco, cringing.

Madeira, crouched in the boat, heaved a sigh of relief as they cleared *Purvis'* side, then caught his breath again as the boat, climbing the face of a water mountain, hesitated and swung to port, starting to broach before the curling crest.

The coxswain, unable to gain more speed, put his wheel hard over and gritted his teeth. Behind them was an immense precipice. Ahead and above, deadly foam.

The boat hung, seemingly suspended in time, then slowly turned and burst through the crest, thrusting her bow into the screaming air. As her stern reached the crest, the bow plunged down the wave's windward slope into the great trough that followed.

Exposed once again to the wind's fury, diving toward the base of yet another awful wave, Madeira felt the same terror as his companions. He'd never been in a small boat in seas like these and doubted any of his crews had, either.

How could they possibly survive, much less reach and board the buoy? His fear for what might have happened to the station, and to Susan, drove the terror of the great crashing waves and bitter tearing wind from his mind, leaving only a residue, a terrible doubt that they'd be able to board the buoy.

Clutching a walkie-talkie in one hand and hanging on for dear life with the other, he found himself observing the coxswain and evaluating his performance, almost as if he were scoring an exercise.

The man was tense, his face having aged twenty years in the last fifteen minutes, but he had the situation as much under control as seemed possible. When the boat was in the trough of the waves, or climbing their mountainous sides, he was heading at an angle to them, in the direction of the buoy. As he approached their often breaking crests, he turned directly into them.

The coxswain noticed Madeira watching him and responded with a questioning look. Madeira replied with a thumbs-up sign and forced his numb face into a reassuring grin.

After twenty minutes of its roller coaster, crab-like passage, the boat was halfway to its destination. Almost directly ahead, the buoy was a great, yet still indistinct, orange mass. Astern, and off to one side, *Purvis*, pitching and rolling, loomed through the swirling snow and sleet. In the boat, overlaid by a whitish scum, almost two feet of icy water was sloshing from side to side.

"Bail!" shouted Madeira, realizing that the boat's self-bailing system was unable to handle the deluge.

While passengers and crew bailed with anything they could find, the coxswain, using full power and full concentration, was able to creep into the lee of the buoy. Although the boat was now shielded somewhat from the dreadful wind and seas, it had found no haven. The waves, only slightly smaller, were curving around the buoy's mass and now coming from two directions, attacking the boat from both sides.

Madeira felt the coxswain tapping him on the shoulder.

"We're almost there, sir."

He grabbed a heavy belt with rings attached to it. After buckling the belt around him, he clipped the walkie-talkie, a chipping hammer, and a long tether to it, then unsnapped the short lifeline and crept forward to the bow.

With the added weight forward, the boat plunged even deeper into the seas, drenching Madeira and filling the boat with a great sheet of icy water, almost swamping it.

As the boat's bow approached to within a few feet of the orange buoy, Madeira sprang toward the row of handholds welded to its side. After what seemed like an eternity in the air, he felt his hands wrap around one of the holds as his face smashed into another. Waist deep in the raging water, he scrambled to find another hold for his feet and felt the buoy roll toward him. He looked up just as his head went under the water.

The fucking thing's going to roll right over me, he thought in a near panic, holding his breath as his head started to throb where it had smashed into the buoy.

Deeper and deeper he was driven, the buoy's barnacle-encrusted bottom now cutting through his drysuit and into his flesh.

"Give me some slack," he shouted silently as he felt the tether dragging him away from the barnacles, but also away from the buoy itself.

His lungs bursting, his grasp of the handhold slipping, he waited. The roll stopped, then slowly reversed itself. As he rose, while still underwater, he found a foothold and started to climb.

He was lifted clear of the water in a small burst of spray. Climbing frantically, oblivious to his aching head and the cuts and bruises he was receiving, he made it to the buoy's deck before it reversed its roll again.

Panting, he checked his belt and unsnapped the tether that could as easily have killed him as saved him. The walkie-talkie was still there and appeared undamaged, although he'd have to try it to make sure. It was supposed to be waterproof, but everybody knows there's really no such thing. The water will always win.

"*Purvis One*, this is *Purvis Two*," he said into it as he clipped his lifeline onto the buoy's antenna tower.

"Roger, *Purvis Two*. Are you okay?"

"Affirmative. Send the next man."

The boat approached again and another diver, Chief Gunner's Mate Rand, who was Madeira's second-in-command, jumped for the handholds, was dunked, and finally made it up, with Madeira tugging him the last few feet. In all, three divers joined Madeira, leaping from the slush-filled, wildly pitching boat to the icy, wildly rolling buoy.

"*Purvis*, this is *Purvis Two*."

"Roger, *Purvis Two*," replied the Blue Crew XO.

"We're all aboard. The phonebox is covered with ice. We're presently chipping it off. Unless otherwise directed, will have *Purvis One* standby in buoy's lee."

"Roger, *Purvis Two*."

After four sets of mixed gas diving gear, as well as the snatch block, were passed from the boat to the buoy, Madeira directed the whaleboat to pass a line to the buoy, then to drop back on it. Even with the line, the coxswain had to keep forward way on to keep from capsizing.

With the boat more or less secured and Chief Rand and another diver pounding feverishly with chipping hammers on the ice-covered phone box, Madeira worked his way over to the edge of the buoy to take another look at the ladder running up its side.

"Man overboard," shouted one of the divers. Chief Rand spun and looked in the direction the diver was pointing. The orange lifejacket, and its passenger, were being blown rapidly downwind, into the snow.

"It's Captain Madeira," said the diver. "He was freeing his lifeline, it got tangled, and he just disappeared."

"Shit!" cried Rand.

"The boat, Chief?"

"No. Too dangerous. It'll have to be *Purvis*."

He raised his walkie-talkie to his raw face. "*Purvis*, this is *Purvis Two*. Man overboard! Man overboard! It's Captain Madeira. Drifting rapidly toward you . . . Upwind of you . . . Off your port bow. Do not believe *Purvis One* can recover."

When he heard the Chief's words, DeFranco grabbed his binoculars and jammed them into his eyes. Barely breathing, he finally spotted the orange speck as it rose up the side of a wave.

My God! he thought. How in heaven am I going to recover him alive?

"Sound 'Man Overboard'," he shouted into the pilot house. "Man the port whaleboat."

Looking around at the gray chaos, he realized he was about to sacrifice another boat crew.

"Prepare the port whaleboat and make all preparations for a ship recovery. Prepare to stream a recovery line."

Should he risk three more men to save one? Or should he try to snag Madeira and haul him aboard like a hooked tuna?

If he chose to fish, Madeira would almost certainly be cubed steak by the time he reached *Purvis'* deck, pounded and diced by her hull.

If he sent a boat? The starboard boat had survived, so far, but he still couldn't understand how.

He gave himself two minutes to decide.

THIRTY-FIVE

THE NORTH ATLANTIC—
DAY TWENTY

So preoccupied was Madeira's mind with the details of re-establishing contact with Cabot that he was not truly conscious of falling into the raging maelstrom until the first passing wave lifted him almost twenty feet to its top, then curled and rammed hundreds of gallons of foaming brine into the small area of face not covered by the dry suit hood.

Gasping and choking, buried in the churning mass, he yanked at the life vest inflation lanyard. The near freezing water felt warm against his cold-numbed face although given time, it would steal his body's heat far more efficiently than the much colder, wind-tortured air.

His vest inflated with a barely audible pop, just as Madeira emerged from the wave's crest and started surfing down its windward side.

His first reaction to the changed state of affairs was one of total astonishment—astonishment that he was overboard, since he didn't remember falling, and astonishment at his own carelessness and stupidity. He obviously had to unhook his lifeline to untangle it but only an utter fool would do so without rigging a temporary replacement, no matter how quickly he believed the untangling could be done.

He looked around and discovered that all he could see in

all directions were great, gray waves towering over him, racing at him, threatening to overrun, crush, and pound him.

From his lowly perspective there was no sign of either *Purvis* or the buoy, and his astonishment turned to anger. He cursed that same carelessness and stupidity that had astonished him but a moment ago. Then he cursed the weather, the Russians, the waves, the Navy, fate, his own stupidity again, and finally the stupidity of the whole human race.

Only after being buried under five or six cresting waves in a row did it occur to him to be afraid.

He rubbed his bruised forehead. Wasn't there something he could do? Swim, maybe? Swim upwind, toward where the buoy should be? He tried flapping his arms and kicking. With the life vest inflated, that was all he could do—flap ineffectually. Even if he could swim it would have been a waste of time and energy. The wind, the waves were so much more powerful than he would ever be.

If only he could live! If only he could live he would—what? Light a candle to the Virgin? Nothing wrong with that but he seriously doubted he'd actually do it.

Resign? Move ashore to someplace where they didn't know what a ship was? Start over again, freed somehow of all his burdens, of all the baggage he'd accumulated over the years? Never repeat all the mistakes he'd made in the past? Change the direction of his life? Dedicate it to helping the poor, the disabled, the homeless, the hopeless?

Nothing wrong with any of those ideas but he knew he'd never do them either. If he lived he'd shudder, take a deep breath and undoubtedly go back to what he had been doing, to being what he was.

What about running to Susan, if she was still alive, and asking her to marry him while he still had the chance? Seizing whatever happiness, whatever release she might offer before it was too late?

He wouldn't even do that. Neither was ready yet.

If he wanted to live, and he did, he wouldn't swear any extravagant oaths or make himself any promises. What he'd do was everything possible to keep himself alive for as long as possible, give DeFranco as much time as possible to recover him, and hope, pray, whatever, that DeFranco could do it.

Just as Madeira started to cross his arms, as best he could, in front of his bloated chest, something smashed into his back with near-bone crushing force, driving him into the face of the next awful wave and knocking most of the breath out of him.

THIRTY-SIX

THE NORTH ATLANTIC—
DAY TWENTY

Chief Gunner's Mate Rand clutched the antenna tower and watched Madeira drift off into the murk. He'd seen a lot of shitty weather over the years and he'd seen a lot of shiphandlers try to deal with it in various ways, and he didn't think Madeira was ever going to be recovered. DeFranco was pretty good, he thought, but not good enough. Nobody was!

He hefted the walkie-talkie, planning to report that he was ready to continue the operation whenever DeFranco wanted, even if Madeira was lost.

"They've got him!" shouted Frank, one of the other divers. "The porpoises have him."

The Chief lowered the walkie-talkie, his eyes following Frank's pointing arm. Sure enough! Madeira had stopped drifting away and seemed higher in the water. His movement into the wind and toward the buoy soon became apparent. The Chief exhaled a great sigh of relief. Well God damn the little buggers!

"*Purvis. Purvis Two.* The porpoises have our man overboard and appear to be returning him to the buoy."

"Roger, *Purvis Two,*" Pierce's voice glowed with relief, "we saw it."

Chief Rand, continuing to hold onto the antenna tower,

watched tensely as Madeira rose to the crest of a huge wave, and then disappeared from sight into the trough in front of it before reappearing on the next. He was holding onto the dorsal fins of two porpoises, being towed through the wild waters. Within a few minutes, the cetaceans had him in the lee of the buoy, having made the trip much more rapidly than the boat ever could have.

"Give him a hand," shouted the Chief.

"Aye, Chief," responded Frank as he and Suarez, the other diver, started down the handholds.

As they approached the buoy, one porpoise dropped back and started pushing on Madeira's life vest. Then the other slipped under him. At just the right moment, the two porpoises pushed forward and up so that Madeira was able to grab a handhold. As the buoy started to roll away from him, the Chief, Frank, and Suarez grabbed his vest and dragged him up onto the buoy.

"You okay, Captain?" asked Rand. Madeira lay panting, and shaking slightly, on the buoy's slick, rolling deck.

"Yes. Just winded. I'll be okay in a minute."

They all watched as one of the porpoises dove through a wave, then shot into the air and did a flip.

"I wish, we had a fish or something to give them," remarked Rand to no one in particular.

Although slightly dizzy and still winded, Madeira struggled to his feet and raised his walkie-talkie, which had somehow survived. *"Purvis, Purvis Two.* Man overboard recovered. No serious damage."

"Roger."

Then, his smile blown away by the bitter, howling wind, he continued. "Will now call down to Cabot."

"Roger."

Tired, battered, and drained by the cold and the tension, Madeira felt increasingly pessimistic as he shuffled across the treacherous deck to the phone box. Nobody, he felt sure, would be there to answer his call.

With shaking hands, he raised the phone and pressed the buzzer button.

No response.

He buzzed again, staring out into the storm as he waited for a reaction.

On the third or fourth buzz, he heard a click at the other end.

"Cabot," he shouted into the mouthpiece, "this is Madeira."

There was a pause, then, "Captain. This is Sonneberg. We thought you'd never get here."

Thank God! thought Madeira, his pessimism blown away by Sonneberg's words, slurred and halting though they were.

"What's the situation down there?"

Another pause.

"Ten dead . . . I think it's only ten . . . it's dark and so cold it's hard to be sure . . . Submarine and Porpoise Sections flooded . . . need heat, air, and water . . . we're licking condensation off the bulkheads . . . more injured and sick . . ." The voice remained slurred and listless. It was almost a whisper.

"Can you use the escape pod?"

"No. Pod's destroyed."

"How about the buoyant escape gear?"

"Can't get at 'em."

Madeira looked around, felt the icy wind tear at his raw face and decided that non-buoyant ascent was not going to save what was left of Cabot's crew.

"We can't get you out until *Procyon* arrives in another eight or nine hours. . . ."

"*Procyon?* . . . Eight hours?"

". . . but we're going to get air, heat, water, and food to you in the meantime. There's one hell of a storm blowing up here."

"Roger. Is there anything we can do to help?" Sonneberg's voice had developed a little more snap, thought Madeira. I'm getting through to him.

"Just stay where you are," he replied, not immediately recognizing the humor in his order.

"We're not going anywhere, Captain," replied Sonneberg.

Madeira replaced the phone, raised the walkie-talkie and reported Cabot's situation to *Purvis*.

"Out-fucking-standing," shouted Pierce when he heard that most of Cabot's crew was still alive. He reported the news to DeFranco who smiled slightly and, without removing his eyes from the compass repeater, ordered that the news be broadcast over the ship's PA system.

"We're ready to receive the air line," continued Madeira over the walkie-talkie, "and pack as many thermopaks as you can, along with ten gallons of water and some rations, in pressure canisters. I want to send them down with the divers."

"Roger, *Purvis Two.*"

Madeira lowered the walkie-talkie and, still feeling dizzy, picked up the phone again and pressed the buzzer.

"Cabot."

"Sonneberg! I'm glad you're still there."

Sonneberg managed a loud "Ha!"

"*Purvis* is maneuvering to deliver an air line. What's your status now?"

"Same as before, Captain, although morale's higher. We're all jammed into Central Command."

"What happened?"

"Frazier lost control of *Molly* and she rammed the Subsection. Then the watertight door gave way."

Madeira looked around him at the churning madness, rubbing his forehead as he did. He brought his gloved hand down and was surprised to see what looked like blood. Shit! he thought, realizing that the cut must have occurred when he hit his head on the buoy. He had an essential question to ask Sonneberg and he couldn't put it off any longer.

"You said you had ten dead. Who are they?" His stomach knotted as he spoke.

"Hammerstein, Frazier, Dobieski, the XO, Jamison, Dumont, Pell, Arnold, Gomez, and Doyle."

"Is Dr. . . ."

"She's okay, Captain. As okay as any of us. To be honest, I figure that within another six hours, we would have lost another ten. There are two or three that may still slip away any time now."

Madeira slumped slightly, then straightened up again.

"Very well. We'll have some air down to you shortly, then thermopaks, water, and maybe some food."

"Roger."

While Madeira was on the phone, Chief Rand was securing

the snatch block to the base of the buoy's tower and DeFranco was edging his ship up to the buoy.

When *Purvis* was about fifty yards downwind, a whistle, inaudible to Madeira on the buoy, sounded on her forecastle. A loud crack followed as a gunner's mate fired his linethrowing gun. The orange-colored messenger flew on an arcing path through the gray air, was caught by a gust of wind and fell about three yards downwind of the buoy, just out of reach.

As the first messenger drifted away, the whistle sounded again and a second gun cracked. Again, an orange streak arched through the air, higher this time, and well to windward. It drifted down and caught on the antenna tower about thirty feet above the buoy's deck.

Madeira stared up at it.

"Frank, can you get that?"

"Yes, sir."

"Be careful!"

"*Purvis Two*, this is *Purvis One*."

Madeira looked at the whaleboat, still pitching and rolling at the end of the long line. He could see the coxswain grimly hanging on, using the engine to keep his bow into the waves, while the crew bailed.

"Roger, *Purvis One*."

"Request permission to return to the ship. We can't keep up with the water. Will return to buoy when you need us."

"Roger, *Purvis One*. Permission granted. Return to the ship."

"Do you copy, *Purvis*?" he added.

"Roger," replied Pierce. "Send the boat back."

While Frank made his slow, careful trip up the ice-covered tower, Madeira watched the boat charge up to the buoy. The knowledge that once it left, they would be alone and isolated made him a little nervous but, at the same time, if the boat swamped it would be of no use to anybody. Better to have it safely hoisted aboard *Purvis*. They could always launch it again. Maybe.

Having recovered its painter from the buoy, the boat turned quickly in the buoy's lee and surfed back toward *Purvis*.

After an extremely fast trip, and just before ramming *Purvis*' bow, the coxswain turned slightly, passing under the first orange messenger, still hanging down from the frigate's bow, and into *Purvis'* slight lee. There it was quickly hoisted aboard.

Aware that the cold, dark night would arrive within a few hours, Madeira looked up at Frank just as an especially huge, breaking wave thundered in and struck the buoy, dousing the deck and driving it over at an alarming angle.

As the buoy rolled, the wave surged around it. Frank lost his footing and dangled by his arms, flopping like laundry hung out in the storm.

Madeira held his breath as the wave surged past. Somehow, Frank maintained his hold.

As the terrible wave rose triumphantly to leeward, the buoy rolled back, forcing Frank against the tower. He regained his footing and continued to climb.

When he reached the messenger, he found it hopelessly tangled around the tower. Using his diving knife, he cut it and started back down.

He was about halfway down when another huge wave hit. As Frank grasped at the tower with both hands, the messenger slipped away and blew downwind, lost.

Madeira waited until Frank, whose shouted obscenities could almost be heard above the storm, had reached the relative safety of the deck before lifting the walkie-talkie again.

"*Purvis*, we're going to have to try again."

"Negative to that," replied Pierce, "the porpoises appear to have retrieved the first messenger."

Madeira scanned the waters and shortly sighted the orange, plastic messenger projectile moving rapidly through the water in the mouth of a porpoise.

"I hope he doesn't get tangled in it," Madeira remarked to Rand.

"Amazing little buggers, aren't they?" replied the Chief.

"Get a long lifeline around Suarez and have him take the messenger from our amazing friend."

Five minutes later, the thin, orange messenger was aboard the buoy. While the porpoises did more flips, Madeira and his crew, sweating despite the cold, hauled on the thin, braided line until what looked like three one-inch nylon lines appeared. In fact, it was only two lines—the bitter end of one and the bight, or middle, of another.

After untangling the two lines, they secured the bitter end of the one to the buoy for use as a transfer line, while the bight of the other was run through the snatch block so that it made a giant loop, running from *Purvis*, through the block and back again to the frigate.

"*Purvis*, *Purvis Two*," said Madeira into his walkie-talkie. "Send over the air hose."

"Roger, *Purvis Two*."

On *Purvis*' wave-swept forecastle, one party of sailors heaved around on one end of the looped nylon while another fed a wire rope, secured to the other end of the nylon, over the ship's side. Married to the wire, and marked every fifty feet with a small, waterproof strobe light, was the air hose.

Madeira stood watching the hose snake its way slowly toward the buoy.

Jesus! It's cold, he thought.

Aboard *Purvis*, DeFranco, stiff and sore from the cold and the intense concentration required to keep station, glanced into the pilot house just as the wind shifted slightly. Thanks to his brief inattention and fatigue, he was a second or two late in responding as his ship's bow started to spin rapidly downwind.

"Right full rudder. Port ahead flank. Starboard back full," he bellowed.

The ship shuddered but continued spinning off the wind.

"Twist, you mother, twist!"

The bow continued to fall off.

"Come around, Goddamnit!"

Despite his bitter rage, DeFranco recognized the futility of his efforts and acted to limit the damage.

"Emergency breakaway! Emergency breakaway! On the forecastle, heave around smartly. I don't want that crap damaged, or caught in the screws."

As Pierce repeated "Emergency breakaway" into the walkie-talkie, a seaman on the forecastle, armed with two ping-pong like paddles, waved them rapidly back and forth horizontally, making the visual signal for a breakaway.

Even before hearing the signal, Madeira had seen what was happening and had his crew casting off and freeing up the messengers.

As *Purvis* spun away, Madeira watched the messengers follow her, splashing into the water and being carried away.

A bitter fury welled up in him, a rage at the sea, at life, at fate. A rage fed by cold and fear, pain, and desperation.

He forced himself to calm down.

"Very well, Chief. We're going to have to do it all over again."

"Aye, aye, sir."

He raised the walkie-talkie to his raw lips and was struck dumb at the realization of what a stupid bastard he was, what creatures of habit they all were.

"We're going to do it again," he said to himself, "but we're going to be a little smarter this time."

THIRTY-SEVEN

THE NORTH ATLANTIC— DAY TWENTY

Was it already starting to get dark? he wondered, or was it just his imagination? Madeira looked at his diving watch and decided that the sun, wherever it was hiding, still had a way to go before it reached the horizon. This sure as hell is turning into a typical salvage job, he thought as he looked out into the snow at *Purvis*. All screwed up!

Before speaking into the walkie-talkie, Madeira paused to phrase his words carefully. He could imagine full well how DeFranco felt at the moment.

"*Purvis*. This is *Purvis Two*."

"Roger, *Purvis Two*. Captain DeFranco apologizes for blowing that maneuver."

"No apologies necessary. Since these porpoises appear to be ours, I recommend that we get them to deliver the messenger this time."

DeFranco, who now had *Purvis* back under control, listened while he maneuvered to insure that the hose and messengers continued to tend forward.

"Sounds good to me," he said to Pierce without taking his eyes off the hose, "I'm not embarrassed to ask for help. Can we get them to do it?"

"I think so, Captain."

"How do we get them over here?"

"Transmit Papa on the sonar. They'll come."

"Then we drop 'em the messenger?"

"Yes, sir, and I'll have one of my handlers on the forecastle to tell them what to do with it. We should have thought of this before."

DeFranco glowered at him.

"I didn't mean it that way, sir."

"Why not? You're right, we should have."

The gyro compass, on which DeFranco was hanging, started emitting a rapid 'tick, tick, tick', marking every degree as *Purvis*' bow fell rapidly off the wind.

"Shit!" growled *Purvis*' captain. "Right full rudder. Port ahead full, starboard back full."

Then he turned back to Pierce. "Tell Madeira that as soon as I finish recovering this gear we'll approach again and have a porpoise make the delivery. You get your handler up here and tell him what we want done."

"Aye, aye, Captain."

Madeira watched *Purvis* drift back into the snow and then called Sonneberg and told him what had happened.

"Captain, I'm almost glad I'm here and not there. If I were, you'd undoubtedly be all over me about something."

Madeira laughed, forgetting momentarily about his throbbing head and roiling stomach.

Fifteen minutes later, the hose and messengers now totally recovered, *Purvis* commenced her new approach. When she was about one hundred fifty yards from the buoy, her Sonar started transmitting PPPPP in Morse Code. Less than a minute later, the two porpoises appeared off her port bow.

With the ship still creeping forward, the messenger was dropped over the side and the handler, held by two seamen, leaned out over the life line and signaled the porpoises. Before the messenger even reached the water, the smaller of the porpoises leaped up, grabbed it, and shot off toward the buoy.

"Frank," said Madeira as they hauled the end of the hose over the buoy's side, "you and I'll take the hose down. After we hook up and get back, Chief Rand and Suarez will take the canisters."

Frank nodded.

"Chief, can you and Suarez get the rest of the hose aboard?"

"Affirmative, Captain."

While Suarez and the Chief hauled in and coiled over four hundred feet of stiff hose, Madeira and Frank donned and tested their mixed-gas diving gear, which had been lashed to the tower, and crawled to the edge of the heaving buoy.

"All right," said Madeira, panting slightly. "I've figured an absolute maximum of twenty-five minutes for this dive with decompression stops. On the way down, I'll pull the hose. Frank, you bring the wire straps and rig one every fifty feet of anchor chain."

"Roger."

Seal-like, the two divers slipped over the side and down the handholds into the thrashing water, dragging the hose behind them and trying to avoid the buoy's lush growth of barnacles.

They quickly found the anchor chain which they followed down into the heavy darkness, securing the hose as they went, heading toward the huge anchor assembly. The deeper they descended, the safer they felt and, except for two brief stops to allow Madeira to equalize the pressure in his ears and relieve the sharp pains they were inflicting on him, the dive was nearly perfect.

Nine minutes after leaving the surface, they came to the anchor assembly. Two minutes later, they spotted the blurred white of Cabot's side in the narrow beams of their lights, and in another two minutes they were at the Central Section's emergency air cock.

After banging twice on Cabot's side, and securing the hose to the cock, they headed up with over eight minutes to spare. Frank stopped at ten feet to decompress while Madeira continued on to the surface, where he signalled the Chief. He then rejoined Frank.

"We're all hooked up and ready to start," said the Chief into the phone to Cabot.

"Roger," replied Sonneberg. "We heard you banging. As

soon as we feel fresh air, we'll start venting. Once the atmosphere's cleared a little, I'll get everybody moving around here."

"Roger."

Then, into the walkie-talkie, the Chief said, "Commence pumping."

The hose twitched once. The Chief waited, the phone to his ear.

"Shit!" said Sonneberg over the phone. "Where're you getting this stuff? It's even colder than what we've got here."

"Can't have everything in this man's Navy."

"Who is that?" asked Sonneberg, apparently just realizing he wasn't still talking to Madeira.

"Chief Rand, sir. From the Blue Crew."

"Okay, Chief. Glad you're here."

"It's a pleasure, sir. Now, here's the situation. It's getting dark up here and your CO and one of our divers are making a decompression stop right now. As soon as they come up, another diver and I will be headed down with thermopaks and water. We're only going to be able to make one trip so I don't think we'll be able to get any food to you."

"That's okay. We can wait for that."

"They're on the surface, Chief," shouted Suarez, trying to be heard above the shrill wind.

"They're on the surface, Mr. Sonneberg. I'm going to help them up."

"Roger, Chief. We're looking forward to your arrival."

Frank, then Madeira ditched most of their diving gear and were dragged aboard the buoy. Madeira lay on the deck a few minutes, feeling totally exhausted and frozen. He wanted to rest his battered body there forever, but knew he couldn't. None of them could until they were finished and had returned to *Purvis*.

"Your turn now, Chief," he grunted, trying to sound positive. Standing, he picked up the walkie-talkie. "*Purvis, Purvis Two*. How many canisters are ready?"

There was a pause.

"*Purvis Two*, twelve are ready. Five with thermopaks, four with water, and three with food."

"We'll only be able to make one more dive, so just send

eight canisters, five with thermopaks, three with water, and rig them in sets of two."

"Four sets of two?"

"I'm hoping the porpoises will be able to get the other four down."

"Roger."

"*Purvis Two*, the canisters are on the light line. Heave around when ready."

"Roger," replied Madeira into the walkie-talkie. Then, turning to the next two divers, he said, "You two start checking your gear while Frank and I haul these canisters in."

While Chief Rand and Suarez examined and tested their diving gear, Frank and Madeira hauled on the light transfer line until the canisters were a few yards from the buoy. Once the canisters were secured, they turned and helped the divers into their gear.

The Chief and Suarez clambered clumsily over the side and down the handholds, worked their way out along the transfer line, unclipped two sets of canisters and returned to the buoy. After signalling to Madeira, they headed down.

"Are Rand and Suarez there yet?" demanded Madeira into the phone a minute or two after they had arrived.

"Yes, Captain, they just put four canisters in the lock."

"Okay, Frank," shouted Madeira.

While Frank used a wrench to tap PPP on the buoy's side, Madeira heaved the four remaining canisters aboard.

When the two porpoises appeared, Madeira lowered the canisters into the water and pointed down. At first, it didn't appear that the porpoises understood the signal.

It's almost dark, thought Madeira, worried and unsure how to communicate with the porpoises other than by visual signals.

Suddenly, as if by magic, the canisters disappeared, like bobbers on a fishing line grabbed by a stripped bass.

"I hope they can figure out the program," said Madeira. "They've got to find Rand and Suarez . . ."

"I think they will, Captain," replied Frank.

"So do I, but they sometimes act so damn dense!"

"You mean like sailors?"

Madeira, scowling, waited, his fingers crossed, hoping the

porpoises really did understand and would continue to cooperate.

"Rand and Suarez just put four more canisters in the lock," reported Sonneberg. "And they're there, too."

"Signal them to get their asses up here. We've got to get off this buoy. *Procyon* will be here in a couple of hours to get you."

"Roger."

Madeira looked around at the fast darkening madness. DeFranco couldn't possibly launch the boat again, not with *Purvis'* maneuverability restricted as it was by the hose. He'd anticipated this problem but that didn't make the solution any more palatable.

When Chief Rand and Suarez reappeared, Madeira told them to ditch their gear, inflate their life vests, and hook onto the light line where two of the canister sets had been. Then, he and Frank also inflated their vests.

"*Purvis, Purvis Two.* We are hooking onto the light line and intend to work our way back to you along the hose. Request you take up the slack as we go."

"Roger. Good luck."

Dropping the walkie-talkie, he followed Frank down the side of the buoy.

"Turn on your lights," he shouted as they were blown downwind along the hose.

Before they had been in the water thirty seconds, one of the now-invisible waves rose up and slapped Suarez hard, heaving him away from the hose and breaking his grip on it. Frank, caught unprepared by the violent tug of the line on his waist, followed his shipmate on the short, mad ride into the night.

"Hang on!" shouted the Chief into Madeira's ear. "I think Frank and Suarez are adrift."

Thanks to Rand's intuition, both had firm, two-handed holds on the hose when the violent yank clawed at their waists.

With Frank and Suarez floating out on the transfer line, dragging them downwind, Madeira and the Chief attempted to work their way, hand over hand, along the hose.

"Chief," shouted Madeira after a few long, painful minutes, "I don't think we can keep this up much longer. I'm going to try to loop the end of this line around the wire . . . see if we can use the loop to slide along it."

"Okay," answered Rand. "I'll hold on while you do it."

After two tries, Madeira succeeded in getting the line around the hose and its wire consort. At first, the loop served its purpose, allowing them to glide downwind along the wire toward *Purvis*. Then they came to a sharp halt as the loop hung up on one of the bindings securing the hose to the wire.

"Goddamnit!" mumbled Madeira, salt water filling his mouth. He yanked on the line and the loop parted where the wire had chafed through it.

Only the Chief was holding on to the hose, and he with only one hand. The instant the loop parted, the four men started to blow rapidly downwind, along a path which led down *Purvis'* side and ended in the vicinity of the frigate's razor-sharp, frantically counter-rotating propellers.

THIRTY-EIGHT

COLORADO—
DAY TWENTY-TWO

Admiral Williams sat hunched forward, elbows planted on his desk, holding his face, and massaging his forehead. It was almost two AM and he was tired. He dearly wanted to go home, to be in bed, but instead he was sitting in this Goddamn windowless office feeling even older than he was.

Damnit! Just when he was getting a handle on the problem—and getting some action—it had exploded in his face.

Ten dead. At least ten. *Procyon* had reported that two or three more might not make it home.

He'd failed and there would be retribution. He hoped there would be, anyway. The people—the press—would demand it.

At least it was over for the survivors. They were all safely aboard *Procyon*, headed home.

Unless something happened to *Procyon*. . . .

He noticed a sour stench in the air and realized it was him. He'd been sweating in these clothes for almost twenty hours and they showed it.

He took a deep breath and spoke into his intercom. "Find Captain Ring and ask him to come in here."

"Aye, aye, Admiral."

When Ring entered, he couldn't help but notice the admiral's pallor.

"Are you feeling all right, Admiral?"

"No, I'm not, but we have work still to do."

As he spoke, Williams noticed that Ring's shirt looked as clean and freshly pressed as it had the day before. Obviously it was a different one. He'd changed. But he couldn't have put on a fresh face, too. How the hell did the man always manage to appear fresh and alert, no matter how long he'd been up?

"Jim, we're going to abandon Cabot. I don't believe it can be repaired. It'll have to be replaced. A complete new station will have to be built."

"It may never happen, Admiral. Where will the funding come from?"

"That's a problem you and whoever relieves me will have to solve."

Three months to go, he thought as he paused.

"How do you anticipate maintaining SOSUS in the meantime?"

"I'm hoping to borrow a sub from ComSubLant, one that can be rigged to carry worksubs. We'll man them with Cabot's Blue Crew, and what's left of the Gold Crew after they recover, and operate her out of Portsmouth."

"That'll be very awkward, Admiral."

"I know it. Do you have any suggestions?"

"No, sir."

"Very well. Now, back to the Siren. They must continue on and recover it! No matter how sick we may all feel at the moment and how inadequate their resources."

"To be honest, Admiral, I'm not sure I understand the rush. We know it's Russian. Wouldn't it make more sense to wait until the ice clears and we can assemble a more complete salvage force?"

"No! The President still wants to know why it's there before he signs the Agreement—which is still scheduled for One May—and we must know *how* it got there. ASAP!"

"I gather this has become a domestic political matter as much as anything else. There may well be nobody to sign the Agreement with him. According to the intelligence I've seen, they're pouring troops—ethnic Russians—into the Ukraine and Georgia again and are calling up every European reserve they can find to reinforce the borders with China."

Williams sighed.

"Assuming civil war *is* breaking out again, who's going to win? The Communists? The Christians? The Social Democrats? The Fascists? The Mongols?"

"It would appear to me. . . ." Williams cut him off.

"It doesn't matter! Whoever wins will control a technology that apparently enables them to sneak past SOSUS and we can't permit anybody—not even the Royal Navy—to do that! We must recover it before they decide to do so themselves."

"I understand, Admiral."

"*Purvis* is to rendezvous with *Falcon* and transfer both Madeira and the deep-diving vehicle to her. *Purvis'* CO is senior, so he'll be Officer in Tactical Command. Based on his performance at Cabot he seems to be able to work with the Bubbleheads. And I still want Madeira to be Salvage Master."

"He's in *Purvis'* sick bay at the moment."

"He'll be out in a day or two. *Purvis* is to escort *Falcon* to Zebra 403 and protect her. I'll arrange underway replenishment for them as necessary."

"I'm sorry to keep harping on Madeira, Admiral, but he'll need time to prepare for the inquiry. It looks to me like both he and Ozawa are going to have serious trouble with that."

"He's better off at sea for the time being. We'll address the inquiry after we finish with the Siren. Madeira's going to be very busy with it and I don't want other considerations to interfere until he's done."

"What about the Soviets?"

"What about them? Let's hope they're as preoccupied with their own problems as you seem to think they are. That's why I want to move quickly."

"I'll get back to preparing orders, Admiral."

"And when you're finished, I still want you to go to Portsmouth. You're to assist Captain Robertson in the coordination of whatever support proves necessary for the salvage operation. Of equal importance, you're to collect whatever communications and operating logs *Procyon* is bringing back from Cabot, along with any supply and maintenance documents they may have. Then I want you to get the same from Portsmouth."

"Aye, aye, Admiral."

"And Jim, I didn't notice anything in *Procyon*'s message about Cabot's cryptographic materials. Did they remember to retrieve or destroy them? All of them? If not, they're to go right back and attend to it."

"I'll contact Schwartz immediately, Admiral."

"I'm going home now. Call me if anything comes up."

THIRTY-NINE

THE NORTH ATLANTIC— DAY TWENTY-FIVE

Madeira could hear the Siren calling him even before he stepped out of *Falcon's* Combat Information Center in search of fresh air. He could feel her alluring song in every cell of his battered and bruised body. He *would* recover what was left of her. Come hell or high water and whether they tried to stop him or not. He had a plan; and if it didn't work, he'd come up with another.

The Siren's recovery had grown, for him, into something far greater than a matter of national defense or preventing the world's new order from unraveling; it had become, even before its realization, an integral part of the flow of his life, of all that had happened to him and all that might. It was old business that had to be completed before any new business could even be considered.

Pausing next to the ship's funnel, Madeira listened to the throaty roar of *Falcon's* diesels exhausting high over his head, echoing the furious, ceaseless pounding of her iron heart as she was driven north at maximum sustainable speed.

To the west the sun was dying, eulogizing itself with a spectacular, scarlet display. To the east, in the direction of Greenland, the first stars were becoming visible against a blue-black field. The seas were almost eerily calm, the winds light and the air bitterly cold.

One mile ahead, *Purvis* idled along, her captain pacing his bridge, alert and worried. They'd been passing drift ice for two days. At first, it had been an occasional white slab or a bergie bit bobbing sluggishly in the long swells that had replaced the horrendous seas of the storm now dying to the south. The further north they progressed, the closer they came to their objective, the denser the ice became until both ships now found it necessary to twist and turn regularly to avoid its deadly kisses.

Madeira shifted his glance from *Purvis* back to the western horizon. Almost three hundred miles in that direction lay Labrador's unwelcoming coast. In between lay an immense carpet of ice, the partially unraveled eastern edge of which they were steaming through now.

Lowering his gaze to the tarnished pewter sea, his thoughts turned to Susan. Once the Siren was recovered, and it would be, he assured himself; he'd be headed home, to Susan. Whatever other good reasons might exist to complete the recovery quickly, he had a personal reason for hurrying.

He felt the vibrations of a long forgotten vitality, youth, and optimism running through him. A mixture of almost childish excitement and anticipation at the thought of Susan and of the Siren swept over him. He'd regained a sense of freedom that he'd misplaced long ago. No longer was he limited to deciding the lesser evil. Now he could make positive choices, he could pursue opportunities. His life was one of motion, of change, of expanding horizons rather than of bare survival and stasis.

Then, with almost psychotic speed, his mood changed as the thought of Cabot echoed in his mind.

What choices did many of them have now?

Recognizing the danger, Madeira forced his thoughts away from the disaster itself, away from the faces of the dead, and onto the mad horror show that had been his own final moments there.

After the line had chafed through, they had been blown rapidly downwind, pounded without warning by invisible, breaking seas, unable, except for occasional glimpses of *Purvis'* working lights, to see more than a few inches in the snow- and water-filled dark and totally helpless to do anything to save themselves.

He never doubted for a minute that they'd make it back to *Purvis*—but would they be alive when they were hauled aboard?

Choking from continuous immersion, numb from fatigue, bruises, and the bitter cold, fearful of the eternal darkness, he had almost given up hope when he felt a sharp tug on the line. Then, there had been a second, sharper tug. The two porpoises were back, performing the lifeguard duty that seemed to come naturally to them.

While *Purvis'* deck force, lashed by their petty officers' snarls and temporarily oblivious to their own cold, wet misery, heaved around frantically, the porpoises kept the castaways clear of the propellers. Eventually, the nightmare ended when the divers were yanked, one by one, out of the water, up and over the ship's side, and then stuffed into the portable re-compression chamber as a precaution. Surprisingly, only one of them, Madeira, was seriously injured. He, however, was so happy to be alive that he never really felt much pain from his broken arm.

He had lived but eleven had not.

"Enough of that shit!" he mumbled to himself, veering rapidly off the subject. Now wasn't the time to rehash Cabot. There'd be plenty of time for that later. Stick to the job at hand!

FORTY

DAVIS STRAIT—
DAY TWENTY-SIX

Madeira stood on the fantail in the feeble, early morning light watching as the fly-away deep-diving rescue vehicle, transferred from *Purvis* shortly after dawn, was prepped for operation and its almost toy-like external arm reinforced for the heavy salvage work ahead.

Tiny in comparison with Cabot's worksubs and limited in range, endurance, and capabilities, she was not designed for salvage work, but she would have to do.

Falcon was now north of Labrador, roughly abreast of Baffin Island's southern end, and about midway between the latter's desolate shores and the equally cheerless ones of Greenland. The weather remained calm but bitterly cold.

"The target's ten miles away, Mr. Madeira, and the Captain requests your presence on the bridge, sir."

Madeira turned to the messenger, who had managed to walk up behind him without being heard.

"Very well. I'm on my way."

Lugging his left arm and cast in a sling, Madeira arrived on the bridge several minutes after the messenger. Waiting for him was Captain Melvin, a thin, elf-like man, at least ten years older than Madeira, with a large, weatherbeaten face adorning a round, almost hairless head.

"This ice makes me damn nervous, Madeira," said the elf with the gnome's face in an accusing tone. "If the wind shifts and we get trapped in there. . . ."

The ice doesn't make you nervous, Captain, though Madeira as he studied the slightly senior lieutenant commander, it scares the hell out of you—with damn good reason.

"I couldn't agree with you more, Captain. We've got to get in and out quickly. The satellite says its fairly open over the Siren right now but if—when—the wind shifts . . ."

"Very well," replied Melvin, continuing to eye Madeira skeptically. "By the way, what did you say they told the Canadians we're doing?"

"Through-ice laser communications research, Captain."

"Christ Almighty! Those fucking people think everybody's as stupid as they are!"

While *Falcon* completed the last few northerly miles of her passage, *Lion Fish*, alone now that her Soviet playmate had gone home, continued to serve her time in Purgatory making endless box turns around the Siren's wreckage.

"Captain," announced *Falcon's* XO, "based on *Lion Fish's* posit for it, the Siren's now twelve miles away, bearing Three-Zero-Five. We should come left in six minutes."

Melvin nodded in acknowledgement. He then eyed Madeira's cast, then his XO, then the Officer of the Deck.

"We really should have a helo to spot for us," he said. "But since we don't, I'm going to conn from the masthead, so secure the radar, it's not doing us any good right now, while I bundle up. Check with *Lion Fish* to make sure they're ready to vector us in. Just in case their posit's off."

Melvin was soon bundled up from head to foot, looking even more gnome-like than before.

"Radar secured?" he demanded of the Officer of the Deck.

"Yes, Captain."

The gnome stepped onto the bridge wing and down a short ladder to the signal bridge.

Madeira also stepped out onto the bridge wing, watching Melvin's bulky form start up the handholds welded onto *Falcon's* mast. Any envy he might have held for Melvin's command melted away. The son of a bitch certainly was about to earn the few paltry perks that came with his office.

Three minutes later, the gnome, armed with a walkie-talkie, binoculars, and a hand compass was in position, perched high in the cold air on the radar antenna platform.

"View's much better up here. Mr. Madeira would like it. I'm sure he'd want to be here if it weren't for his arm. Very well. What's the course to the target?"

"Two-Seven-Five, Captain," reported the XO into his walkie-talkie.

"Come left to Two-Seven-Five, speed five. Tell the Bosun to make sure those timber balks are all prepared for lowering if we need them. From what I can see here, the ice looks considerably thicker to the west."

"Left to Two-Seven-Five, speed five," replied the Officer of the Deck as the XO called the Bosun to insure that the large bundles of timbers rigged along the forward portions of the ship's sides were ready to lower.

For the next four hours, while *Purvis* waited at the edge of the frozen carpet, Captain Melvin guided his ship through increasingly dense rafts of white ice spread across the blue-white sea, all rising and falling gently with the swell.

"What's the bearing to target now, XO?"

"Three-Zero-Zero, Captain."

"Very well. Right to Zero-Five-Five. As soon as we get around this monster I think I see a lead that runs in the right direction."

Back and forth and around, once in a complete circle, they went, the exposed tip of Melvin's nose becoming more and more painful, despite frequent friction from his mittened hand.

Within half-an-hour of turning left toward Canada, Melvin ordered the balks lowered as the ice closed in and during the next three-and-a-half hours he used them to nudge relatively small ice flows and bergie bits out of his way, holding his breath every time he watched the potentially lethal ice approach the sides of his ship. After steaming almost twenty miles, *Falcon* made good slightly over five toward its target.

"Captain," reported the XO," *Lion Fish* reports the target is about five miles west of us."

"That's too damn bad. This is as far west as we're going to get today."

"Yes, sir."

Melvin looked around, wondering how the hell he was going to make it down the mast in his present stiffened condition. The sun was on its way to Labrador, the temperature only slightly above zero. His eyes, despite his sunglasses, hurt like hell from the glare and there was a seemingly limitless layer of ice right where his ship was supposed to be.

Shit! he thought. We don't have time to wait for anything to change.

Five minutes later, shaking, one leg badly bruised from a misstep on the way down, Melvin was standing on his bridge drinking coffee and wondering if his legs would ever work correctly again. His ship was stopped five hundred yards east of the solid ice, in a lead he was sure would close up any minute.

"XO, I want a responsible petty officer up where I was keeping an eye on the ice. Use quartermasters and signalmen, I think. No more than half-an-hour at a time. What I just did was stupid."

Then, turning to Madeira, he continued, "We don't have much time. The sun's already headed south and so are a couple big flows just north of us. You've only got a couple hours. Are you sure a detailed survey is necessary? Absolutely necessary?"

"Yes, Captain. As I said before, this isn't a simple clearance operation. We're here to get data, not just junk, so we have to go about it the way an archaeologist would. Before we touch anything, every fragment has to be charted and photographed in detail. Some may be damaged or lost when we try to recover them."

Captain Melvin, who was not happy about having to take the advice of a Salvage Master junior to him, looked irritated.

"You really think we have time for that? We've got this ice problem—and the Soviets may arrive any time to fuck us up. I also doubt this weather will hold for long."

"Everything you say is true, Captain, but if we just snatch and run we may end up doing their job for them."

As he spoke, Madeira looked to the east where *Purvis* was visible, beyond the ice, sharply defined but small. At least DeFranco wasn't further confusing matters. In fact, he was being totally reasonable. He'd made it very clear that while he reserved the right to take charge at any time, it was his intention to let Madeira and Melvin attend to the business they knew best.

"Very well," said Melvin, surrendering. "Let's get to it. Are you going in the vehicle on the survey run?"

"Yes."

"You'd better get aft, then. And remember, we may have to move at any time. You may have to chase us all the way to Greenland when you return. I want you back well before dark," he added, eyeing the high, feather-like clouds trailing in to the north and west.

Accepting Melvin's almost parental admonition, Madeira headed aft towards the fantail, taking great pains to avoid slipping on the icy deck.

Much to his surprise, he had little difficulty climbing up the side of the vehicle. It was getting in that was the problem. Although the fit was tight, his chunky, already-bruised frame fit through the hatch relatively easily but his cast-encased arm took a little twisting.

"Hatch secure," he heard Hale, the vehicle's operator, report to *Falcon*. Madeira slumped into one of the seats in the passenger compartment and, using his good arm, secured the seat belt.

"Am commencing pressure test," continued Hale into his microphone.

"Roger," replied both the second operator and *Falcon's* CIC.

As he spoke, Hale pressurized the interior of the vehicle. They then waited.

"Pressure test satisfactory. We have a seal," reported Hale to *Falcon* as he vented the space down to one atmosphere. "You can drop us when ready."

"Roger."

Madeira felt a bump and shudder as *Falcon's* deck force heaved around on the towing machine, lifting the vehicle up and out of its jury-rigged cradle, and swung it over the ship's side. An almost electrical jolt ran through him as he felt the tiny submarine settle into the deep, almost mystically blue waters. Was it excitement? Relief that the final phase of the operation was now underway? Anticipation of action? Or was it fear? Fear of the unknown, of failure, of death?

He neither knew nor really cared.

"All hands check for leaks," ordered Hale as the vehicle settled into the icy waters.

Madeira crawled around the passenger compartment. "Passenger compartment secure," he finally reported.

"Roger . . . *Falcon*, all secure. Cast off."

The hook securing the vehicle to the wire whip on which it had been hoisted was tripped. Immediately sensing their freedom, Hale ballasted down and the vehicle glided into the depths, diving to five hundred feet, just to be safe, before heading under the ice.

"Mr. Madeira. You want to come up here and take a look while there's something to look at?"

"No thanks, Hale. I'll wait until I can see the bottom."

The instant they reached five hundred feet, Hale turned northwest and increased speed, commencing the long commute from *Falcon* to Siren.

For the next hour, while Madeira rested in the passenger compartment, the vehicle sank slowly through the southerly flowing Labrador Current, then through a slightly warmer, and much slower, northerly countercurrent. Below the countercurrent they found an almost stationary water mass that extended most of the way to the bottom.

"Got anything yet?" asked Madeira when he heard the second operator report one hundred feet to the bottom.

"Not yet, sir. But I think I see the bottom."

Madeira crawled forward, stuck his head into the tiny operators' compartment and concluded that the next few hours were going to be hell. With only one arm to lean on, he was in an impossible position.

"Shit!" he groaned.

The second operator turned and looked at him. "Hell, sir. You can't stay like that! Let's trade places."

"I'd love to but I'm not checked out on the charting and photometric equipment. I'm just going to have to make do."

As he spoke, he turned on his side, leaned on his good elbow and groaned.

"I'll rearrange myself from time to time."

Hale turned and looked at Madeira's face, then at his cast, then at his face again. Shaking his head slightly, he turned back to his controls. There was no way the bastard was going to be anything but miserably uncomfortable.

"*Lion Fish* says steer Two-Eight-Nine. Range to target about three hundred yards," reported the second operator.

Hale diddled the controls and the vehicle turned left, its TV camera still pointed at the flattish, unremarkable bottom.

"There! I see it," said Hale, a muted note of excitement in his voice. "Right where *Lion Fish* said it would be."

"As advertised," remarked Madeira, his left leg now totally asleep. After watching the TV monitor a few minutes, he continued, "It seems to be in three big pieces a few yards apart, and a shitload of small fragments." As he spoke, he shifted position and, almost immediately, his left leg burst into the most excruciating pain as circulation was restored.

"All right, Hale. Let's get to work."

"You sure you want to do a full survey of these things?"

"Don't want to. We've got to."

"Yes, sir. Still want to do a relative plot using that big piece as datum?"

"Unless you can get that photometric gear," he pointed at the black box that wasn't normally carried in a rescue vehicle, "to interface with your navigational computer we have no other choice."

"We can get it to interface, sir. I'm sure of that. But it'll take time."

"We don't have time," replied Madeira. He wondered where the Russians were.

"So we do a relative plot." Hale smiled, hoping Madeira didn't think he'd been smart-assing him.

After dropping a sonar beacon, to hasten the many return trips Madeira expected the vehicle to have to make, they commenced charting the wreckage, criss-crossing the deep bottom waters, a slow-moving mass of supercold arctic water oozing south towards the abyssal depths of the Labrador Basin. With every second that passed, Madeira, twisting and squirming, discovered again that there were no limits to true misery.

Even before the vehicle reached the Siren, conditions on the surface started to deteriorate, slowly at first and then with almost blinding speed.

[211]

Three hours into the survey, Captain Melvin called down to the vehicle.

"Madeira, I'm afraid that's it for now. The weather's turning to shit up here and the ice's moving fast. We can't hold position. We've got to head for open water. I want you to secure and head for home. Otherwise, it may be too rough to recover you."

Madeira temporarily forgot his physical misery as he grappled with this new dilemma.

"Can you give us another half-an-hour? We're so close to completion!"

Melvin walked out to the wing of his bridge and eyed the darkening sky and the encircling masses of ice whose motion, relative to each other, would now be obvious to even the most careless observer. He then grunted to himself and returned to the pilot house.

"Thirty minutes, Madeira. Secure in thirty minutes whether you're done or not. I'm heading for open water so home on my signal. I hope to God you remembered to bring your Swimmies."

Twenty minutes later, the survey of the wreckage, forty seven pieces in all, was complete. Madeira crawled aft and, with a shudder of relief, stretched out in the relatively roomy passenger compartment as Hale headed the vehicle eastward and up in search of *Falcon*.

While the vehicle scooted through the cold but still waters, Captain Melvin was back aloft, hanging on with all his strength to the exposed radar platform. As icy blasts of wind buffeted him, he piloted his ship out of the danger into which he had guided her a few hours before. His face and feet were numb, as were his hands.

Christ! he thought. I wish I was back in the Carribbean.

He clutched instinctively at the slippery steel as *Falcon* started to roll, all too aware that the slightest carelessness would result in his falling over eighty feet to a very cold death.

Melvin recognized his own misery and fear but his mind had little room for such distractions. He concentrated instead on saving his ship, and then recovering the vehicle and its crew. As *Falcon* twisted and turned among the groaning, heaving masses of deadly ice, the only distraction he did allow himself was an occasional volley of curses directed at Madeira, not because he really felt Madeira was the cause of his problems, but because it was infinitely more satisfying to curse a real person than to curse the insubstantial fates that Madeira had damned on Cabot's monster buoy.

Fairly early in *Falcon's* flight, Melvin guided her into a wide, east-west lying lead that, thirty minutes later, turned out to be closed at the other end. Cursing loudly, he turned and looked aft.

"All Stop!" he shouted, his eyes growing wide.

"All Back Full! This fucking thing's closing up behind us."

For the next hour, unable to turn around and considerably less maneuverable backing than going forward, *Falcon* weaved from side to side, her timber balks grinding against and, at times, forcing aside great slabs of ice as her captain frantically backed her out of the lead and back into the interior of the ice pack.

Dusk was fast falling when *Falcon* finally reached the relative safety of open water and found *Purvis* pitching and rolling with increasing violence.

"Where the hell's the vehicle now?" demanded the frozen gnome the minute his feet touched the pilothouse deck.

"One thousand yards astern and two hundred feet down, Captain," replied his XO, thinking as he did that Melvin looked dangerously pale.

His eyes glazed from the cold, Melvin looked around at the solid overcast, at the ice off to the west and at the rolling—now starting to crest—seas.

"Tell them we're going to come to Zero-Four-Zero and try to hold position. They're to surface ASAP as close as possible off our starboard beam. There should be some sort of lee there."

"Aye, aye, Captain."

"Are the swimmers ready?"

"Yes, Captain."

"I want two—make that three—tenders on each swimmer's life line. And I want a workboat swung out and manned."

"Aye, aye, Captain. And how about some coffee?"

"Jesus! XO," replied Melvin, stamping his feet to see if they were still alive, "I thought you'd never get to that."

The instant the vehicle surfaced, about twenty-five yards off *Falcon's* starboard quarter, Melvin was in action as two swimmers, dressed in full exposure suits, leaped from *Falcon's* bullworks into the heaving waters. Dragging a nylon line, they drifted down on the vehicle and secured the line to it. They then climbed onto it, the seas sloshing and breaking around and over them. One swung his arm in a great circle and aboard *Falcon*, a boatswain's mate bellowed "Heave around!"

Throughout the recovery process, Madeira and his companions in the vehicle could only hang on as their vessel rolled and hope that the vehicle wasn't smashed to pieces against *Falcon's* side.

As the tiny submarine was dragged slowly closer to *Falcon*, a wire-lifting whip was passed to the swimmers, who secured it. Then, after the nylon line, and another just like it had been rerigged as guy lines, the vehicle was drawn against the fenders rigged along the ship's side and quickly snatched clear of the water during what Melvin hoped was a lull in *Falcon's* increasingly violent rolling.

When, with the assistance of several boatswain's mates, Madeira emerged from the vehicle onto *Falcon's* flood-lit deck, he ached all over and his stomach was empty and grumbling. He wanted food but he wanted to see Melvin first.

He slipped, skidded, and stumbled over the slick, rolling, windswept deck toward a door into the ship's superstructure. Using his good arm he was able to open the heavy steel door, slip through, and close it again before it took command of him.

Two short passageways and two ladders later, he was in the pilothouse. There, in near-total darkness punctuated only by the red light illuminating the chart table and the feeble white glow of the compass, he searched for Melvin.

"Captain," he said in a low voice once he'd located the gnome, standing in a corner eating a sandwich, "thanks for giving me the extra time. That was one hell of a ship-driving job you did today."

Melvin, enjoying the very personal high of a man who knows he has just met and overcome a very difficult challenge, replied in kind. "Thank you, Salvage Master. I'm sure now that between us we can pull this operation off."

The small task force, signal lights flashing, then turned

east, away from the densest ice and in search of any protection that might be afforded by the sheer cliffs towering over Greenland's southwestern coast.

The next five days were filled with the wet, cold, stomach-wrenching enforced idleness that has, over the centuries, driven whole fleets to mutiny and madness. Unable to return to the site and unwilling to seek refuge in a real harbor for fear of missing a break in the weather, Captains Melvin and DeFranco paced, waiting for *Lion Fish* to report the return of the Russians, or when not holed up in their cabins participating in the almost non-stop card games that broke out in their respective wardrooms.

Madeira tried to rest his battered body, all the while endlessly studying the survey. Eventually, having memorized the data and succeeding in acquiring more bruises from *Falcon's* pitching and rolling, he gave up and joined the card game, even though he neither liked nor excelled at bridge.

The third afternoon, he received a pleasant surprise, a letter faxed from Susan:

Dear Al:
Thanks for your get well message. I'm fine now, although still a little shaken.
You didn't mention your being injured but from what I understand you had to do, you must be a little worse for wear. I hope you're feeling better. Thank you for coming back for us.
I've decided to leave for Kam Station on the 9th, partially because I want to finish up this project—it really is very exciting—and partially because I want to get up again on the horse that threw me. With any luck, I'll be back in Boston in three weeks.
Speaking of luck, good luck with finding your Siren.
   Love,
   Susan

Around the fourth or fifth reading of the letter, Madeira's elation became tinged by irritation. Kam Station was almost ten thousand miles away and God only knew when she'd get around to returning. Based on her performance at Cabot, it could be months.

Unfortunately, he couldn't blame her. She'd caught sight of glory and had raced off after it. And, he really had no idea when he'd be back himself.

On the morning of April eighth, the gale finally showed signs of breaking. At 0900, the ships turned west and headed back toward the Siren. Then, at 1123, *Purvis'* signal light flashed through the slowly lifting murk:

FALCON FROM PURVIS / SOSUS REPORTS UNKNOWN
SUB APPROACHING RAPIDLY FROM EAST /
INTENTIONS UNKNOWN / BT /

FORTY-ONE

DAVIS STRAIT—DAY THIRTY

"What're they doing now?" asked Madeira as he stepped into *Falcon's* pilot house.

"Same as before. Paralleling *Lion Fish*, occasionally making a run toward the wreckage. *Lion Fish's* managed to stop them every time so far. Then back to running parallel," responded Captain Melvin.

Madeira shook his head. "Those fuckers are getting on my nerves."

Melvin shrugged his shoulders. "That's probably the idea."

"I just hope they stay clear of the vehicle. I assume they won't risk killing the crew. A little property damage is one thing, but some deaths might wreck everybody's current good feelings about each other."

"That makes sense. Which doesn't mean it's true. Luck *does* seem to be running our way, for a change. That storm moved a lot of ice. I think I can get *Falcon* to within about three miles of the Siren."

"Outstanding!"

When Melvin turned and walked out onto the port wing of the bridge, Madeira followed. They stood silently for a few minutes. The seas, although still choppy, were nothing like they'd been the last few days.

"You told Admiral Williams we'd have it up by the twenty-fifth. You really think we will?"

"I hope so. We have to, sooner, if possible."

"You're damn lucky it turned out Chief Rand and that other Cabot Blue diver are qualified to operate the vehicle. At least we'll be able to operate 'round the clock."

"As you said, luck seems to be with us. If the Russians will just leave us alone. . . ."

The gnome grunted. "Barometer seems pretty steady, though the temperature's still rising."

"We may get a day or two of decent fishing weather soon. What passes for decent around here, anyway."

Melvin rolled his eyes. "You still plan to go after the big piece first?"

"Yes. The one with the cylinder and what looks like most of the berthing and control compartments. That's the one with the answers! If we get the chance we'll go after the rest but I think we can identify them pretty well from the videos."

"So you're going to snatch and run, eh?"

He just couldn't resist, could he? thought Madeira.

Three hours later, *Falcon* and *Purvis* arrived at the edge of the packice. The seas were five to six feet, the wind stiff, though dropping.

Melvin looked out at the undulating white surface fifty yards to the west. The massive slabs of ice, glowing with crystalline coldness in the bright sunshine, alternately rose and fell, ramming and riding over each other. He turned to Madeira. "This is as far as we go for now. I know I promised you three miles but four-and-a-half will have to do until these fuckers calm down."

Madeira started laughing. "Four-and-a-half's fine with me. I thought you were crazy to do what you did last time we were here."

"XO," shouted Melvin, "prepare to launch the vehicle; and rig extra working lights on the fantail. We'll be working all through the night."

For the next sixty hours, the vehicle shuttled back and forth between *Falcon* and the Siren, transporting huge wire straps and wrapping them under and around the fragment Madeira intended to recover first. Although, as the weather moderated, Melvin was able to shorten the commute by creeping into the ice during the day, it was a long, slow task since the vehicle could only work with one strap per four to six hour trip. In some cases, especially when a water jet had to be used to get a strap through the ooze under the wreck, two trips per strap proved necessary.

Despite his compelling desire to get the job completed, Madeira's thoughts drifted far from the Siren as he dozed in a chair in CIC, the close, dark quiet broken only by the muted conversation of the watchstanders and an occasional report from the vehicle.

What *did* Susan want from life? Fame? A family? Him? A little of each? All of them? None of them? Did she even know?

Too bad he'd never asked her.

Did he, for that matter, know what he wanted?

Once he had known—or thought he had—but things had changed over the years. He'd changed, hadn't he?

Did he still want to shout at the wind and prove he was tougher than the ocean? Probably not, he decided. He'd lost interest in that while doing time at Cabot. If so, why did he want the Siren as much as he thought he wanted Susan?

He tried to imagine her face and sat up with a jolt. He couldn't.

He could remember the beauty, he could feel desire, but he couldn't visualize the details. They were hazy and unclear, like so many other things.

What the hell did it mean? Why couldn't he remember her face clearly? Was he losing it?

No! he forced himself to conclude. He'd just been away too long and there was too much other crap sloshing around in his head at the moment. He probably couldn't even visualize his own mother.

"Christ Almighty!" he half shouted, jumping to his feet and scaring the hell out of the others in the compartment.

I'm crapping out on the job, he thought. I need some fresh air.

Throwing his jacket on, he stepped out into the black night and walked aft, his vaporous breath glowing in the ship's working lights.

At 0300, just as the vehicle was positioning the twelfth of the twenty-two straps, Sam Peacock aboard *Lion Fish* was awakened by a messenger.

"Captain, the XO reports the Russian is trying to get at the wreckage again."

"Very well," replied Peacock as he leaped out of his bunk.

"Right full rudder," ordered the XO as Peacock rushed into the Control Room. "Captain, he just stopped his motors and is turning right. I think he's trying to cut behind us so I'm circling around to meet him."

"How far are we from the wreckage?"

"Six miles, Captain."

"Intercept course is Zero-Seven-Three," reported the navigator, wondering if they'd ever be allowed to go home.

"Very well," replied the XO. "Shift your rudder," he continued to the helmsman. "Steady on Zero-Seven-Three."

"I'll take it, XO," said Peacock. "This is the Captain. I have the conn."

For the next two hours, while Madeira sat in *Falcon's* CIC holding his breath, Peacock twisted and turned, backed, dove, ascended, and rolled in a successful effort to keep *Lion Fish* between the Russian and the wreckage.

"He's really pressing us this time," said the XO to Peacock. "You think he's after the vehicle?"

"Don't know, XO. At least he hasn't gotten by us, but we're damn close to the wreckage—and to the bottom."

"Captain," reported the sonarman, "he's just goosed it and turned ninety degrees to port. He's headed directly away from the wreckage."

"Very well. Left full rudder. All ahead full."

"*Falcon*," reported Hale in the vehicle, "I think I just saw one of the subs."

"Are they that close!" snapped Madeira, on his feet now.

"Affirmative. I think he just turned away. I think that's his stern I can see. . . ."

"Goddamnit! Tell me they're not!" shouted Madeira to no one in particular. To lose it now!

"Sir?" asked the petty officer supervising the CIC watch.

"Do you see the other sub?" Madeira asked Hale, disregarding the petty officer.

"Negative, *Falcon* . . . Holy Shit! The sub's prop wash must've just hit the bottom. There's a dense cloud of ooze headed right for me."

"I was afraid of that. You'll be getting a second dose from the other sub." As he spoke, Madeira snapped the hapless pencil that had the misfortune of being in his hand at the time.

The water surrounding the vehicle, and the wreckage, soon turned a dense, impenetrable black.

"Falcon. Request instructions."

Madeira threw the broken pencil into the garbage can. It made a loud clang as it hit. It would, he figured, take at least an hour for the water to clear. Maybe two.

"Return to *Falcon.* We're going to have to wait for the water to clear."

Having recalled the vehicle, as much to keep it out of trouble as anything else, Madeira walked over to the weather deck door and opened it. Looking out into the increasingly dense night he calculated—times, depths, displacements, dates, possibilities, probabilities, and consequences. He then closed the door and picked up the phone to the bridge.

"This is Mr. Madeira. Give me the Captain."

"Captain Melvin."

"This is Madeira, Captain. The Russians suckered *Lion Fish* again."

"What did they do this time?"

"They pressed them in close to the wreckage, then turned away and made turns. *Lion Fish* followed and the whole area is now filled with ooze and silt. I'm willing to bet *Lion Fish's* prop wash did more damage than the Russian's. Visibility's zero. I've recalled the vehicle for now."

Captain Melvin, already bent under the load his ship and her crew were bearing from the extended, 'round the clock operations, groaned and cursed *Lion Fish's*, for him, faceless, and obviously moronic, skipper.

He heard Madeira continue, "I want to send a message to *Lion Fish* describing exactly what they did to us and asking her to keep the Goddamn Russian away from now on—if they can."

"I'll handle that and I'll alert what's left of my Deck Apes to stand by to recover the vehicle. You get your people back in there as soon as you can."

FORTY-TWO

COLORADO—DAY THIRTY

"Lane? Is that you?"

"Yes, Kate," shouted Admiral Williams, closing the front door behind him and hanging his coat in the closet.

"You're home early. Are you all right? Is something wrong?"

"No, dear. I'm fine. In fact, I'm feeling particularly good today, for some reason. I decided to knock off early, to get us both used to the idea."

Kate Williams, a petite woman with pleasantly well-defined features, a glowing smile and blonde hair that was only beginning to show evidence of gray, appeared at the head of the stairs wearing jeans and a red sweater. After examining her husband from afar, she hopped down the stairs and kissed him.

"You look all right to me. I hope you don't think this new life bit means you're going to be allowed to hang around the house all the time once you retire. We both have any number of things to do."

"No, dear," laughed Williams, "I don't think that would be good for either of us, but I do want to practice living like normal people, like having a quiet cocktail hour, just the two of us, before dinner. We can shoot the breeze and do whatever people do, whatever we used to do when we had time."

Standing on tiptoes she kissed him again. "It's a date, sailor, the first of many, I hope. Can you give me half-an-hour?

I'd like to finish packing some things I'm sending to Bitsy, for little Lane, then I want to freshen up."

"Half-an-hour. In the family room."

"Roger, Admiral."

Admiral Williams clumped up the stairs to the bedroom and changed quickly into soft, worn khaki trousers, a sport shirt, and loafers.

On his way to the family room he detoured through the kitchen where he grabbed the afternoon paper. Then, returning to his original course, he proceeded on to the family room and, settling into an easy chair in front of the picture window, opened the newspaper. It took him no more than a few seconds to find a column of interest.

CABOT STATION:
NEGLIGENCE AND ARROGANCE
by Allen Reginold

It has been almost three weeks now since the still-unexplained tragedy at Cabot Station, the naval undersea station off the Labrador coast.

Although all of the evidence isn't in yet, I have reason to believe that the story behind the tragedy will likely prove to be one of almost criminal pigheadedness and negligence on the part of one high ranking naval officer.

While little information concerning the disaster has been released, my associate Packi Irundi has had the opportunity to examine certain Top Secret documents that shed considerable light on the matter. According to our sources, the disaster was caused by the failure of a watertight door that allowed the station to flood. These same sources indicate that the personnel at Cabot Station had attempted for some time to get a replacement for the door, but were stymied by Admiral Laneland Williams, Cabot Station's immediate superior.

Admiral Williams, a Brasshat widely known for his taste for personal power, was apparently more interested in spending money on new unproven technology than insuring the safety of those serving under him. Indeed, our sources report that Brasshat Williams, considered by some an arrogant martinet, developed a personal dislike for Commander Alfonso Madeira, Cabot Station's Commanding Officer at the time of the accident, as a result of the latter's repeated requests for additional resources. These sources further indicate that, shortly before the accident, the admiral ordered Commander Madeira to leave Cabot Station and report to him in Colorado for the sole purpose of receiving a spiteful rebuke. There are many who feel that by this act, the admiral may have sealed the fate of Cabot since it is entirely possible that, had Madeira been present, instead of cooling his heels in Williams's anteroom, the outcome might have been very different.

It's also been suggested that Williams attempted to prevent Commander Madeira's being sent to lead the rescue effort. Thanks to intervention by still higher authority, Commander Madeira *was* sent and is now credited by insiders with having done an almost miraculous job, and in the process prevented much greater loss of life.

Having done his best to prevent Cabot Station from protecting itself, Admiral Williams continues to shroud the whole affair in secrecy—to the point of concealing the location at which Commander Madeira is recuperating from injuries received during the rescue operation. Of even greater concern, Williams has succeeded in preventing the press and members of Congress from learning the details of this disaster.

Williams laid the paper down, wincing and chuckling at the same time. It wouldn't be long, he thought, before they indicted him for contempt of press. At least there was no hint of any problem with SOSUS.

"I don't like that column one bit, Lane. Why are they raping you that way now? You're not some high level courtier. You're not involved in that sort of game, are you?"

Williams looked up into his wife's concerned face.

"Just this once, I'm afraid. Do you believe it?"

"Of course not. That's not you they're writing about."

"Good. The funny thing is the son of a bitch hasn't even gotten the leak right."

Kate sat down in the chair opposite him, her face considerably calmer.

"You don't seem worried about this so I won't be. All the same, I can't wait until your papers come through."

"You're going to see a lot more of me soon," he said as he got up and headed toward the bar. "Right now we've got some important things to discuss; like where we're *really* going to live, whether we *really* want a boat, and when we're going to do all those things you want to do."

"Will we have to change our name?" she asked, a conspiratorial grin skipping across her face.

"That may not turn out to be a bad idea."

"Good evening, Admiral," said Williams dutifully into his telephone.

"Evening, Lane," replied the CNO.

This doesn't sound good, thought Williams. He only shifts into that chummy, first name mode when somebody's putting real pressure on him.

"Lane," continued the CNO after a pause, "what the hell are your people doing about that Siren? The President is very serious about knowing what it's doing there. He swears he won't sign the agreement until he does, and he must know by the end of the month!"

He really is worried, thought Williams, and when he's worried he turns into something of a weasel.

"Admiral, I feel they're making excellent progress, under the circumstances."

"Are the circumstances really that impossible?"

"They do have very limited resources, and the weather in Baffin Bay is usually awful. The important thing is that I have total confidence in Lieutenant Commander Madeira, and I also have good reason to believe that Captains DeFranco and Melvin are both excellent seamen and very solid officers. They are on the scene and I am not. I will not second-guess them."

"I'm not trying to second-guess them or you, Lane, I'm simply trying to *emphasize* the importance of this operation and of the time factor. The President must have this information."

"I understand that, sir, and so do they."

"DeFranco—He's *Purvis*, isn't he? The OTC? The destroyerman?"

"Yes, sir."

"He should be able to keep the Bubbleheads moving in the right direction."

"I'm counting on that, Admiral," lied Williams.

"There was a National Security Council meeting this morning. All hands were very concerned about the situation in the Soviet Union and I was in a very difficult position on this. The concensus was that the Navy is fucking around. It was embarrassing. . . ."

Fuck the consensus, thought Williams. "I'm truly sorry you were put in that position but I can assure you we *will* recover the Siren, or enough of it for our purposes, in time."

"You'd damn well better."

"Admiral, this is one operation you don't have to worry about. We'll produce."

Damnit, thought Williams as he hung up, I enjoyed that! I loved hearing that slick bastard squirm. I just hope I don't have to eat my words.

FORTY-THREE

DAVIS STRAIT— DAY THIRTY-ONE

"He wants it up by the twentieth?" demanded Melvin, his voice reflecting more than a hint of disbelief." What makes him think it can be done?"

"I've often wondered what makes Admiral Williams think the way he does. All I do know is that he has an amazing knack for getting his way."

"If you say so, and if the Russian doesn't return. I just don't read the bastards on this. Are they seriously trying to stop us or are they just fucking with us?"

Madeira shrugged.

Fifty hours later, the Russian still hadn't returned and the wire straps were finally all in place, wrapped around the Siren, both ends shackled to a massive steel plate, creating a steel cocoon in which Madeira hoped to lift the wreckage intact.

"That's it," he said looking at the videos of the cocoon. "You two do good work," he continued, looking at Hale and Rand. "Next we place the sinker."

"No break, sir?" asked Hale, feeling numb from inadequate rest.

"No break 'till we've turned that pile of scrap over to the technicians."

It took slightly more than one complete, 'round the clock

day to implement the next phase, the placement of a sinker assembly composed of four oil drums, each filled with about one thousand pounds of concrete and miscellaneous scrap, and a long wire strap. One end of the wire was shackled to the top of the cocoon, to the thick steel plate, while the other end was shackled to one of the drums. The remaining drums were secured at roughly equal distances along the strap's length.

"He's back," said Captain Melvin to Madeira as the latter finished briefing Hale and Rand on the placement of the lift bags.

"The Russian?"

"Affirmative."

"What's he doing?"

"Just watching. For now."

"As long as he leaves us alone."

"Even if he does, you've only got six to eight hours. A real howler appears headed our way."

"Oh hell!" He could easily imagine the storm lasting for days, destroying any chance of meeting the deadline and further delaying his quest for Susan.

The vehicle was launched immediately and one of the five rubberized lift bags, each ten feet in diameter and capable of generating about 30,000 pounds of lift, was towed down to the cocoon and secured to the steel plate.

"Now set the heavy weather detail," blared the PA speaker beside Madeira's head as he watched a party of stiff, cold, thoroughly exhausted boatswain's mates clumsily prepare to once again recover the vehicle.

While the storm never proved to be the terror that Melvin expected, it did prevent them from launching the vehicle again until early the next morning. Fourteen hours later, the remaining four lift bags were in place and Madeira noticed a new tightness in his gut.

If this didn't work, he could look forward to another month waiting for the ice to break up over the wreckage. If he blew it, if he'd miscalculated, he could easily destroy what was left of the Siren, ending any chance of learning its mission.

That, he thought with a touch of paranoia, was why the Russian was there now—to watch him blow it. They must have figured what he was going to do and decided it couldn't be done.

Shortly before dawn, with the deck-shaking "barooom" of *Falcon's* fog horn assaulting him and a cup of coffee in his good hand, he headed aft. When he reached the fantail, he found Melvin waiting for him in the dense, dripping fog.

"Perfect weather for recovering sunken treasure," he mumbled to *Falcon's* Commanding Officer.

Melvin laughed as the two turned to look at the vehicle resting in its cradle, glinting in the working lights, while the ship rose and fell gently in the long, oily swells. "Let's hope it lasts," he replied after a long pause.

Madeira called the two vehicle crews together.

"Based on my calculations, our little treasure weighs between sixty and seventy tons. It should start to rise at some point after the fourth bag's filled. So Rand, you're going to fill the first three bags while Hale gets some sleep. Then Hale and I are going to fill the last two—and hope we stop before we lose control and the whole mess blows up and plasters itself against the bottom of the ice."

"Roger," they both nodded.

While Hale and his second operator headed off to their racks, extra high pressure air cylinders were loaded into the vehicle and hooked up to the external air injection system, normally used to provide air to crippled submarines. Shortly thereafter, Chief Rand and his second operator squeezed in, sealed up, were hoisted overboard, and set out to fill their quota of lift bags.

Eight hours later, as the vehicle was again sealed and dropped into the almost slushy waters of Baffin Bay, Madeira strapped himself into his seat and leaned back. Breathing deeply, he felt the tension flare up again in almost nauseous waves. He could imagine everything that might go wrong, every little misstep that could snowball into disaster. During the next few hours he would either succeed—or utterly blow it.

With his feet propped up on one of the recently installed high pressure air flasks, he leaned back and tried to relax, to clear his mind. He thought of Susan, and of how much he didn't know about her, and wondered if she ever thought of him. He closed his eyes and concentrated on big bags of air.

"Bags're in sight, sir."

He opened his eyes.

"Roger. I'm on my way."

He released his seatbelt and slithered over the air flasks until he reached the padded, couch-like device he'd had fabricated aboard *Falcon*. It was no chaise lounge but it did offer the possibility of considerably less discomfort than he'd experienced during the survey.

As he settled himself into the custom couch, his body remaining in the passenger compartment while his head and shoulders protruded into the operators' compartment, he studied the video display. There, on the bottom was the shadowy cocoon. It reminded him more of the cocoon built by a spider around a captured fly than that of a moth or butterfly. Floating above it, hovering menacingly in the creeping bottom waters, were the three even-more-shadowy bags. It would be a simple matter to become entangled in them or their bridles and a simple matter to die as a result.

"You two concentrate on the vehicle and the air nozzle," said Madeira as he wormed his way forward to reach the video camera control. "I'll use the video to keep an eye on the wreckage."

"Roger. Which bag do we start with?"

"Number five. Leave four for last. Otherwise we may get tangled in this mess."

"Roger."

Hale turned the vehicle and descended, finally settling gently on the bottom, up-current and slightly to one side of bag number five.

After waiting for the small cloud of suspended ooze they had created to dissipate, Madeira trained the video camera around onto the cocoon while the second operator, using the vehicle's feeble working arm, extended a long, probe-like air nozzle forward and under one edge of the bag.

"Commencing pumping, sir," reported the second operator.

"Very well," replied Madeira, glancing up from the video and out the viewing port.

At first, the bag showed no sign of life. Then, one side started to rise slowly. As the amount of enclosed air increased, it pushed its way to the top and the bag righted itself and bulged up from the bottom, undulating slowly.

Despite the crucial importance of keeping an eye on the cocoon, Madeira found himself sneaking quick glances out the viewing port. He watched as the dark bag grew out of the ocean bottom, then slowly broke free and rose, expanding all the way, until air started to bubble out of its open bottom.

"Securing pumping," reported the second operator.

"Damnit," grumbled Madeira, studying the video display, "that's sixty tons of lift and the damn thing still looks like it's cemented there."

"Madeira, how're you doing?" It was Captain Melvin. "That cold front's about six hours to the west of us now and the seas are beginning to kick up."

"We've got four bags inflated and the damn thing's not budging."

"What do you intend to do? We don't have more than a few hours. Do you want to try towing it as it is?"

"No. Not yet. If it doesn't lift cleanly we're going to end up dragging it across the bottom and destroying it."

"The other bag, then?"

"Affirmative."

Just as Madeira took his eyes off the video display to watch bag four, now partially filled, start to lift off the silty bottom, the second operator glanced down at the video.

"It's light, sir!" he shouted. "I just saw it twist a little."

"Stop pumping!" responded Madeira, also shouting. "I don't want to lose it."

As he spoke, he returned his full attention to the video display and looked for confirmation of the operator's observation.

There it was! The wreckage rolled slightly.

"You're right! It's light. It couldn't weigh more than sixty-five tons after all." He felt beads of sweat forming on his forehead. This was it! This was his opportunity to blow the whole operation, to waste weeks of work, to over-inflate just enough to send the whole mess rocketing up toward the ice.

"Pump for ten seconds, no more."

"Ten seconds, sir."

The bag inflated a little more and the cocoon rolled again.

"Ten more."

"Ten more, sir."

The cocoon hopped a foot or two down current, raising a small cloud of ooze.

"Ten more, quickly! Before it pounds any more."

"Ten more, sir."

The cocoon rose gently off the bottom and started to drift slowly, trailing the sinker assembly, one of which was now suspended off the bottom, leaving three firmly in the ooze.

Madeira took a deep breath and wiped his sopping forehead. He had to inflate just enough to get two of the three remaining drums off the bottom. He needed another two thousand pounds of life—thirty cubic feet of air . . . maybe less.

"Five seconds this time."

"Five seconds, sir."

Madeira watched, his physical discomfort totally forgotten, as one of the drums rose off the bottom . . . then another . . . and then the last?

Was the last one rising? Had he over-inflated and blown it?

Thank God, no! It was very, very light but it was still on the bottom, being dragged in tiny fits and starts through the ooze.

Jesus Christ! It was almost perfect! He couldn't have wished for, or even dreamed of, any better!

The whole array had only a couple hundred pounds of negative buoyancy. Even the vehicle's feeble motors could now tow it out from under the ice to open water where *Falcon* could hoist it to the surface.

The one remaining danger was bag number four, which was still only partially inflated. If, for any reason, it managed to rise, they could still lose control. If the ocean bottom sloped up or if they ran into a pocket of increased salinity or temperature, the bag might rise and, as it did, the volume of air within it would increase slightly, increasing the bag's lift and starting the treasure on a disasterous romp upwards.

"Secure pumping," ordered Madeira. "Secure the nozzle."

"Roger."

Then into the communications speaker he reported, *"Falcon,* it's working like a dream. Am taking array under tow at this time. ETA open water, two hours."

"Roger, vehicle."

"Okay, Hale," said Madeira, his voice bordering on jubilation, "Let's see if you can snag that tow line."

"Roger, boss."

By midafternoon, almost precisely on schedule, *Falcon* was able to confirm that, with the assistance of the deep current, the vehicle and its tow were almost a mile beyond the edge of the ice.

"Roger, *Falcon*," replied Madeira to the news. "Unless otherwise directed, I intend to cut away bag number four and return to *Falcon* for hoist wire."

"Roger, vehicle," replied Melvin. "You're cutting it damn close again."

"Take her in, Hale, and trip number four."

Hale dropped the tow wire and turned the tiny submarine into the current to approach the tow—which had come, in Madeira's mind, to resemble a giant, dark bulbous plant rising up from the ocean bottom on the slenderest of stalks. He slowed as he approached the base of bag four and the second operator reached out with the mechanical arm and tripped a giant pelican hook. The cocoon settled slowly into the ooze, the four remaining, fully inflated bags waving gently above it.

Bag number four now looked like a giant, brown jellyfish. Surrounded by frothing white water, it broached two hundred yards to the east of *Falcon*.

While a boat was sent across the whitecap-flecked water to recover the bag, the vehicle appeared alongside *Falcon* and was passed the better end of the hoist wire.

Forty minutes later, with the wind and seas still building, Madeira, his eyes glued to the video display, called up to *Falcon*, "Hooked up and ready to heave around."

At first, while the winch took up the slack in the three thousand plus foot-long wire, there was no change to be seen on the video.

Suddenly, the wreckage was a few feet off the bottom. On the surface, the lift wire was quivering, bar-hard, and *Falcon* was listing noticably to starboard.

Madeira held his breath, expecting the wreckage to bounce down and off the bottom as *Falcon* fell into some wave's trough—but it didn't. As the wreckage continued to rise, huge bubbles rolled out the bottoms of the bags and headed rapidly for the surface.

By the time the pale sun reached the western horizon, the vehicle and boat had been recovered, the bags replaced with four steel pontoons and *Falcon*, escorted by *Purvis*, headed east, slowly towing her treasure to Greenland.

"Just in time, Madeira," remarked Melvin as he looked out over the rapidly building chop. "In two hours we'll have ten foot seas."

"We've had a great run of luck the last few days."

"Don't start counting our chickens yet. We've still got to deliver this little gem. You know anything about Godthab?"

"No more than you. It's the capital of Greenland and there's some sort of shipyard there. . . ."

". . . and nobody we know ever goes there on vacation."

Madeira laughed.

"You think they're going to send us back for the rest?"

"I don't think so," replied Madeira. "I think we've got what we need."

Smiling, Madeira gazed out at the sky, which was gray but clearing as the big, high pressure system to the east made its influence felt. There was a solitary gull circling and crying in the cold air. The gray and white wanderer glided down as if to land on *Falcon's* mast but disturbed, perhaps by her snapping ensign, stretched its wings and circled three more times, then swooped down and landed on the choppy water. Now more boat than bird, the gull shook its wings twice, folded them neatly away, and hunkered down to watch the salvage ship plow past, rolling as she went.

Madeira found himself mentally framing and composing a photograph of the gull. Using the big telephoto lens, he would close in on it, close enough to show clearly the bird's fiercely bored expression, yet not so close that its reckless, epic solitude, alone and adrift on the ocean's great, looming expanse, would be lost.

It would be an excellent shot—the crystalline glow of the gull's white feathers, the silvery sun reflected on the pewter sea. It was an image of great power and strength, he thought, but it was also so very cold and hard, so metallic. The same sharpness, hardness, and clarity, the somber, metallic glow that would for many provide a fantastic and eye-opening contrast to the everyday, made it all too real and lifelike for him.

All oceans aren't as persistently miserable as the North Atlantic, he decided. If they were, there wouldn't be many sailors around any more.

"I assume there's an airport at Godthab."

"Has to be something. How else can they get the technicians in?"

"Do you have any objections to my asking Admiral Williams to give me a couple weeks of leave and fly me right out of there?"

"Not at all . . . though it *has* been fun! Going home?"

"To Hawaii. I want to see if I can arrange to meet a friend of mine there before I have to get back for the Cabot inquiry."

"Good luck."

FORTY-FOUR

COLORADO—APRIL 26

"Jim, we were a hundred eighty degrees off about the Siren," said Admiral Williams, leaning back in his chair.

"It wasn't a masking device, Admiral?"

"It's a masking system, all right, but it isn't designed to mask the boomer's presence. It's a mask that can be worn by any submarine and makes it look like a boomer. It's a decoy system, an emissions generator. That damn cylinder contains an electromagnet to generate a magnetic field similar to a boomer's, a set of small signal generators to provide miscellaneous other electronic emissions, and some air guns to generate shock waves which seem to mimic everything from a screw beat to the pressure wave generated as the submarine moves through the water."

"Do the technicians think it works?"

"I damn well know it works. When the Siren was first reported to me, Pendleton said two Soviet boomers had been in Zebra 403 and one was still southeast of Greenland."

"The Siren was the second boomer?"

"I think so. I should have caught it at the time, but I didn't."

"I'm still surprised they let us get it."

"Maybe you were right about their being preoccupied with their own problems. It's also possible they may have decided, after a while, it wouldn't be the end of the world if we did learn about it. They know as well as we do that a well advertised minefield is generally more valuable than a secret one."

"Now we'll never be able to trust SOSUS?"

"I think that may be the idea."

"Of course, now that we know about it, we can look for something that will give it away."

"We have a meeting with the computer programmers this afternoon to look into that."

"What's the President going to do?"

"He's not signing. He's going to tell them he wants to know who authorized it. If the present government admits it was them, he's going to want to know why he should trust them further. If they say it wasn't them, he's going to demand to know who's really in charge."

"Admiral, you seem almost cheerful about this."

"I am, Jim. I don't like unsolved mysteries. I'm also very pleased with the way the operation was handled. Madeira and *Falcon* completed a difficult task with the usual limited resources."

"About the inquiry?"

"I've spoken with the CNO. He's going to convene it in a month. Admiral Howard will preside."

"A month! That's not going to give Ozawa and Madeira—especially Madeira—much time to prepare!"

"They won't need much time because you're going to write the preliminary report so the facts are obvious to the most hopeless moron."

"Admiral, the true situation was that the command and support system failed. Cabot was pushed and squeezed too far."

"That's my understanding of it."

"That will never satisfy the media. They're going to want a hanging . . ."

"And they'll get one! Jim, who was in charge of Cabot's command and support system?"

"Oh!" mumbled Ring with sudden understanding as he sat, uninvited, in one of William's chairs.

"Will a gesture like that really do any good, Admiral?"

"It'll shake up the right people for a while. And that's all to the good. Then, of course, the old inefficiencies will creep back in and it'll have to be done all over again."

Ring took a deep breath. "Admiral, do you have any last requests?"

"Yes, Jim. I want Madeira to do me a favor. I want him to go back to the real Navy for a while. For his next job, I want him to put in for one that'll do his career some good. If you talk to him before I do, tell him that."

"Aye, aye, Admiral."

"The man deserves a medal—but an intact neck will have to do for now."